BLOOD HERRING

Book One of the Blood Herring Trilogy

To Uncle Bear,
Who sat up with me several nights to keep me company
while I ranted about my imaginary friends and watched every
possible cheesy vampire movie with me.

We miss you.

CHAPTER 1

GABE

Paperwork. All the technological advances and they were still burying me in paperwork. Each of my knuckles ached from the typing. I leaned away from the faux wood desk and pushed my hands through my hair. Off to my right, Sanders tried to coerce a witness into coming back. Sadly, none of this served to distract me from the case at hand.

This much typing should be considered cruel and unusual punishment.

In reality, I just wanted to avoid the rest of my report. I'd joined this department to help people, yet *people* were my biggest problem. Another case where humans were the perpetrator. Sadly, the stale ceiling tiles didn't offer any condolences, no matter how long I stared.

"Yo, Collins!" The shrill whistle of my partner made me jump from my chair.

"Jesus, Harper! You trying to get my attention or call back some hunting hounds?"

James Harper sat on my desk, holding a small stack of papers in one broad hand. His dark head shone in the bullpen's fluorescent light and pale flakes of Pop-Tart crumbs littered his bushy beard. "Sorry to scar you for life, buddy, but the captain just handed us a fresh one."

I groaned and eyed the already swelling inbox on my desktop. "My hands are cramped just thinking about the reports I gotta file tonight."

Harper smiled, shifting his big brows and burly beard, and spilling some of his breakfast onto my desk. "If only you had a partner to help with all those, eh?"

I stood, reaching across my desk to brush the pastry crumbs away. "Yeah and one that could groom himself."

My partner realized the mess he'd made and moved his big frame like something had bitten him. "Oh, shit, sorry, man!"

He dusted off the few crumbs I'd missed.

"Don't sweat it. Not many could brag about surviving the dreaded crumb attack." I shrugged as I finished flicking the last bits away.

Harper barked a single laugh.

My lips twisted up at the corners. "So, what's my next report?"

"Uniforms were responding to calls out in Rockwood when they found a body," he said simply.

My eyebrows knitted together. "That's not exactly uncommon for the area, what makes it one of ours?"

Violence, drugs, working girls. All of these were fairly normal for Rockwood, and we hardly got calls from the residents. We'd once had a woman who'd rammed her car into her boyfriend's truck repeatedly. The next day, he'd dropped the charges, and I caught them making out in our lobby. Very classy place.

Harper handed me the stack of papers. "Read the calls."

I took the pages and began flipping through them. The skin between my brows pinched as I read the first anonymous 911 call. "Well then."

"Keep going."

I read on, practically shoving my nose through the paper. "Three different calls over four days, but all the same—"

"Yep," Harper smacked his lips on the *p* for emphasis. "And I guess the condition of the body was pretty gnarled."

I grimaced at the mental picture and handed them back to him. "Okay, let's go see if this is another fake."

Twenty minutes later, we were driving through Rockwood, and I was waiting for the twang of noir music to start. Or maybe my eyesight would slowly drift to grayscale as we descended into poverty. The bright yellow dandelions escaping through cracks in the sidewalk begged to differ. As did the expensive cars mixed among cheap lawn ornaments.

My breath turned into an exasperated sigh.

Harper flicked his gaze to me. "Something on your mind, partner?"

I debated letting out a good rant. The politics here made it so people had a hard time getting out. But then I would end up talking about the same people refusing to call the cops because many were criminals themselves. After that, I'd descend into rambling about the poor innocent kids who were quickly being taught that crime was the only way to survive and the endless revolving door of bad priorities and horrendous politics.

It would have been nice to blow off steam, but Harper had heard it all before. I decided to switch topics. "Nah, just thinking of the forms you left on my desk."

Harper let out one of his harsh laughs. "Hey, I bought coffee. Doesn't that earn me some kind of break?"

Harper turned down Lincoln Avenue and eased off the gas. Fast enough to move smoothly with traffic, but slow enough that we could watch for anything worth reacting to.

"A single cup isn't going to cut it this time. At this rate, you might as well buy me a new machine. Maybe one of them fancy ones with a timer?" The distraction was nice, even if it was temporary.

"Oh, and while I'm at it, I suppose you'd like it to be a fancy latte' thing with something for your— Ah *man*!" Harper pulled over and groaned.

A crowd had already gathered, some dancing on the asphalt in their pajamas or slippers, and even a few wearing house robes I prayed didn't fall open. This day was ugly enough as is.

"At least the news isn't here." I tried to give Harper a sympathetic look. Neither of us really cared for audiences.

"Yet," he grumbled as he climbed out of the car. "You take the scene and ME."

I got out and scowled over the roof of the car. "You're just trying to unload more work on me."

"Nah, I want to talk to the uniforms, see what they got." Harper walked off, politely elbowing his way past the onlookers and hailing one of the uniforms by name, "Hey, Johnson!"

I pulled a similar, though less successful routine, trying to smile my way through the crowd. Pretty sure someone called me a cracker, but it wasn't worth addressing. Instead, I rolled my eyes and ducked under the crime scene tape. It gave a soft *twang* as I let it fall back in place behind me and nodded at the nearest uniforms.

"Hey, Stevens, how's the missus?"

"She's taken a liking to ghost pepper pickles." He shivered in exaggerated disgust and waved me in. "How's Michelle?"

I shrugged. No need to talk about that here.

The garish light of the ME van and a couple of cruisers tried to compete with the sun in thick red and blue waves. The body was partially shielded under a red-splotched shroud as a stubby little man examined it. It didn't stop the putrid smell of death from wafting my way.

"What do we got, Dan?" I pulled a small notebook from one pocket, yanking the pen from the spine.

"I'm afraid it's the real deal," the medical examiner greeted me in kind.

"You sure it's not a fake, like last month?"

"Certain." The tail ends of his huge mustache danced under his mask like a couple of deranged squirrels while the tubby old man looked at me through his round spectacles. He pulled the shroud back and pointed at our victim's neck. "Though the shoulder wound is huge, there are four distinct drag marks from the fangs. That's almost impossible to fake. Plus, this bite is the wrong shape for most animals."

It was hard to keep my neutral face for the crowd. No matter how many times you see a dead body, it's always horrible. The poor kid, couldn't have been more than twenty, was all black and purple like he'd been beaten before he'd been killed. His skin was stretched too tight over his face, like he'd tried to scream in his last minutes, but just couldn't.

Scenes of past victims swarmed my mind, trying to claim my attention. A girl missing an arm. A man being pulled at like a dog toy between two vamps before being torn apart. A mound of human pieces too mangled for me to identify.

I closed my eyes and breathed, forcing my brain back into the present.

"See, right here." Dan pointed to twin drag marks, the kid's neck sliced into big ribbons just before a softball-sized hole sank into the flesh. Blood had gushed in a reddish-brown torrent, making a nauseating congealed puddle on the blacktop.

"Damn, Harper's not going to like this."

"And you do?" Dan eyed me as he covered the kid back up.

It wasn't like I was thrilled it was a murder, but having an actual vampire case, that was exactly what I'd joined this team for. Not hunt down husbands who'd killed their wives with a damn deli fork. But the bloodsuckers hid their dirty business well, and I was stuck with a pile of human-posers. I sidestepped the question, "Any ID?"

"That was handled by uniforms."

Nice way of saying, *Not my problem.*

I took additional notes and shoved the pad back in my pocket. "Alright. Thanks, Dan."

Dan looked back to the victim. "Wish I could say it was a pleasure to see you."

I shrugged. "Come beat Harper at poker next time we get together. Maybe you'll finally have a chance."

Dan shook his head. "No offense, Collins, but I think I'll pass on hearing shop talk after hours."

"See ya next time, Dan."

He wished me well as I left. It took a minute to tiptoe back around the crime scene techs and the tiny yellow markers to make my way back to my partner. He was waiting for me inside the tape.

Harper blew out an exasperated sigh and combed his beard with his hands as I gave him the news. "Man...I was really hoping it was just another dog bite."

"Hey, at least now we know those 911 calls weren't fakes."

"Always looking on the bright side, 'eh partner."

Harper probably would have done all the paperwork from now on if I offered to go solo on this one case. But I needed him with me on this one. God knew what I'd find working a real case.

"We had to expect something bad when multiple people claim folks are disappearing right off the street."

It had only been two years, but in that short time, a lot of murderers had tried to fake vampire crimes to get away with it. God knows how many had succeeded, especially during the original panic. It took months for police departments to train their officers and medical examiners to properly sort the twisted fakes from the real deal. Sadly, most of my calls were for human-on-human murders.

"Well, Johnson—" Harper pointed to the uniform in question, "says they didn't find any ID and most people were pretty hush-hush when they canvased the neighborhood."

"Shocking."

"Yeah, but a few were a bit more adamant than others. They thought we should try those."

"Wanna see if *detective* puts the fear of God into them?" I lifted the crime scene tape to allow my partner through.

As it fell back in place, local news pulled up, the brakes barely applied before two men rushed towards the scene, giddy at their early arrival.

"Yeah, gotta start somewhere." Harper scowled at the new-comers. "Wonder why they left the body out in public. They usually seem to clean up after a meal."

Sad but true. We rarely found vampire victims just lying around, that was kind of the problem. Vampires might eat like rabid animals, but they were smart. They knew how to cover themselves. Probably from centuries of practice, though that was just speculation.

The last time we found actual vampire victims, it had been a pile of working girls located during a drug bust. Their arms had been littered with track and fang marks alike, their pale and bloated bodies piled in a room for later disposal. That scene still clung to my dreams. The fact that we still hadn't brought in the ones responsible didn't help.

"I don't know. Maybe we got lucky and it's a young one." We walked up the street to the first of many houses.

"Yeah, I feel real lucky right now." Harper rang the first doorbell. Six slammed doors, a crazy old cat lady, a hoarder, and one house of screaming children later, Harper and I sat next to each other on a rather clean floral couch, sipping tea.

We both thought tea was a bit too frilly unless you counted the sweet iced kind. However, we'd both learned a long time ago that if someone let you in and you turned down their drink offers, they'd spend all their time asking repeatedly if you were sure instead of focusing on your questions. People's manners could be a damn nuisance.

So, begrudgingly, we both tried to smile and sip from our frail cups. "Ah, excellent, Miss Stafford. Thank you."

"Why thank ya, dear." The old lady's brown cheeks lifted in a smile. The tone complemented nicely the gray bun on the back of her head. "Now what'd you boys wanna ask about?"

Harper sipped again before starting. "Well, ma'am, we've received a few calls about unusual violence in this area."

"I imagine you already know that's not unusual 'round here." There wasn't any shake in Angela Stafford's voice but it had lost its sweetness. "It's one of the reasons I don't invite my children down here more often."

When I was a little kid, I'd thought of detectives as real-life superheroes. They could crack any bad guy like magic. But then I grew up, joined the force, and started getting into the routine of interrogations. We don't have any superpowers, but the best detectives are damn good lie detectors. It could be as simple as a rushed word or a quick bite of the lower lip, but it didn't take much to set off our inner polygraph.

Something about this woman, how she talked about her kids, set the little bulb in my head off, bright red and on alert.

"Yes, we do. However, these reports were a bit more specific." I took another swig as I spoke. "We're part of the Vampire Police Bureau."

Miss Stafford's eyes darkened. She set her cup down on a doily covering the coffee table between us. "What are the vamp cops doin' here?"

"The VPB got word that there were a lot of disappearances at night with no traces." Harper put his cup down. It was well over half-full. "And I don't know if you noticed all the commotion down the street."

"Afraid I didn't. I tend to keep to my own here. I'm sure you understand. Little old thing like me in this area, I do best if I'm ignored altogether."

At her age, you only lived in this area because your budget wouldn't allow for anything else. Yet, when uniforms had come by, nobody had answered. The bulb in my head blazed brighter, but I kept quiet all the same, not wanting to upset the flow Harper had set.

"I'm afraid a body was discovered." Harper paused, trying to let that sink in. "We don't have a name, but the time of death was sometime last night."

"Ya mean to tell me a corpse done showed up in the middle of our street and y'all just now found it?" She looked mildly displeased by that, yet the volume of her voice didn't raise.

"It was a few hours ago ma'am," Harper continued.

She let out a *hmph* and sat back. "I suppose you can't watch this area twenty-four seven." She picked her saucer back up and began sipping idly. "I'm really not sure how I could help. Like I said, I mind myself."

"And we respect that, of course," I tried to sound reassuring. "We understand life in this area requires special precautions."

She eyed me and Harper over her cup, pausing on each of us, then nodded. "What do you boys want to know?"

"Did you hear anything? Maybe around nine or ten last night?" Harper took the reins again.

"I hear plenty every night. Guns a-blazing, little hoodlums yammering on at all hours. Just last night there was some hollerin' over there." She placed her cup back on the saucer and waved her weathered hand in the general direction of where we'd found the body. "Course, one could hardly call that out of the ordinary."

Harper and I nodded. He tried to prompt her further. "Any specifics stick out? Even just single words or names."

"There was a lot of cursing, yelling. I had to turn up Family Feud just to drown it out." She tilted her head and squinted her dark eyes at a distant point behind us. "I don't think I've heard that much cursing in my life."

I'd abandoned my teacup, making quick notes as Harper kept the questions going. "Any other details aside from the foul language?"

Miss Stafford pursed her lips and twisted her brows, trying to replay something in her mind as she spoke slowly, "Well...they hollered on about soda at some point."

Harper wrinkled his nose, and I stopped writing. "Soda?"

"Yeah, before I finally gave up and cranked up the volume, I heard one yell something about Cherry Coke. Thought that was weird."

Harper and I looked at each other. He looked as bewildered as I felt. We stood in silent agreement. "Well, Miss Stafford, I think that's all. But if you think of anything else, let me leave you my card."

"Nah, just write your number down."

Best guess, she didn't want to have a detective's card sitting around where her neighbors might see it. I obliged, tearing a page from my notebook, and handing it to her on our way out.

As we turned back to her on the stoop, I spoke loud enough for any eavesdropping neighbors. "Thanks again for the tea. Be sure to let us know if you do see anything."

She smiled. "So sorry I couldn't help but thanks for giving an old bird some company, boys."

With that, she shut the door. Harper and I shared a knowing look and walked away. We waited until we were back on the sidewalk to talk. Harper's dark eyes shifted back towards the old lady's window as he spoke. "Seem odd to you?"

"Yeah." I kept my eyes on the gray slab underfoot. "She didn't hear our ambulance arrive or a bunch of people talking over each other. But that old crone picked up on that argument no problem."

CHAPTER 2

LILY

"**I** paid you to tell me what she was up to!" Mr. Anderson was starting to resemble a pufferfish. His already bloated cheeks bulged in an indignant shade of red.

"No." I pulled out his contract and pointed to the sections I'd highlighted. "Ya hired me to figure out where she was goin'. Never once did ya ask the activity."

He picked up the contract, flipping through the pages and slapping them on my desk as he finished. It was shocking that he didn't rip them. After a little further arguing and me pointing out a few more highlights, he unhappily paid for my services and left.

I leaned back in my chair and chuckled to myself, "Hope ya enjoy the show."

It was just too bad I wouldn't get to see the look on his face when he found his daughter singing on stage, instead of whatever he'd thought she was up to. The elevator dinged and my disgruntled client kept grumbling in the hallway. "Know-it-all little bitch."

He'd slammed my door and I got up to make sure he hadn't busted the glass panel. After so many years behind it, I could easily read *Strictly Confidential Investigation*s backwards through the frosted glass.

He called me a few more choice phrases as he left the building, and I laughed again. Seeing as he didn't realize I could still hear him, I couldn't hold it against him. I glanced at the card transaction on my phone. Hell, as long as he paid me, he could call me anything he wanted.

The phone vibrated in my hand and *Funky Town* blared through the speakers. I blinked in disbelief, watching my adoptive sire's face light up the caller ID.

It kept ringing, the song's chorus becoming more insistent with each repetition. On the third time around, I had to accept this wasn't an ass dial.

"Shite." I swiped my thumb to answer. "Ivan?"

"Hey, kid." My old boss' distressed accent leaked through the line. His was far harsher than my own, given that it was old Russian. He sounded unusually exasperated. "You busy?"

Little hairs danced on the back of my neck. I debated lying, but it was Ivan after all. I swallowed my pride. "Nope, just finished with my latest client. Why?"

He hesitated. "We're having issues in your area."

"What kind of issues?" I locked the door and turned off my light. No reason to invite some new client in.

"People have been turning up in the ER with vampire blood in their noses."

"Goddammit..." I leaned my forehead against the cool glass. Why didn't I just lie and say I was busy?

"Yeah, not my favorite news either, kid. Luckily, no one's died." The implied *yet* hung between us.

I ran a hand down my face and tried to keep my tone level. "Those fuckin' cabbages just don't get it, do they?"

"Doubt it."

I went to my desk, pulling open my drawer for notepads. "Police involved yet?"

"Not very. There's one concrete attack but no ID yet. What do you call that area again, the slummy one?"

"Rockwood's not that bad." Okay, it was. Most of my case-work was a partial result of something from Rockwood. I scrawled out some tester squiggles from my third pen before I continued. "Do ya have the name of the other victims?"

Ivan gave me a list of seven people, four men and three women judging solely by their names. I noted their birthdays and anything else he could tell me, which wasn't a lot.

"How'd you find out about them?"

"They were dropped off in different ERs, high as kites and hard to restrain."

Considering what was coursing through their bodies, that was probably an understatement. Shit, if that kept up the human population would be onto us within a week.

"You got the police names on ya?" I wrote detective James Harper's name next to Gabriel Collins, drawing a line between them and the victims to keep the groups separate. "And what makes ya think the death's connected other than fang marks?"

"They found vampire blood in his nose during the autopsy."

Yeah, that sealed it. "And why does she want me?"

Ivan paused. For far too long.

"Out with it, Boss. Ritti never calls me in unless there is a unique need. Why not just send you or Cyrus?" I hated arguing with him, but there was no way I could let Ritti land me with another shit gig. "Spill."

"The hospital records..." He grumbled slowly.

"What about 'em?" I twirled my hand, waiting for him to get on with it.

"Anna signed off on a number of them."

"What?" I stuffed a curse back into my mouth. Of course, that little maggot was involved. This was just one more time the queen could stick it to me. "It's been forty years. Is she really that petty?"

"We both know that's not the only reason to send you."

True, there was a certain rationale for sending me. The queen and I may not be BFFs or whatever, but I could see her reasoning.

"Kid?"

I chewed on the idea of hanging up before speaking, "It'll cost ya."

Ivan sighed. "How much?"

I stated the hourly rate and the down payment. Plus expenses.

"And if it takes a month?"

"Then you're paying me for a month. I could make more than that trying to catch some cheatin' spouse." Okay, that *was* a lie. But in the time this case would take, I'd be too busy to take on new ones. Ivan was lucky he'd caught me in a slow spot. Otherwise, I would've demanded the Court reimburse my lost casework too.

He grumbled Russian obscenities under his breath.

"I can't hear ya, Boss."

"Fine," he said a little louder. "You know she'll bite my head off for this."

"Tell her I forced your hand." I let my tone soften a bit. "She's always ready to blame me."

With that, we said goodbye and hung up. I changed my voicemail and taped a message over the logo on my door. Both referred any potential new client to Peter Andrews, another local PI two blocks down. He did the same for me when he took any time away or when his caseload was too heavy.

Even if I hadn't agreed to an amount to cover my bills with one case, I still would've dropped to just the one. If these idiots kept dealing in the area, they would expose the vampire population of Portland. I might not be living at Court anymore, but I still didn't need the cops on higher alert.

I grabbed my coat and helmet, locking the door on my way out.

———◆———

I set up shop in my living room, my mass of blonde hair tied in a big bun to keep it out of my face. I wasn't worried about my roommates interfering. They knew the drill when I worked from home. Plus, hours of research were much easier with a glass of whiskey on my couch than in my cramped uptown office.

Granted, using my PI license gave me access to some pretty cool tools on that computer, but using those would also risk drawing attention to myself. Police could easily see when I ran a background check or any other information for work. I needed to keep my human alias intact. So, I did things the slow way starting with Googling the crime stats in my city.

It was easy enough to find a pie chart from the city outlining various types of crime from drugs, violence, and other nonsense. The last slice was labeled for known vampire crimes. That part of the pie chart showed eleven percent. Whoa. That was high.

I mean it was probably lower than the actual number since we tended to clean up our own messes. However, humans usually had that number in the area of six percent; I'd seen eight once. Now it was almost double the normal figure. I leaned against my couch and sipped my drink, contemplating how that may affect my work.

If the percentage was already high, then the police may already be on high alert as it was. That would mean a lot more tip-toeing around the humans to avoid being noticed. I swirled more whiskey through my mouth before putting the glass down to add the statistics to my notes for future reference.

"Alright." I cracked my neck like I was going into battle. "Let's check Facebook."

Was I just too damn old to get it? Back in my day, kids ran around outside, dammit. Okay, back in my day, kids did farm work, but still. Why the hell did everyone feel the need to share *everything* online? Whatever happened to talking?

Yep, definitely showing my age.

Adrian St. Claire had his account set to private so I wrote a question mark next to his name. Sadly, his profile photo didn't give me any hints about his lifestyle, it was just a very close-cropped selfie. It made him look more like a shadow than a man. I made what little notes I could about his appearance since it was all I was getting. White, probably thin, hooked nose, and dark hair. Then I moved through the rest of my list.

Two of the profiles yielded very little but at least there weren't any food photos. Most of the victims were taking photos at parties with their *homeboys* or *girlfriends*. Various language and slang, along with their photos told me they probably were in high-risk areas. Easy pickings if you were a vampire trying to juice the population without getting noticed. I made my notes about each of their appearances, including a party that both of them had on their calendar for tomorrow, address included. Thoughtful of them.

Four of the profiles made me wish I could puke. They were either up to their eyeballs in debt or in a completely different social circle from the others. There was a man with an exorbitant number of photos of him and his Corvette, along with various upgrades he'd made to the machine. Each picture he posed, trying to look sexy, I think. He looked silly to me, but most people trying to look hot didn't seem to accomplish it. There was even one where he was kissing the hood of his car.

Don't get me wrong, I loved my motorcycle and it'd been some time since I'd gotten some action. Still, making out with my bike was not high on my to-do list. I rolled my eyes and jotted my notes before moving on. I didn't see any links between him and the other victims. I even spent an hour scrolling through their friends' lists, but there was nobody in common. Nothing so far, but if I was this high class, I certainly wouldn't shout about my ghetto friends either.

"And society thought they got rid of the class system." I snorted

One of the girls was my worst nightmare. This girl and her friends' drama filled the screen, various declarations of rage and excitement over petty things.

Bitch, he was mine first!

Those posts were only split up by photos of the girl and every meal she ever ate.

MMMMM, scones!

"Why the hell do people insist on photographing their food?" I grumbled and scrolled through a little faster. Granted, my particular meal plan may have influenced my preferences, but I just didn't see the bloody appeal.

Okay, so I had one unknown, two clearly lower class, and four in upper middle class or better. A shared party plan, but no other obvious friendships between them. I couldn't call that result shocking. Multiple choices with no big obvious connection could be the result of multiple culprits or just very careful planning to hide the crime.

Still, weird that the rich kids were showing up in the hospital more than the kids from Rockwood. I'd have to look into that.

Next were the two cops, just to see who I might need to steer clear of. Gabriel Collins rose in my estimation when I couldn't find a profile for him, not even a private one. Though that also annoyed me a bit, since it meant he could run into me at any time, and I wouldn't know it. Hopefully, his partner would prove more social.

I'd crossed paths with the police more than once. Mostly after one of my clients got violent with their spouses or my investigation turned up a crime I had to report. It didn't happen often, but it wasn't unheard of in my line of work. I'd cooperate, hand over my case notes, and make myself as forgettable as possible. The humans still didn't know how to properly kill us, and I was not interested in lining up as the first guinea pig, thank you.

James Harper did not disappoint. It took a few wrong clicks, but I found one man in Portland old enough to be the right guy. His profile was set to private, but his picture was clear. Two men. One was beefy and dark, built like a stereotypical biker with a long dark, Santa style beard. His head was either shaved or bald, but based on that beard I was thinking the former. His black eyes twinkled with merriment.

A scruffy man had his arm around the beefy one's shoulders while holding a brown bottle up in cheers. The lean one was a little taller than his friend but only an inch or two. His arms showed muscle but it wasn't thick. Maybe a runner. His dark hair curled around his ears and was more than a little messy. It didn't look intentional or gelled, but it also didn't take away from his features. His chin was flecked with the same midnight-colored hair, just a little longer than a five-o'clock shadow.

It was the scruffy one's expression that grabbed me. He had his camera smile on as he raised his beer, but it didn't reach his eyes. They were more determined than happy, and I couldn't quite suss out the color. Maybe blue?

I leaned away in thought. Well, one of these was probably Harper. If I was lucky the other would be his partner. As I began noting their appearances, the back of the couch sagged behind me.

"He's not bad."

I smiled up at Alex, not bothering to ask which one he meant. It wasn't like it mattered. "Ya better watch Darren doesn't hear ya say that."

He was leaning against the back of the couch, using his arms to support him. He rolled his obsidian eyes. "Please. If Darren was the jealous type, he'd just be another meal buddy."

"True," I acknowledged. Darren had his weird quirks, evidenced from the stack of conspiracy rags we got in the mail every week, but he didn't fret window shopping. "Ya'd still better get a move on it if ya want to keep him around."

"Not your business, Lils." Alex twisted his lips in annoyance before nodding at the screen. "What's up with the two guys anyway?"

I decided to let it go and turned back to my screen, gesturing to the photo. "If I'm lucky, they're the detectives I need to avoid while on my next job."

"Oh, got one of our cases, huh?" Alex leaped over the back of the couch and landed next to me. His scrawny body barely even shifted the cushions.

"Yep." I looked over at him. "Apparently, some humans have been popping up with evidence of red cocaine in the area."

CHAPTER 3

GABE

"**I**n his nose?" I stopped writing and looked at Dan, waiting for the punchline. He didn't deliver one.

"Yeah, I might've missed it if not for the procedure to type all blood against vampiric markers." Dan showed me the sample he was logging into evidence, as though that somehow cleared up the issue. The ME's mask muffled his words, and I had to strain to hear him anytime he turned away.

He'd found cocaine in our victim's nose, which didn't surprise me. The red tint, however, had warranted the usual labs to check if any blood on the scene was human or undead. Something about certain markers or amino acids not being present in vampire blood made it easier to type and log it into evidence. I didn't know the weird science, and I wasn't paid enough to remember.

"Okay, I get the drugs. But what was the blood doing up there?" I used my pen to point at John Doe's nose.

Dan shrugged, putting his gloved hands up in the gesture. "Not a clue. I didn't find any around the nose or anywhere else on him for that matter. The rest of the blood collected from the scene was all his."

He pushed the corpse back into the drawer of the morgue wall, shutting the cabinet door with a thick suction sound. I tapped my pen against my temple in thought. "Have you ever seen anything like this?"

"Not that I can recall." He shrugged again before removing his mask. "I've started making some calls to other MEs and hospitals. We'll see if anyone has noticed anything similar."

"Yeah, it might be nothing but it's just too weird not to look into. I'd appreciate any updates whenever you can. I know you have other cases in need of your help." I gestured to indicate the rest of the drawers near me.

"No trouble, I'll let you or Harper know if I find out anything."

I turned to leave and grunted a goodbye to Dan. The temperature raised slightly with every linoleum-covered step as I ascended towards the bullpen.

At the top of the stairs, I saw Harper hunched over his computer, clicking away. I turned to our break room, grabbing two disposable cups from the cabinet, along with some cream and sugar packets. I pulled at the tie around my neck out of habit.

One of these days, I would just wear bike leather, like Harper. I scoffed and shook my head at the mental image as I filled the two cups from the tepid coffee pot. I didn't even feel right wearing jeans in the office, let alone what Harper wore. When I turned back to the floor, Harper sat back in his chair with a look of triumph on his face.

I made it over to his desk, handing him one cup and dropping the sugar packets off. "You first, my lead is just weird."

Harper grabbed three of the sugar packets and shook them vigorously from one end before dumping the contents into his tiny cup. He took a satisfied chug and turned his screen to face me. "Meet our Mr. Doe. Fingerprints came back a few minutes ago."

I hunched down. Sure enough, it was the same face as the corpse I'd just seen in the morgue. Hooked nose and brown hair.

"Adrian St. Claire, booked last year for assault and battery." The rap sheet next to the photo showed a list of his other charges, petty theft and drugs among them. The poor kid was only seventeen. It had been hard for me to guess his age from his body's bruised and chewed condition. "Any known associates or family?"

"His last known address is about a block north of where we found him. Shows he lived with his mother."

"Wanna head over and deliver the news?" I'd have to give Dan a warning, in case the family wanted to see the body. We never suggested looking at a family member after we identified them, but some people felt they needed the closure.

"Yeah, we can get that over with. I'm waiting on the subpoena for his Facebook to come back anyway." Harper reached into his desk for his keys. "What was your lead?"

"The kid had vampire blood in his nose." I downed the contents of my paper cup before tossing it in the trash.

"Come again?" Harper stopped halfway through shrugging his coat on.

"I told you it was weird." I walked over to my desk and flung my coat over my arm, and we headed out.

❖

Adrian St. Claire had died only one block from home, a dingy green ranch with curling shingles and a busted picket fence. The faded door loomed in the distance.

Be careful what you wish for.

I'd finally gotten it, a legit vampire case. I could finally make a difference. And I was scared of a door. I just didn't want to see the look on their face. Delivering the news had never been fun. I'd had people slap me, collapse in tears, and slam the door. One even broke into laughter asking where the hidden camera was. But I had no idea what to expect this time.

Harper paused, giving me a moment. "You sure you want to do this, buddy?"

"Yeah it sucks, but I signed up for it." I had to get through this. This was why I'd requested assignment to the Vamp Queue. "Let's get this over with."

I forced myself forward to ring the cracked doorbell.

"Coming!" A peppy voice called from somewhere far in the house. Footsteps thumped rapidly towards the door. The thick oak squeaked open, and I immediately knew where Adrian had got those forest-colored eyes.

The tiny woman on the other side of the screen dried a dish as she glanced from me to Harper. "Can I help you?"

I tried to speak a couple of times but Harper beat me to it. "Annabell St. Claire?"

"Yes." The curvy woman took a step back from the door.

I coughed once and tried again. "I'm Detective Collins. This is my partner, Detective Harper. May we come in?"

"Oh, no." Her eyes grew wide, and she stopped rubbing the bowl with the rag. "What did Adrian do this time?"

"I think it's better we speak inside." I restrained my expression, trying to remember what I'd wanted from folks when it was my turn.

Whatever I did, it was the wrong thing.

"No." She backed up again, tossing her brown curls side-to-side. "What did my son do?"

Dammit. I hated when they took the news through a screen door. It never went well.

"Ma'am—" Harper took a deep breath, "I'm afraid we're not here because of what your son did."

"No..." The bowl dropped with a thick *thud*, but it couldn't compare to the heavy fall of the woman on her floor. "No..."

It took everything in me not to yank the screen door open. Years of practice. We didn't have her permission to enter and, even if we did, it wasn't like I could do anything for her. I let her rock on the floor, ringing the dishtowel in her hands until the skin was red.

After the tenth rendition of *no*, her voice shook with the words, "I knew he wasn't coming home this time."

The whole scene took about five minutes. It took her another moment to edge the screen door open in invitation.

"How?"

"Vampires." I squatted in front of her, not bothering to lower my eyes to hers. She would just look the other way.

"Figures." She snorted, the breath sending one of her slow tears sputtering off her lips. "This neighborhood may as well get a big sign that says *Drive-Thru*."

That was a bit of an exaggeration but I didn't say anything. I didn't have any reason to defend those parasites.

She swallowed and sat up straight on the floor. The pain was evident on her face, but she also looked almost numb to it. "What do you need from me?"

"Maybe it'd be best to move to the couch." Harper offered a hand.

"Yes, of course." She shook her head more slowly this time and stood, ignoring the offer. It took her several tries to pick herself up. "Can I, um, get you something to drink?"

"No, ma'am, we're fine."

"Please, water maybe?" Her eyes quaked and swelled.

Harper opened his mouth, but I beat him this time. "Water would be great, thank you."

Annabell nodded and plodded off towards the kitchen. Harper waited until the water was running to mutter, "Why'd you take it?"

"She needed something else to focus on." I was already examining pictures on the wall.

He grunted and came to stand next to me. "Is that what you needed?"

"Not a lot of pictures of Adrian lately." I gave him a warning look. "And I don't see any pictures with the rest of the family."

There was Adrian on a bike, smiling the big, gap-tooth grin of a proud child learning to ride. There he was again, his collar popped looking happy the way only a teenager can when they look that ridiculous. There he was with his mom in a photo booth, his hair dyed black and chewing cotton candy in each frame. Nothing that looked older than fifteen. Nothing more than him and his mom.

"None on file." Harper sighed and gave me an exasperated look. At least he didn't push the subject.

"Where's his father?" I swallowed like I could take the last word back.

"He heard I was pregnant and lost my number the next day." Annabell walked back in holding two glasses of water. Her nose was red, and a wadded tissue protruded from her pocket.

"Must've been hard." I drank my first sip and suppressed a grimace. The water wasn't filtered very well. And it was warm. But now was hardly the time to judge her hosting skills.

"Not at first." She motioned towards the couches. "My parents helped a lot. But then my dad lost his job, and he couldn't support us anymore. We ended up here."

We sat and I finally took in the whole room. It wasn't manicured, like Ms. Stafford's place had been. This felt more like a home; a jacket thrown over the back of a chair, some of the older wallpaper peeling at the corners, and mismatched furniture that was worn and dented. But nothing was flat-out dirty or out of place.

The walls were littered with more pictures of Adrian, but not many of her. Birthday parties, skating rinks, a couple of assorted sporting events that dwindled as the boy got older. Each one in a set in matching frames with precision and care, despite obviously being taken by an amateur. This woman sitting across from me loved her son, yet the tears slid down her cheeks in slow, controlled patterns.

"What do you need from me?" She clasped her hands and let her eyes roam over the gallery. "I don't know any of Adrian's enemies or the people that might want to hurt him."

Well, that was an interesting answer. Harper pulled a notebook and pen from his pocket and leaned back, giving me room to take over. Witnesses were his territory, but family was mine.

"So, he did have enemies?" I wanted to start with something that would let her ramble. Family members didn't usually divulge the best information on purpose, it was while they mourned and couldn't really keep their thoughts organized. Not always because they were trying to hide things. Most of the time we didn't even know what was important until we heard it.

"With what he's been up to." She snorted and pulled the tissue from her pocket. "*Was* up to. Yeah, he had enemies."

"And what was that?"

"It started when he was about fourteen." She glanced at the photo booth shot and a tear escaped her eyes as she whispered, "I knew this was coming."

"What started?" I wanted to know how she knew, but I figured I would get the answer to that later.

"He started skipping school. He started lashing out and stealing alcohol out of the cupboard. I stopped buying any, but I kept finding bottles in his room when I went for laundry." She blew her nose and finally looked back to us. "The school recommended a therapist, but I just couldn't afford it. I set curfews, made him apply for jobs, I tried everything. But curfews don't keep kids in their rooms. So, finally, I just asked him to call when he wasn't going to be home."

It was odd appreciating every time my mother had grounded me. You never knew what you had until it was gone.

But now, I needed to focus on her. "Did he tell you what he was doing when he called?"

"Not exactly, but I got the picture." She looked up at me then down again. "I know I should have reported him to the police, but I just kept hoping he'd grow out of it. I mean, teenagers get into trouble, right?"

She was stalling, probably ashamed of letting it go this far. Her words seemed stiff, like she might have even rehearsed them a time or two. She'd known this day was coming, but she'd held out hope. And this was where that hope had led her.

"What kind of trouble did yours get into?" I hated pressing, but I couldn't help her son if I didn't know what I was up against.

"He started with petty crap. Shoplifting, that kind of thing." She shrugged and it was the most helpless gesture I'd ever seen. "But ever since the massacres, his friends were obsessed with vampires. They went full Renfield."

I wanted to curse, but I settled for a scowl. "How so?"

Even after all the movies and books referring to vampires were blacklisted, Renfields still caused us more casework than the actual vampires. Hell, some of them had begun organizing vampire-human relationship groups. I could only hope this wasn't one of those.

"They thought they could become immortal, get stronger, ya know. The whole stupid kit and kaboodle." She shook her head.

Okay, she was going to keep skating around that. She wasn't ready to admit what her son had been doing. She'd be admitting her own failings. If we kept going at it, she'd just get defensive, and I would get less and less out of her. I needed a different angle.

"Earlier, you said you knew he wasn't coming home." Maybe if I reminded her of her maternal instincts, she'd open up more. It felt dirty, using that against her, but I needed to catch this vamp.

"Yes." She nodded emphatically, still not meeting my eyes. "I couldn't get Adrian to stay home, so I had him call when he wasn't coming home."

I didn't point out she'd already said that. She was talking, no point in spoiling it. I just nodded and tried to remember how she felt. Even the things that weren't her fault, she would blame herself. Hell, I still did.

"He hadn't called as much lately so I started going through Facebook, to see where he was checking in." She blew her nose then got up and walked away. She carried a laptop in her hands when she came back. "Last night was the first night he didn't post any updates. He *always* posts something, even if it's just a quick update."

She set the laptop on the coffee table and logged in, turning for us to see.

"May I?" Harper leaned forward and pointed at the keyboard.

Sure, it was just another Facebook page, but you'd be surprised how much we get from those. Social media might have a short attention span, but it never forgets.

Annabelle waved him forward. "You can take it, it's not like I'll need it anymore."

I pulled a glove out of my pocket and offered it. Harper pulled it on when a calendar notification popped up.

John's party, 7:00 PM tomorrow.

Looks like we had plans the following night.

CHAPTER 4

LILY

They were called bondage pants. In reality, they were just overpriced skinny jeans with straps crisscrossing several layers of metal studs in two diagonal patterns. My long boots hid the bottom third of my trousers, along with some extra artillery. My top half was swathed in a blouse, or so one could generously label the shreds of fabric layered in a way that barely concealed my torso and did fuck all to keep autumn air off my skin.

I'd toned down my natural blonde with layers of temporary red and silver dye and straightened my normal mess of curls, making the mass hang far past the middle of my back. A rub-on tan over my pale skin and makeup that made me look like a reject from a Marilyn Manson music video completed the look.

Alex had snapped several photos for future blackmail while our other roommates laughed before I could leave the house. Not that I blamed them. I'd chosen the goth girl look for several reasons. Chief among them, the excessive makeup made my normal features harder to pick out.

On top of that, if I looked like I used Sharpie for mascara, it tended to make my lack of social skills more excusable. Typically, you stand in a corner, people-watching at a party, and someone tries to approach you. Then the social butterfly gets all pissy when you tell them to shove off, drawing a lot of unwanted attention.

So far, the ugly makeup was doing its job. Everyone seemed to buy the ruse. I was just some bitchy girl with a bad attitude. I overheard someone asking if they should kick me out, but their concerns were set aside because I wasn't bugging anyone.

Still, I got jostled by other partygoers as they danced badly to the obnoxious bass, nearly spilling my room-temp beer as I hunched my shoulders and surveyed the crowd.

So far, all the people surrounding me seemed to have heartbeats, but I could have missed a skip in the thumps with the crappy music. I was a little surprised the rattling windows were surviving. I turned around to check again and almost broke into laughter.

Some poor sod was passed out on the cheap sofa, one of his arms sprawled over his face as he snoozed. A few partygoers stood around him, each with a different shade of Magic Marker as they debated what to do with the kid's face.

"Hey, come on." I stepped forward to tell the group to leave the poor kid alone before he ended up with dicks all over his face. I stopped short when I saw the guy's snoring countenance. I knew that face. Where the hell did I know this guy from?

A kid wearing a do-rag snorted. "This rich jerk should know better than to pass out 'round here."

I looked up to retort but his 'rich jerk' comment clicked something into place, and I looked back down. This was the guy I'd seen macking on his car when I was looking through Facebook yesterday. Had he been in the Facebook event? I scrolled through my memory and almost swore with frustration. I was certain he hadn't been on the list of people attending, even when I had checked this morning. Adrian St Claire had been, though I hadn't seen that distinctively hooked nose yet. Had I missed something? Do-Rag said something, and I shook my head to clear it.

"Huh?"

"You want in on this?" Do-Rag held out a marker, and I shook my head again.

"He's all yours." I turned on my heel and tried to blend back into the crowd of miscreants while making a mental note to do more research on Corvette Guy later.

Anna wouldn't see me until tomorrow, so I'd decided to attend the party tonight. Alex hadn't liked it, pointing out that any vamp here could use their extra senses to scout me in return. It was a risk, but seeing as seven victims had grabbed the Courts' radar, this guy was probably too cocky to think about watching for his own kind.

So, I wandered randomly from one partygoer to the next, listening for the telltale skip in the rhythm of heartbeats. Right as I'd decided I needed a new cup of stale camouflage to sip, I heard the front door open. One set of footsteps followed the loud *thud* of the door closing. Only footsteps. I fought the sudden urge to snap my head up.

The newcomer would have the same predatory instincts. Any sudden motion would make my dark primping a huge waste of time. So, I continued my steady stride to the keg. Once my red cup was refilled, I turned around to take in the whole room before I took in the newcomer.

His appearance almost made me snort. Even two years after we'd been outed to humanity, the warning posters still made us look like supermodels. Their skin was paler than mine and they flashed seductive smiles, a big warning sign about the *temptations*. If only the proprietors of those billboards could get a look at this guy.

The newcomer looked to be in his thirties by modern standards. He was short and had the misfortune of being turned with a potbelly forever frozen to his gut. That alone told me he was most likely young in undead years. Obesity had been rare before the 1950s. His head shined under a bad comb-over that no one was buying. In other circumstances, I would have told him to be bald and be proud, but I wanted to see what he was up to.

I sauntered in another direction to avoid his immediate attention. Newbie though he may be, I didn't know enough about what crown he was under or even if he was the dealer. While chances were low he had just come to relax, I didn't want to assume this was my guy without proof. I needed to wait for evidence. I didn't have to wait long.

Not even ten minutes after I'd spotted him, I learned his name was Joey as he'd accepted several shoulder slaps and all sorts of drunken bro-hugs. Many of the greetings were accompanied by questions about coke or Cheri coke. I nearly rolled my eyes at the lack of originality when I heard the street name. What cabbage had come up with that? Still, at least I knew I had the right vamp.

I kept myself on the edge of the crowd, craning my neck in obvious absorption. Everyone was staring, no need to stand out feigning a lack of interest. Joey started pulling small Ziploc bags of ruby-colored powder from his coat pockets, holding a handful up in each fist for the crowd. Several drunken yells accompanied my shock at this show.

True, I'd figured whoever I was chasing was a novice at trouble-making but this was ridiculous. Couldn't he at least do the selling in a quiet back room or something? Being this blatant wasn't just daring. It was like a fucking billboard! I was glad everyone was staring; I couldn't peel my eyes away if my life depended on it.

Money and red powder began changing hands quickly. It wasn't long before the room split between those partaking in the new entertainment and those not. A coffee table was set with several cherry-colored lines and surrounded by several enthusiasts. I kept reminding myself that stopping tonight's transactions would probably only give the Court an inexperienced pawn. While that was a decent start, it was also easy to stop the trade here and start somewhere else if I didn't get a few rungs higher up the ladder from Joey.

So, I stayed with the crowd of pot smokers and thanked God I didn't need to breathe. The smell alone would've been enough to make me consider leaving or blowing my cover. Luckily, the perpetual 'fuck off' sign I'd erected across my forehead also kept away any offers for hits and dances.

I leaned against the wall, playing one of the games Maria had stuck on my phone and trying to look disinterested. I occasionally paused the game to snap a few photos with my camera. Little colored blobs swirled in and out of existence as I matched them haphazardly and tuned my hearing to the conversations across the room.

Granted tuning out all the other distractions and noise when I chose to use my enhanced ears was a bit of a nuisance. But once I got a mental lock on Joey's voice and slow speech pattern, it was easy enough to filter for the responses. About an hour of low scores and five stale refills later, Joey had negotiated price on a few sales, educated some new users on best practices, and shooed away one guy looking for a free high. Still, he hadn't mentioned anything supernatural like I'd been expecting.

"Come on man, what do you put in this stuff? It's incredible!" This was the fifth attempt at learning the secret ingredient.

Joey donned a poor imitation of a British accent to reply, "If I tell you, I'm afraid you won't even try it."

He followed this with repeated slurps of his tongue to continue the Hannibal Lecter impersonation. I snorted and almost shot beer through my nose.

A real vampire mocking a fake human cannibal, that was fucking brilliant. It would have been great under other circumstances. Joey had turned every prod for information into a joke or redirected the conversation. I was curious what he would do if someone got pushy. Could be worth finding out. And it wasn't like I was doing much else.

Another forty-five minutes later, I was dancing poorly to keep up with the drunk partygoer next to me. His breath was coated in beer and weed; it was pungent even without the need to take in air. Still, I needed him. Not for what he had in mind as he snake-hipped the air near my body, but he did have value.

I'd made it seem like the massive number of drinks were getting to me, slowly peeling the scowl from my face and making myself more inviting. After all, going from cold bitch to 'ooh fuck me' would have been a bit too obvious. After I'd feigned a little shy giggling, Dean had shown me his tattoos in the hopes of breaking the last bit of my ice. He even pretended to be interested in my days in Ireland, but I verbally skated around the topic.

Bloody accent. There were definitely days I thought about learning to talk without it but it was the only thing I had left of home. That and some shitty memories.

As we white-girl-danced, I'd given him a few feather-soft kisses, barely keeping the inner grimace off my face. Acting like I was warming up should have earned me an Emmy right there, but I needed this to go just a little further for what I had in mind. I leaned in for another kiss, lingering in a way that I hoped seemed inviting.

Apparently, it was. Dean leaned in further and stuck that disgusting tongue right on in, gently gripping the back of my neck at the same time. It took all of my energy not to rip my head out of his grasp. Dean's breath had told me he'd indulged too much, while his kiss told me he had no clue how to use a toothbrush. Come on, even the undead could keep good dental hygiene

Revulsion slithered through every nerve in my body, and I fought a shiver crawling up my spine. I counted to ten to make sure the kiss was long enough, chanting to myself, *Fake it 'till you make it.*

I pressed on, moaning softly, hoping it sounded like I was enjoying the moment. Another Academy Award apparently, because Dean started slipping his hands through the holes of my shirt to caress my skin. I pushed at his hands, barely remembering to check my strength to chipmunk levels.

My room temp skin hadn't given me away, but he'd probably noticed if a girl who looked about fifty pounds lighter than him was somehow stronger. Still, no way in hell I could let him reach below my blouse. "Can we go somewhere more private?"

"Hell yeah, we can!" Dean gripped my hand, telling me that my blood circulation really sucked. I stifled a laugh, grateful the music swallowed some of the noise. He led me to the back of the packed house and some obvious bedrooms. The first door had a couple behind it who'd forgotten to lock the knob. The smell of sweat and some soft groans had given me that first tidbit while Dean opening the door to a surprised shriek had told me the second. After another door that was properly locked, he edged the last door open with more caution, pulling me close for another kiss. We were still in view of the party, so the show must go on, but I couldn't wait for Dean to lock that door.

The minute Dean turned back from the lock, I gave him a direct stare. A look of shock crossed his features right before his jaw went a little slack and his eyes glazed. I knew without looking that my eyes would look like the pupil had swallowed all the color. I smiled, thankful my seduction was over and wishing desperately for a breath mint.

I didn't feel too bad about using Dean. Once I was done with him, I'd wipe his memory and give him a new one of the drunken passions he'd been angling for. The least I could do was leave him with some fake whoopie, right?

"All right, you're going to get some of that Cheri Coke outside and bring it back to me." I kept my voice low to avoid Joey overhearing my directive. Between my whisper and the loud party music, I should be okay. He hadn't even glanced my way all night. "You'll just know ya need it to loosen up your date. Once you're done buyin', ask the dealer what makes it so powerful. If he tries to not answer ya, ask again but don't push him if he gets angry."

Dean nodded, still looking a bit like an extra from the *Walking Dead*. My grin widened as I let the color slowly come back into my gaze. "Okay go out there, and remember the sooner ya come back the sooner ya get lucky."

As soon as I shut off my power, Dean blinked and looked natural again. He smiled crookedly and leaned over to give me another quick kiss. "Don't worry baby. I gotcha covered."

He opened the door and slinked out. I didn't bother putting my ear to hollow wood; it wouldn't help. The door would suppress noise for me about as well as tossing a wet blanket over my head.

I shut my eyes and sifted for Joey and Dean's voices. I learned through the inane chatter that there was a line for the red cocaine. Thank God my directive to hurry back hadn't resulted in Dean cutting in front or pissing people off. A little bit of small talk and some blah blahs later, I finally got the conversation I was hoping for.

"Hey, man. I need something to loosen the little lady in the back." Dean's voice.

"Ah...gotta give your girl some incentive?" Joey chuckled with his reply. "Good timing, I'm down to two bags. One for each?"

Dean's response must have been a nod or something because Joey kept talking like he'd said yes. They talked price for a bit, and I reminded myself to pull a few bills out of my wallet to replace what Dean was losing. Ivan could cover it.

Joey made sure Dean knew how to use it, even had him do a sample to get the hang of it. With his proper tone, Joey could have been selling insurance. Hell, I got less professional with some of my PI clients. After the sales pitch was over, Dean came to the main question. "Dude, you gotta tell me what makes this stuff so powerful!"

"Never ask a magician to reveal his secrets, my friend—"

A loud crash announced something breaking open at the front of the house, cutting Joey short. The following bellow identified the literal party crashers.

"Police! Everyone down!"

"Shite!" I dropped my concentration and cracked the door to peek out.

Sure enough, armed men came in with their guns drawn. "Nobody move!"

Of course, the command didn't work for everybody. Half the people stood still with shock or rage on their faces. The other half bolted for the open windows or back doors, giving our new company a little extra work.

I groaned, "Double shite."

On one hand, I didn't want the cops getting those last two bags Joey had or putting them into evidence to test them. On the other hand, I needed to get out of here before my cover was blown. If I got arrested at this party and fingerprinted, they'd find out who I really was, even if none of them had ever met me at my day job. And that didn't even cover what I was. Dean hadn't figured it out when he touched my chilly skin, but he was drunk and horny. Trained police were another matter entirely.

As I saw the approaching officers come down the back hallway, I made up my mind. At least if my cover wasn't blown, I could warn the Court we were about to have another media nightmare before it happened. I shut the door as quietly as I could, and then switched to my normal speed. My rushed movements disturbed the bedspread and curtains like a strong breeze as I threw the window open. In my haste, I managed to break some glass from the bottom pane. I winced at the instant guilt but climbed out right as I heard someone make demands for me to open the door I'd just locked.

Once outside I sprinted to the other side of the yard and out of sight from the open window. I heard the sound of wood splintering from the room I'd left followed by the static of a hand radio as the officer advised his team that someone had gotten away on the north side of the house. I didn't wait for anything else. I hopped the back fence, glad I hadn't brought my motorcycle. The engine would have grabbed everyone's attention for miles, and I couldn't have left her behind.

I slowed to my human speed on the off chance anyone was back here to see me. It sucked I had to leave the drugs behind, but I didn't need anyone witnessing my own vampire activity. I just had to hope Joey got out too, maybe with the rest of his stash in tow.

I was halfway down the block when a car turned the corner ahead of me, headlights blinding me. Blue and red emitted from the top of the vehicle and a loud whoop sent a wave of cold panic through my skin. The larger man from Detective Harper's Facebook photo got out and told me to freeze.

I held up my hands. "Triple shite."

CHAPTER 5

GABE

S omeone had finally staggered out and tried to drive home drunk. We waited until she was about a block away before pulling her over to prevent the other partygoers from noticing. Even while we were arresting the twit, she told us all about her wild party night and the *amazing new drug*.

Bingo.

A few quick calls later, we had the rest of the Vampire Task Force assembled and were going in. Three cars stayed outside to get stragglers, Harper and me in the one we'd been using for our stakeout.

The call came that someone had gotten out through the back of the house, and we headed towards the alleyway. Sure enough, a blonde woman ran down the block. She looked like a homeless person who'd swam in some tar. Harper got out and told her to freeze. For a split second, her face flushed with annoyance while she held up her hands.

I put the car in park and radioed in that we had the runner before leaning over the passenger seat, shouting through the open door. "You got her?"

"Yeah, I got her." Harper's light was still trained on her, and his other hand over his holster. "Okay, ma'am, turn around with your hands on your head."

The woman let out a weary sigh. "Officer?"

"Yes?" Harper's tone became curious but no less authoritative. He didn't want to spook the woman, but he wasn't taking any risks either.

"Can ya please reach into my back pocket?" Her voice carried a distinct lilt, but I couldn't quite place it over the thrum of the idling engine.

Harper looked back at me for a moment before responding. "What for?"

"I got somethin' back there that may clear this up." She placed her hands on the back of her head and turned around. "On the left."

Harper walked forward, crunching a few leaves under his feet. He dug in the pocket she'd indicated, his cheeks darkening with blush as he did. He pulled something out and aimed his body so the headlights of the car caught it better. Was that a billfold? Harper barked out a loud laugh. "Hey, Collins, we got ourselves a lady dick."

The woman turned around and arched a brow at Harper. She still kept her hands on her head. "Really?"

I finally stepped out and walked forward, the autumn air brittle against my face. "What are you talking about?"

Harper handed me the wallet. I pulled the heavy flashlight from my belt and clicked the back button for a better view as Harper escorted the woman back to our cruiser, using her elbow for guidance. She dropped her arms to her side and walked peacefully next to my partner. I saw a driver's license for Lillian Edwards in a clear ID pocket.

I could see her face more clearly in the beam of my flashlight than I had in the headlights of our car. Apparently, she didn't always look like a Hot Topic junkie. Her hair was bright and full in the photo, covering the width of her shoulders in wild curls that looked like they would break any standard hairbrush. Her face was oval and sharp, her nose just a bit too pointy, like an elf. One of her cheeks was dimpled as she smiled for the camera, making her cheekbones appear sharp. Her smile seemed a bit off. It was pretty enough, but it felt hollow.

I moved the wallet to see the other side and saw what Harper had been snickering about. A second plastic pocket held a tiny blue certificate about the same size as a social security card. Stamped on the top was 'State of Oregon: Department of Safety Standards and Training.' Below this was Miss Edwards' name, same as her license. Below that was her PI-ID number; the number I would use to confirm if she really was who she said. The car door slammed, and I looked up at Harper, shaking my head. "She's right, you know, about the dick joke."

He crunched back towards me through the dirty alley. "Been a while since we got to question a private investigator."

<hr />

Miss Edwards rocked on the back legs of her metal chair. She looked directly at the window, the heavy makeup deepening the shadows under her eyes. The gray bricks behind her almost swallowed her in their deep color, but for the various hues littering her hair. She had her boots propped up on the table and her hands crossed over her stomach while she made little popping noises with her lips.

Her eyes were fixed directly on mine like she somehow knew where I was behind the two-way mirror. That couldn't be...could it?

I held two cups of coffee in my hands as I assessed her. "So, how do you want to play this?"

"I don't know." Harper sipped at his own cup and grimaced. "Needs more sugar."

"We're out, I checked."

"Great, it'll be a week before they bother to order any." He shrugged and took another sip. "Let's try playing this one straight. She's the most interesting lead we have, aside from all that red powder they've got evidence testing. Besides, she's not likely to be an idiot. Good cop bad cop probably won't work on her."

"I agree." I'd only ever interviewed one PI, but the guy had been sharp as a tack. I'm sure there were dumb investigators in the world, but I didn't think the eyes staring back at me belonged to one of them. "Want to bet that red stuff has something to do with the vampire blood in Adrian's nose?"

"You already take enough of my money at poker, bud." Harper thumped me on the back, making the contents of each cup try to crest over the edge. The liquid settled back in place, and I followed him into the tiny concrete room. Harper took the farthest chair from the door. Miss Edwards didn't change her posture, but her sky-colored eyes darkened with interest. I put my cup on the table and placed the second one in front of her as I sat.

She eyed it with a bemused grin. "Ya could just ask for my prints."

"That's okay." I smiled at her and pointed at the cup with a pen I pulled from my pocket. "You can take that cup with you. I'm not logging it into evidence."

"Really? Here I thought the ol' glass of water trick was still all the rage." Without the engine, I could more easily hear her accent. Irish, maybe? It didn't quite sound like what I'd heard in movies, but that was my closest guess.

"Nah. Your ID checked out. Besides, that's coffee." I fished in my pocket and handed her the wallet. She took it, barely shifting her legs as she did.

Harper placed a paper file and writing tablet on the metal table in front of us and crossed his burly arms over his beard. "So, what brought you to the party tonight?"

I pulled the pen and paper over to me. Miss Edwards took a swig from the cup and sneered at it, sticking her tongue out a few times like she tried to clear it with the flats of her teeth.

"Do either of ya have a mint or somethin'? Sadly, that's only the second-worst taste I've had tonight."

I fished in my pocket, more for show than anything. If anyone would have candy, it was Harper. And he hated mint.

"Sorry, no. Do you want some actual water?"

She looked down at the coffee with more intense thought than it deserved and shook her head.

"Nah, thanks though." She wrapped her hands around the paper cup as she turned her attention back to Harper. "As to why I was at the party, I have a private client who's certain his kid is doin' drugs. I found the party on her Facebook calendar and didn't have any other solid leads to follow tonight."

"And the getup?" I motioned to her whole body with my pen.

"Or the hardware we found in your shoes?" Harper added, giving her boots a pointed look.

"The ugly makeup tends to keep people away from me so long as I glower at 'em." She gave us such a look, and I could see why people would avoid her with that face on. Her face relaxed as she pressed on, "As to the second part, ya carry a gun for work, right?"

We both nodded.

"I also like protection."

"Why not carry a firearm then?" Harper leaned forward on the heavy table.

She shrugged. "Knives are easier to hide and I'm more skilled with them. Besides, they don't require a con-ceal-to-carry."

Her answers made sense but something was bugging me. The tiny lie detector was going off in my head, but I just didn't know why. I looked across the table and her blue eyes were locked on mine.

"Am I free to go?" She was snippy, but that wasn't uncom-mon in the interrogation room. Hell, violence wasn't uncom-mon in there.

"Just a few more questions, if you don't mind," I said it like a statement. She could leave anytime. She hadn't done anything unlawful except run. That was hardly worth pressing charges unless she had more valuable information she wouldn't spill. Plus, Harper was right, she could be a good lead. I tapped the pen against my pad in thought. "Did you have any interaction with the guy who was selling the red powder on the table?"

"Ya mean that Cheri Coke shit?" She shook her head, the motion jostling her long hair. "No, why?"

I gave Harper a confused look. The PI had pronounced it like *Cheri* instead of *cherry*. Had the old lady misheard it?

"Unfortunately, we didn't catch him, and we've been getting fairly vague descriptions of him all night." Harper twirled his hand next to his head in a slow motion, his big fingers dancing with the gesture. "Most of the people who interacted with the guy are all fuzzy about the details. We thought a trained PI might remember him better."

Miss Edwards looked at the coffee as she spoke slowly. Like she was picking through the details. "He was a bit pudgy around the middle. And he talked like he was selling windows or somethin'."

"Windows?" I looked up with interest.

She worried her bottom lip with her front teeth then nodded. "I've come across a few dealers in my work. They're usually kinda brisk with their clients, because they can be."

"It's an illegal substance, so who's the guy going to complain to when the dealer's rude?" I asked. "That what you mean?"

"Yeah, like that." She nodded again, appreciation lighting her eyes. "But this guy, he acted like he was everyone's buddy, even if ya weren't buyin'. Then, he actually had a sit down with his clients and talked with each one to make sure they knew the right procedure so they wouldn't overdose. It was like he cared they had a good experience or somethin'."

I scribbled notes as Harper leaned away again. "Anything else?"

She worried her lip again and it looked like she was weighing something before she spoke. "Yeah, I think I broke a window when I was tryin' to get out of the party. Can someone help me get in touch with the homeowner? I'd like to pay for it."

My eyes widened, and I laughed in surprise. I guess she had done something worth note. She glared at me, her expression darkened further by her makeup. I held up a hand as I fought for control. "I'm sorry, Miss Edwards..."

"Lily." She snapped it out, but her tone wasn't unpleasant. She was just stating a fact.

I nodded and got myself under better control. "Apologies, Lily, it's rare that someone in here *asks* for a bill. I think we can let the homeowner know that you're willing to cover the damages if you leave your card behind."

"Speaking of which." Harper tilted his head. "Why'd you run anyway?"

Miss Edwards squirmed and hunched her shoulders. "I didn't want to spend all night in here instead of workin' my case. I'm a little behind on the payment for my office space and could really use the client's payments sooner rather than later. It was stupid, I know."

Something about how she said that set another alarm ringing in my head again, and I reminded myself to look into it later. Harper gave me a look, and I nodded. We stood, and Harper stuck out his dark hand. "Thank you for your time, Lily."

She gave his hand a wary look but let go of the cup and shook it. I offered her my hand. Her fingers were warm, and I felt a strange urge to keep holding her hand a little longer, like I'd learn something from a bit of prolonged contact.

I mentally shook myself and tried to smile as I released her fingers. Relief flooded her face as I did so, and I felt my brows try to meet in the middle. Did she really want to leave that badly? "Do you need anyone to drive you back to the party? I assume your car is still there."

"Nah, I took an Uber to the party. I didn't want to risk someone messing with my bike."

"Wait." Harper stopped, his hand on the knob. "You *ride?*"

I barely stopped my eyes from rolling. This woman was obviously pretty when she didn't use asphalt for makeup. She seemed clever and had her own PI business. Now she's just admitted she had a motorcycle. Harper was going to fall in love. badly? "Do you need anyone to drive you back to the party ma'am? I assume your car is still there."

"Nah, I took an Uber to the party. I hadn't wanted to risk someone messing with my bike."

"Wait." Harper stopped, his hand on the knob. "You *ride?*"

I barely stopped my eyes from rolling. This woman was obviously pretty when she didn't use asphalt for makeup. She seemed clever and had her own PI business. Now she's just admitted she had a motorcycle. Harper was going to fall in love.

CHAPTER 6

LILY

The smell of burnt eggs and too much pepper flooded my nose. Guess Alex had been taking another cooking lesson.

I locked the front door and leaned my back against the heavy oak, burying my face in my hands. My palms barely muffled the noise as I shrieked, berating myself in a jumble of incoherent words.

"What a mess." My frustration deflated enough to focus, and I stood straight, snapping the back of my skull against the solid surface behind me. "Ow."

"Bad night?"

I peeked between two fingers.

Maria was sitting on the sectional. I always liked my live-in help's style, it was whimsical and colorful. Something I could never pull off. She was still wearing the same gypsy skirt and black blouse from when I'd left. She'd brought her thick mass of braids into one large twist, which she draped over a dark shoulder. Teal and blue beads peeked out from the construction, matching perfectly with the fading hues of her long skirt. Her shoulders were hunched in concentration, and she had her feet tucked under the hem, probably for warmth.

I snorted and collapsed next to her. "You could say that."

She tapped the screen of her tablet as she spoke, little pats emitting between her words. "Your score on *Jelly Splash* is awful."

"Is that what I was playin'?" I propped my feet up on the coffee table, bending my knees to make removing the boots easier. "I was just tryin' to blend in with the crowd."

Maria tapped the screen a final time and put the tablet aside. "So, what happened?"

"Got picked up by the cops."

She waited like there was a punchline before grimacing. "Ew."

"That's one way to put it." I placed my boots on the side of the couch. "The party got raided and they caught me on my way out."

"Why didn't you just black-eye them into letting you go?"

"One of them radioed in that they had me before I could." I shrugged. "There was already one vamp at the party. I didn't want to make it evident there was another if they caught him."

"Yuck." She shook her head, then her face darkened with interest. "How'd you keep them from figuring out what you are?"

"Luck." I let out a short chuckle. "They gave me a cup of coffee. It was disgustin', but at least it was warm. I gripped that thing the entire interview. Apparently, it was enough to throw them off."

"Lucky you. That chilly skin of yours probably would have been enough for them to ask for a blood test." Maria nodded and reached for her tablet again. "So, what's the plan?"

"Call Ivan, get yelled at." I ticked the task off on my thumb, holding up a new finger for each item. "Then start diggin' into some of tonight's leads. I'll see if any pan out before I meet Anna later tomorrow."

Right as I ticked off my last task, a heavy thump and the gasping sound of suction emitted from the kitchen. Alex strolled out from our walk-in pantry, stretching his long limbs and yawning. He brought his arms back down and his eyes landed on me and Maria. He checked his watch and then gave me a look.

"You're home early for a stakeout." I gave him the cliff notes version of my night, and he whistled. "Ivan's gonna be pissed."

"Thank you." I glowered. "I'd never have guessed that on my own."

He gave me an apologetic look, but it was edged with amusement. "You want to kick my ass at Xbox?"

"Maybe later." I got up and stretched. "Right now, I need a hard drink and a hot bath."

"Do you want any blood?" Maria tossed the offer over her hunched shoulders as I headed towards the kitchen.

"Nah, I'm alright," I shot back, grabbing a bottle of whiskey from the cupboard, and heading up the stairs. I heard Alex grumble something after me but paid little attention to it, heading towards a long bath and bed.

Cardiac monitors beeped, their rhythms out of sync and monotonous. I stared at the ceiling tiles and tried to think about anything but unplugging the life-sustaining machines around me. Unfortunately, the only thought that immediately came to mind was the scent of hospital air. Vomit, antiseptic, and a variety of other bodily fluids overwhelmed every other scent, including the coffee machine I'd camped myself next to as a precaution.

Out of the corner of my eye, I saw a little girl with a broken arm in a purple cast. She kept eyeing my helmet like it was a plaything. I placed both arms over it protectively. It wasn't the first time children had mistaken it for a toy. It wouldn't be the last. The little girl still stared at my helmet, her butt on the edge of the plastic chair across from me.

I sank into my own fragile seat and grumbled, "She just had to ask me to meet her at work."

"She could have just told you to take a hike." I ripped my eyes from the ceiling. A nurse stood before me, her thick black hair pulled back in a large bun at the nape of her neck and her copper eyes pinning me to the waiting room chair. She put her hands on her hips and raised both brows. "I still can, you know."

"Heya, Anna." I gave her a wicked grin. "How's tricks?"

She pinned me a moment longer before turning on her heels, the rubber of her shoes squeaking with the quick gesture. I gripped my helmet and followed her, trying not to have a seizure at the fluorescent pattern of hearts and cartoon kitties on her scrubs. The deep olive tone of her arms contrasted heavily with the hot pink material, making it appear more garish than it already was.

She turned her head to make sure I was really behind her. I don't know why she bothered looking. Even with the patients and staff walking next to us, it was easy enough to pick out the squeak of her sneakers or the *thud* of my motorcycle boots in their clipped pace over the linoleum floor.

She turned a corner sharply, and I almost ran into another nurse before redirecting myself. I apologized quickly and caught up to Anna as she turned left into a small room. I entered, and she closed the door behind me, locking it and pulling a blue privacy curtain around us.

She glared up at me, and I almost grinned at the expression on her face. I wasn't a tall woman by any means, but Anna was a shrimp. The combined posture and attitude she projected made me think of Grumpy from the seven dwarfs. I crossed my arms and looked directly down into her eyes.

"Ya sure he won't hear us?" I bobbed my head at the gray patient bed, occupied by an elderly man. He appeared to be fast asleep, but I didn't care to have him wake up in the middle of our conversation.

"Brain-dead." She shook her head and a look of disgust sparked in her eyes before she remembered who she was talking to. "What do you want?"

"Ya treated a few patients recently, people who'd been dosed with red cocaine." I pulled a list out of my jacket and handed it over.

Her eyes scanned the list quickly and her face scrunched in irritation. She looked up and practically shoved the slip of paper back into my chest. "Who says I treated them?"

"Hospital records." I smiled brightly, and her jaw dropped.

"You don't have access to those!"

"No, but one of my roommates does." I reminded myself to pick up some Mountain Dew on my way home. Darren had earned it; being able to tie the hospital records directly to her was worth its weight in gold. "These are only three out of seven victims I have on this list. I find it interesting that all of our victims seemed to be dropped off at hospitals when there were vampires on duty, especially when three of them showed up during your shift."

Her eyes darkened, and she crossed her arms over the garish shirt. "Your point?"

"That either someone knows about the local vampire community and is using it to their advantage—" I crossed my arms again, the leather of my jacket rubbing against itself in a small gasp, "or you and the others are being awfully helpful to the bad guys."

I let silence fill the room, the sharp bleeping of the patient's machine punctuating my sentence. Anna glared a moment longer, and I thought I could hear teeth grinding. "I'm not helping anyone. I smelled the vamp blood on the victims when they were brought into the ER. I had to black-eye half the nurses to erase those paper trails."

"Yet, somehow, they still ended up on file." I ticked an eyebrow up. "All three times."

"It didn't the other five!" Anna snapped it out, then flinched at her own volume before peeking around the privacy curtain.

I gave her a hard look. "*What* other five?"

She let the curtain settle back in place and glared up at me. Her words were clipped as she spoke. "I've treated eight Cheri Coke victims in the last two weeks."

Hot rage filled me, boiling my blood, and steaming my ears. "Didn't occur to you to call the Court about that?"

"Why would I?" She gave a sarcastic snort and placed her hands on her hips. "Your precious Court should be happy I'm covering their tracks at all, after what they put me through."

She said they, but her tone and eyes were both pointed at me. I gave her another malicious grin. "Ya dug that hole yourself. Be happy *they* let ya live, Anna."

Right now, *they* wanted to shove her down a flight of stairs and watch her bones realign.

"Yeah, I'm so lucky. I work in this stinky pit every day and have to sneak sips from patients like him to stay alive." She jabbed a finger towards the guy in the bed.

She turned on her heel and threw the curtain open, a few of the rings ripping from the fabric with a soft slash through the air. She looked up at the shreds and swore softly before she stormed out of the room, the door slamming open with a loud echo into the tiled hallway.

I waited for a beat, giving her some space before retreating from the room. I still wasn't sure if Anna was involved or not, but at least I had more details than before. I'd have to see if Darren could get me a list of the other patients Anna had treated in the ER this month. It would be the proverbial needle in a haystack, but it was one more clue we didn't have.

Besides, now I had something to win back some of Ivan's good graces. He was pretty pissed after the morning news had reported what police had found at the party, not to mention the cops getting a literal interview with a vampire. I looked at the clock on my phone and walked a little faster. Before all that, I was going dancing. And I needed to look good doing it.

CHAPTER 7

GABE

"I'm home." I tossed my keys on the counter and leaned
against the front door, pushing my hands through my
hair.

My parents greeted me, as always, with their perfect grins
from my bedside table, my alarm clock showed 3:12 AM in a
hellish red next to them. Would they still smile if they saw me
now?

Yeah, right. They'd be thrilled to see this place.

I blew out a breath and walked into the kitchen, not even a
foot away from the door. The yellow light of the refrigerator
bathed the entire room before I peered in.

Looked like I had some leftover soup. I picked up the
container and opened the Tupperware lid a fraction before
gasping out a disgusted sigh. "Ah, God!"

I tossed the container into the sink and grimaced. Jesus,
how long had it been since I'd gone through my fridge? I
shut the door and slapped the side of the fridge a few times
before grasping a menu. A tiny black disc flew to the counter.
I grabbed the magnet and smacked it back in place before
leaning against the counter to review my choice. *Hammy's
Pizza, open 'til 4:00 AM.* Never a bad option.

I phoned in my usual, promising a nice tip since I was calling so late. They knew I was good for it. I put the menu back in place and glowered at the moldy mess in my sink. A quick look around my tiny apartment made the decision for me. If I didn't clean the dish now, the whole studio would stink within the hour. My parents continued to smile, but they never would have accepted that kind of mess.

I turned the water on and changed into my pajamas while the faucet worked its way from freezing to tepid. I was still scrubbing when I was summoned to buzz the delivery kid up. I gave him thirty for my twelve-dollar calzone, the smell of pancetta and bacon flooding my apartment instantly.

I shut the door and debated my options. I could read the case notes I'd brought home, but I was worried that might be too much for one day. Several hours of drunken interviews and running several ID checks had me beat, and I had to be up in a few hours to testify for another case. It might be a good time to let my brain latch onto something else. Opting for fiction, I grabbed the Dean Koontz novel off my nightstand and read as I chewed.

I left the courtroom and took a sharp left towards the courthouse entrance, my dress shoes letting soft squeaks out against the marble surface of the floor.

"Detective Collins!"

I stopped and turned my head. Michelle Gibson strode forward, her heels clipping against the floor in a quick pattern. The woman could write Morse code with those shoes. I spun and shoved my hands in my pockets. "Did you still need me, prosecutor?"

Michelle halted in front of me and shook her head, her short auburn locks twisting around her jaw as she lowered her voice. "I was wondering if you found my tortoise brush yet."

I huffed. "I keep telling you, Michelle, it's not at my place."

"Are you sure? You've looked everywhere?" Her silver eyes widened. "You know how I feel about that brush."

"Yeah, I do." I let out another breath to keep my cool. God, this had to be the seventh time I'd made this argument in two months. "Michelle, you've seen my place. It's the size of a shoebox. If your mother's brush was there, I would have found it the first time I looked."

Or the second. Or the third. But I didn't say that part. No use rubbing it in.

She stared at her alligator shoes and let out a sad little sigh. It was the same noise she used to make when I was giving more attention to a book or case than her.

I reached for the first safe subject I could find. "Nice job in court today."

She perked up, puffing out her chest. The motion emphasized the cleavage barely concealed in her blue business suit, just like she'd intended. "You think so?"

I nodded. "Yeah, you put him through the wringer. It's no wonder the jury came back so quickly."

She smiled, her strawberry lips pulling back in a shark-like grin. "You helped."

She reached out to squeeze my bicep, but I pulled back from the long nails.

"I'll see you later." I turned, knowing she wouldn't call after me. Michelle never liked to make a scene, at least not publicly.

I sauntered down the large hallway, the big windows of the courthouse providing a warm glow on my face that was dully cooled every time I stepped into the shadows between them. The flash of camera bulbs lit each window briefly, like shooting stars. If only I could have just wished them away.

I turned towards the giant arch of the entrance. Harper was leaning against the frame of one door, his dark jeans and deep skin turning his whole body into a silhouette against the bright afternoon sun.

He looked up from his phone and grinned as I approached. "I see she left you with your skin."

"I can't testify as effectively if I'm not pretty, right?" I stopped, my body shielded from view just outside the opening. The quick *click* of digital cameras and the loud chatter of monotonous questions filled the air, less boisterous as long as I stayed out of sight.

Harper barked his familiar laugh and pocketed his phone. "Good timing. I was losing anyway."

I shook my head and loosened my tie with a forefinger. "You lose any time you play that shit."

He gave me a serious look, lowering his shiny head. "Never make fun of my *Candy Crush*."

"No need. A name like that makes fun of itself."

"So, how'd the case go?"

"Guilty," I said with a sense of satisfaction. "Didn't even take the jury a full half-hour to agree."

"I was wondering when you texted to come get you. It seemed early."

"Yeah, what can I say? Juries hate when you kill your wife and blame it on the vamps." I shuffled on my feet, not really ready to leave the courthouse. But we had work to do. "How bad?"

"Think zombie hoard." Harper glowered towards the stairs, his face lighting and falling into shadow with each picture taken. "Only instead of *brains*, they're looking for *quotes*."

He drew out the two words with cinematic effect, and I chuckled. There was almost no irony ever lost on my partner.

"Well, best get it over with." I walked into the light of the door and out on the heavy marble stairs. Sure enough, the torrent surged forward, a flood of reporters trying to wash us away.

"Detective Collins, can you confirm that Jack O'Neil was found guilty?"

"Detective Harper, does the VPB have any plans on how to deal with the vampire epidemic?"

"Detective Collins, is it true that..."

"Detective Harper, why..."

Their questions merged into one giant wave, a thick buzz of human curiosity and profit. The courthouse security kept themselves between us and the reporters, forcing the swarm to keep their distance as we silently made our way towards the parking lot.

Someone more important must have left the courthouse, Jack O'Neil's lawyer maybe, because the swarm paused in the questions, and then asked more while walking away, the security team following after them.

"Just another day in the life." I blew out the breath I'd been holding. If I'd let it out, some very unpleasant quotes would have appeared in tomorrow's news.

"It ain't all glamor and diamonds, 'ey, buddy?" Harper looked over his shoulder to see where the commotion had fled to. "Michelle looks pretty comfortable with cameras."

"Of course, she does." I glanced back at my ex. The expression was the same one I'd seen trained on her face at the end of any trial, a practiced mask of pride and justice, with a hint of sorrow for the victims. It was the same expression that had drawn me to her in the first place. It wasn't until months together that I'd realized the expression was false, the sorrow only any act to keep up appearances. She wanted to be *known* as a tireless crusader for the victims, and so she played the part. It was a good act, even fooling her sister. She just couldn't keep it up behind closed doors.

I paused at the blacktop waiting for Harper to point us in the right direction. He stepped up and held his arm high, a key fob clicking lightly in his big fingers. He turned his arm in a few directions, and I realized he'd forgotten where he parked. I scoffed. "Seriously, Harper, how many times do we have to play the parking lot version of Marco Polo?"

Harper glared at me but his eyes twinkled behind that large beard. "As many times as it takes, my friend."

A beep sounded in a far back corner.

He clicked the fob again to be certain, and we headed towards the second beep, a ratty old station wagon awaiting us.

"So, anything new?"

"Yeah, we may have one lead." Harper clicked the fob again, and our car lit up, silent as it unlocked. I went to the driver's side, and Harper tossed me the keys. As I walked alongside the old car, a woman came into the view.

She was leaning against the car door, twirling a pen absently in one hand. She looked ecstatic when we arrived, as though the car's beeping hadn't alerted her to our presence.

"Detectives!" She didn't lift her body off the door, very effectively blocking my way. She wasn't pretty, but she certainly wasn't unpleasant. Her long brown hair pulled back into professional curls that cascaded around her shoulders and her button-up blouse set off the look of a true journalist, despite having been away from professional journalism for over a year now.

"Miss Wright." I shoved back all the snark in my tone. I was representing the VPB, that meant keeping a cool head. "Something we can do for you?"

"Maybe." Amber Wright stood straight but made no move to let me into the car. "I was hoping to sit down with you both some time, get the inside view on vampire crimes."

Harper went to say something, but I cut him off, "Why would we give the leader of V.A.P.E. pointers on how we take down vampires?"

I didn't think the Vampire Allies for a Peaceful Existence actually knew any vampires, but the idea still felt like giving the enemy secrets.

"Oh, I'm not looking for investigative techniques or anything. And, to be clear, you don't take down vampires." She bobbed her head towards the churning mass of reporters still hassling Michelle on the steps. "You take down vampire fakes and run the real ones out of town."

"Your point?" I fought the urge to grind my teeth. True, we hadn't taken one vampire into court. No vampire crimes unit had, not yet. We'd shot a few, but either they really did need a stake through the heart or the bastards were invincible. Here's hoping it was the former, since the death penalty for a species was rather ineffective if you couldn't kill them.

"My point—" her tone was far more pleasant than mine as she dug a business card from her blouse pocket and held it out to me, "is that one day, the public is going to get nasty over your lack of progress. Hell, they might even see my side of things. But even if they do, your team has its uses in this new world."

When I didn't move to take the card or respond, she stepped forward, slipping the stock into my breast pocket.

"One day, you may need someone to give you a favorable face, explain all your many uses. Keep me in mind." She smiled confidently and waved over the car. "Nice to see you again, Detective Harper."

"Ma'am." Harper bobbed his head and opened his car door. I waited to follow until Miss Wright was clear away from the car. I got in and fought every urge to slam the door.

"Traitorous woman," I grumbled, fishing the business card from my pocket, and crumbling it in my hand.

"Don't let her get to you." Harper leaned over and took the card from my hand, shoving the wad in his pocket. "And don't go littering the company car."

"You were saying?" I jammed the keys into the ignition.

"Oh, yeah!" Harper seemed less bothered by the interruption. "You remember that kid with the doodles on his face last night?"

"The doofus with a phone number written on his forehead and a dick on his cheek." I let out a breath and sniffed the air appreciatively. I shifted my gaze to the center console, finding two tall cups of steaming coffee dulling the irritation from the last ten minutes. I took one of the cups and sipped tentatively while searching my memory. No sugar and lots of cream. This one was mine.

"That'd be the one." Harper grabbed the remaining cup and drank. "Anyway, he was bailed out this morning. But before then, I was running his information. He showed up in the hospital last week and was treated for an overdose."

"Overdose of what?" I buckled myself in and looked over my shoulder, pulling the sedan out of the parking spot slowly. I doubted Miss Wright was still there, but I didn't want to risk hitting her if she was lurking. She was only an activist, after all.

"Cocaine." Harper smiled wide, and his teeth practically gleamed in my peripheral vision. "But that's not the good part."

"My breath is baited." I gave him a sarcastic look before turning my attention back to the task at hand.

"Hospital tests confirmed he had the same combo as the stuff we found at the party last night. Same as the crap in our victim's nose."

I stopped the car and leveled Harper with a look. "You couldn't have just led with that."

"Pretty good, eh?"

"It's something, I'll give you that." I shrugged and pulled out of the parking lot, turning into traffic, and heading towards the station. "So, you want to pull him in for questioning?"

"Already done." Harper cracked his large knuckles and gave me a satisfied little smile. "It was easy enough to get him to talk after evidence confirmed what was in the party favors, which I still don't understand."

"I don't know, maybe it's some method for slowly turning a human, get them to take in enough vampire blood?"

"I thought they had to bite you for that. You know." Harper placed his forefingers in front of his mouth. "I wan' to suck yo' blood."

It was his worst Dracula imitation yet. Not that his best would reach theaters anytime soon.

"Not like we know that much about them. We're still sorting out fact and myth." I blew out an annoyed breath. Miss Wright's assertions buzzed in my mind. Our department had a high solve rate, but all we'd brought in were humans related to or faking vampire crimes. My own species was the saving grace in my job, a sick thought when you considered that my whole job was invented to stop vampires. Weeding out fakes had been meant as a precautionary, not the main gig. "God, do you even remember what it was like before we knew they were real?"

"Nope." Harper dropped his hands and turned back to his normal tone. "Anyway, the kid didn't like the idea of his rich daddy finding out about his form of entertainment. His mom's been doing a great job of hiding it."

"So, did he give us a name?" I just prayed Harper said something besides Joey.

"Yep." He smacked the P for emphasis. "But not a person. He said we should try going to Holocene."

Strobe lights writhed over the dance floor; the sporadic movements of the dancers were frantic as they blinked in and out. The black walls made the bright lights and colorful effects from the stage striking as they flickered off the tiny mirrors of the disco ball overhead. The DJ stood at his oversized table and mixed various rhythms to keep the rapid pace. Too many people to count littered the floor, their bodies shifting in convoluted waves and forms.

The heavy bass pounded against my chest, and I stuffed my hands into my pockets just to keep them off my ears. At the bar, various colors of glass lit the back wall, like a mural mixed with the Northern lights disturbed by the occasional strobe quivering through the bottles. An Amazonian of a woman leaned forward, her voice a loud purr as she asked what we wanted. Harper held out his badge. "Can we please speak to the manager?"

The tall woman grunted and nodded as she walked away, swaying her hips in an exaggerated way. Harper stared after her, and I thumped him on the shoulder. "Hey, weren't you just eyeing that PI last night?"

He shrugged. "She was okay but when I drove her home, she became less interesting."

"What, she rides an actual bicycle?" I turned and leaned my body against the bar, surveying the crowd standing on the second-level balcony.

"No." His voice had a touch of reverence in it. "The woman drives a custom 2015 Harley 883 Sportster. Not a great engine, but it's a thing of beauty"

I whistled in faux appreciation. If I admitted I had no clue what that meant, he'd spend the next half-hour comparing it with his Ninja whatever. "So, what was wrong with her, aside from her being a witness?"

"There was that," he acknowledged. "But after the bike talk, it became clear she's not the right lady for me."

I furrowed my brows but kept looking at the crowd, taking particular interest in a great pair of legs attached to a plaid skirt and long boots. "How so?"

"Well, I mentioned I like Candy Crush, and she said her roommate is obsessed with that *shite*." He put extra emphasis on the last word and formed little finger quotes in the air before shaking his large head.

I squinted at the face at the top of the legs and snorted. "Maybe you can ask her for her roommate's number."

Harper turned and let his eyes follow my gaze. He squinted past the light show in much the same way I had. Then he barked out a laugh that made several heads turn towards us. "I'll let you give it a try, buddy."

The PI in question leaned against the metal rails of the top floor, chatting up a guy and playfully pushing at his practically bare chest. Her legs were covered in thigh-high boots that led the eye directly to a red plaid skirt that barely graced her knees. She wore a loose white blouse on top, practically see-through but for the loose tank top she was wearing under it.

I'd almost failed to recognize her with the wild curls of blonde that sprung from under her newsboy-style cap. She was laughing and her face clear of the gunk from the night before. I decided her ID photo hadn't done her smile justice.

"Rock, paper, scissors?" I held a closed fist up in challenge.

"I'll take the manager. You deal with the Candy hater. It'll give you two some common ground." Harper shook his head, his beard shifting in the motion. "Make sure to ask her about her supposedly late rent."

I lowered my fist and pushed back through the forest of human bodies, heading towards one of the corkscrew staircases. I couldn't even hear the thump of my footfalls on the metal steps as I ascended them. The tiny mirrors of the disco ball tried to briefly blind me as I stalked my quarry.

I stepped a little closer and could hear her laughter. It sounded off, hollow somehow. I shook the idea away and stepped forward. "Fancy meeting you here."

Her blue eyes flicked over, and she started to say something before clenching her jaw. Her companion turned his head and glared. The guy crossed his arms over a mesh shirt and opened his mouth to speak, but Lily Edwards placed her hand on his arm, her ice gaze locked with mine.

"Thomas, could ya excuse us?"

The guy gave her a look that was equal parts disbelief and annoyance. She nodded once, a reassuring smile crossing her soft features but her face was still aimed at me. The guy leaned down and whispered in her ear, bleached spikes waving in the various lights. She giggled at whatever he said.

"Of course." She smiled, the expression somehow predatory. Her friend started towards the stairs, and she leaned against the banister, the smile vanishing. "Detective Collins."

"Gabe, please." I leaned against the metal frame next to her. "Come here often?"

"Really, ya couldn't come up with anythin' more original?" Irritation laced her lilt, and she ran the tip of one long finger over the edge of her martini glass, barely missing the toothpick and giant olive with the motion. "What can I do for ya, Detective?"

"That's hardly friendly." My smile was lopsided.

"We're hardly friends."

"I thought you liked to wear disguises while you were out." I gestured to her outfit with a hand. "Hard to forget a woman wearing that."

"Ah, but would ya have remembered my face?" She gave me a wicked grin before taking a sip from the stemmed glass. "Sometimes the best disguise is the one that draws the eyes elsewhere."

I gave her legs an appraising glance. The long boots shaped her flesh, leaving little to the imagination. True, if I hadn't recognized her, I would have remembered the mold of black suede long before I remembered much else. She snorted, and I looked up. One pale brow was arched as she spoke, "So, what can I help ya with?"

"You can start by telling me what you're doing here—" I dropped my smile and pointed at the ground for emphasis, "paying a cover fee when you are *supposedly* struggling to pay rent."

"Checked my finances, did ya?" She tilted her head in apparent interest.

"Yeah, and you just paid two months' worth of your office rent the day before yesterday."

"Fine, I just didn't feel like being in an interrogation room for a few hours. I still get paid more if I work faster."

"The owner of the building said you also asked him to let the cleaning crew in until further notice, something you only do when you're taking time off." I crossed my arms and let my face fill with a satisfied grin.

She leaned forward, her voice at a normal level that became a whisper under the loud pulse of the music around us. "Do ya have a point, Detective?"

"Yeah," My breath bounced off her cheek as I whispered back. "You're not telling us something. That doesn't work for me."

"Tell ya what." She still leaned close, her breath swirling in my ear. "I'll give ya full disclosure tomorrow. Scout's honor."

Like she's a girl scout.

"Why not tonight?" I wasn't sure why she was whispering, but I assumed she had a reason and went along with it. I had to start reminding myself she was a witness. And hiding something from us. It didn't entirely stop the intimate feeling of her proximity.

"Because." She pulled the olive off the toothpick with her teeth and gave me a mischievous grin before speaking again. The olive muffled her words slightly. "You're scarin' away my fish."

I watched her throat work as she swallowed the olive and downed her drink, leaving the empty glass on the banister. I grabbed her thin wrist. I wasn't ready to let her walk off and come up with a new story.

She wrenched free, and her bright eyes darkened with annoyance. I'd grabbed her harder than I meant to, certainly more than was professional of me. It wouldn't have hurt her, but it was still a bad idea, not to mention disrespectful. But those weren't the only reasons I chose to let her go.

That woman couldn't weigh more than a hundred and twenty pounds, but she'd just pulled her knobby wrist from my grasp like it was nothing more than wet paper. And in the brief moment, before she had pulled loose, I could have sworn her skin was cold. Like ice.

CHAPTER 8

LILY

I rushed towards my target, watching the detective out of the corner of my eye as he descended another curved staircase on the other side of the club. He seemed to be watching my every step. I turned and cursed myself under my breath, "Stupid, stupid, stupid!"

Thomas emerged from the swarm of bodies and took my hand, drawing me into the crowd. I plastered my smile back in place, still inwardly smacking myself for my stupidity just now. Stupid fucking reflexes!

Thomas leaned forward; his voice was low, and I had to strain my supernatural hearing to catch his question over the pop song. "What was that about?"

"Not much, he was just butt-hurt I didn't call him back." I shrugged as much as the rhythm of our dance would allow. "So, where were we?"

The pale vampire snorted and placed both hands on my hips, swiveling his body to 'Poker Face.' If I hadn't been worried about the threat this guy posed, I probably would have been enjoying myself.

Thomas leaned in again, his words caressing my ear. "Joey didn't say you'd be so gorgeous."

I had to fight a nervous gulp as I smiled in a way I hoped looked confident. "Oh, what did he say?"

"That you're ruthless." The vampire dipped me slightly and drew me back up to the music. "Also, that I better not try buying your loyalty or I'd end up run through with silver."

I almost blew out a breath, I was so relieved. So, Joey hadn't relayed any details about *me* to my talented dance partner. He'd relayed details about whoever this guy thought I was supposed to be. I still hadn't figured out who exactly that was and it was getting a bit awkward playing a role without any script. Still, it was a far cry better than being outed in my investigation. "Well, Joey doesn't mince words, does he?"

Thomas smiled. "No, he doesn't. It's nice to meet you, Ami."

"And you." I grinned and pressed my body against his.

His silver eyes darkened, and he groaned. "You better behave, or I might start mixing business with pleasure right on this dance floor."

I feigned an innocent smile and put a hand over my heart. "Who, me?"

He turned me so my back was to him. A brief glimpse during the spin told me the detective was back with his partner at the bar. His dark eyes were still locked on me. Shit, shit, shit.

I suppressed a groan and tried to focus. Nothing I could do about it. Hopefully, I could get my target out of the building before he took notice of the cop's attention. Last thing they needed was Joey's crew realizing how close the cops were to the case.

Thomas leaned in, reclaiming my attention. "Let's switch to a safe topic before I do something indecent on this dance floor. I'd hate to offend my customers. What was it like turning in Japan?"

I almost snorted, now understanding the name. Seriously, Irish accent and blonde hair, and somehow this dope thought I was some chick from the Far East. The world didn't lack for fools. Lucky me.

I smiled over my shoulder. "A little complicated. Long story and very boring. How about you? When did ya turn?"

"Pretty recent, but I'm excited to climb the old corporate ladder." He flashed teeth in a grin that almost made me shiver. "I mean this scheme to take over, it's fucking brilliant, right?"

"Yeah, I mean they'll never see it comin'." I nodded enthusiastically, hoping I looked like I knew what the hell he was on about. Seriously. This eejit sounded like the white mouse trying to take over the world.

When Thomas had approached me at the beginning of the night, I'd thought for sure I was busted. Being confused and following poorly laid breadcrumbs wasn't much of an improvement but I'd take what I could get. Especially with how this night was developing.

I decided to dig where I could, asking Thomas if he liked his work and if he and Joey could ever really get together on off-hours. At that last question, Thomas snorted rudely. "I don't hang out with Beer Belly Joey. Hell, I'm shocked you tolerate him."

"He's good at the sales. It's all about the bottom line, right?" I shrugged noncommittally, glad I'd heard his sales pitch at the party.

"Yeah, the fact that he's the boss's kid probably doesn't hurt him either." Thomas rolled his eyes. "Hey, so are we gonna trade product or what? Not that I'm not enjoying your company, but the sooner I can get to my clients, the sooner I can meet my own bottom line. You know?"

For the second time that night, *busted* rang clearly across my brain. I smiled, trying to look confident. "Of course, ya got somewhere we can make the exchange?"

Thomas smiled and offered his arm like some sort of dashing prince. "This way."

I took his arm, and we walked off the floor. I glanced over my shoulder and almost let out a breath of relief. The detectives were talking to a stout man in a cheap suit. Neither of them was watching us as we left. Maybe the universe had decided to stop screwing with me for five minutes. Yeah, and maybe my ass was made of candy.

I followed Thomas through a narrow hallway, past the bathroom, and into a small back room. The beat of the music still thrummed against the walls, but not as loud. Soundproofing, what a lifesaver. He sat down on a couch that encompassed a circular metal table. Thomas gestured to the space across from him.

I took my seat and crossed my legs, flinging my hair back like I had every idea what we were doing. "So, what's your trade?"

"Didn't Joey tell you?" Thomas tilted his head and his brows drew together. I shrugged in return.

"I prefer to hear the offer directly from the source." I squared my shoulders. "You're trying to move up aren't ya? Wouldn't ya prefer to speak for yourself in this matter?"

"Whoa, whoa. I want to move up. I'm just used to the other exchanges being handled before the meeting. I mean, Joey always sets the time and locations. He does all the negotiations on the back end. Frankly, if he wasn't such a fat fuck, the sales for my clients would probably fall to him. He just doesn't get the richies to shell out money with the way he looks." Thomas looked a bit eager, his eyes growing wide.

I didn't care for Joey, but even I thought Thomas calling him a *fat fuck* was a bit much for the potbelly I'd seen. Granted, Thomas looked like he was carved from pure muscle. He must have worked out daily before being turned. Still, I kept my face neutral even as I processed the new info that the dealer had just given me. "Well, now it's your chance to prove you're more than just a pretty face to the boss. So, what's *your* offer?"

"What about this?" Excitement edged his words and Thomas leaned in, placing his hands on the cold table between us. "Lower my commission to ten percent but give me the campus too. I guarantee I'll get more humans on the Coke than Joey has. I bet I can double the women customers by Christmas."

"Double?" I raised a brow and leaned back, my arms spreading over the semicircle of red fabric behind me. "Ya think you can hit that many, that fast?"

"Have you even looked at my numbers?" He looked insulted. "I've got a good seventy regular users in this joint alone."

"True, but your clients are also the ones showing up in ERs around town." I held up my hand, the large black H a beacon against my skin. "The little hand stamps kind of gave ya away."

"Hey, it's not my fault the cattle won't listen!" He ran his hand through his bleached spikes. "Besides, didn't we want the local vamps to notice?"

I opened my mouth to respond when a wispy Asian girl came bounding into the room. "Do either of you fucktards know where Thomas is?"

One look at her outfit, and I groaned. She was wearing a plaid skirt short enough to be a belt and a belly top that was probably supposed to mimic the shirt from a uniform. She'd completed the look by putting her hair into long pigtails. I looked down at my own plaid skirt and button blouse with new understanding. Joey had told Thomas to expect his contact to be a vampire dressed like a schoolgirl. What were the fucking chances?

CHAPTER 9

GABE

A crash echoed from the opposite end of the club and half of the dancers stopped their gyrations. One wall of the back hallway blew apart, a large metal disc tearing the drywall apart like sand. Lily Edwards squirmed beneath what I barely registered had been a table.

A half-naked Asian girl flew through the opening, her hand landing on the PI's throat. She ripped Lily from behind the tabletop, and I saw the PI's face contort in a cry of anguish. I couldn't hear her scream over the panicked howls as people ran for the exits.

"Jesus!" Harper rushed forward seconds before me.

"Police! Everyone out!" I drew my firearm and ran forward. More screams issued and the remaining crowd thundered away. I shoved at the shoulders of a gawker. "Hey, stop filming and move your ass!"

"This is Officer Harper, we have a 10-110 in progress. Repeat, violent vampire sighting in progress at Holocene, send back up now!" Harper's shoulder radio crackled with the dispatcher's response, and we kept moving forward, slowly through the hectic crowd.

Someone pulled the fire alarm and the building shifted in and out of light more rapidly, the alarm lights and strobes competing. Water poured from the ceiling, glowing from the multiple sources of light.

Loud shrieks bled through the still blaring bass of the music, a deranged pulse to the violence unfolding. Lily still twisted in the tiny woman's grip, and I saw her wrapping her long fingers around her assailant's arms. I spread my feet in a shooter's stance, Harper taking the same form next to me. He bellowed in an authoritative tone. "Put her down!"

The tiny Asian woman turned to us, a sly grin spreading across her lips. "Stay there, I'll be right with you boys."

"Fat chance," I shot back, releasing the hammer of my Glock. "Put. Her. Down."

The woman's smile fell, and she glared harder, Lily still struggling against her and clawing at her arm. She hardly seemed to notice the skin tearing away as she ground her gaze into mine. It wasn't until the strobe light flashed again that I realized there was no color. The woman's eyes were so dark, it looked like the pupil had swallowed the entire iris. She spoke again, her words colored with surprise as she yelled over the overwhelming racket. "I said stay."

"And I said put her down." I aimed for the woman's shoulder. "Last warning."

A loud crack broke the air and Lily fell to the ground. She landed hard on the floor and the smaller woman screamed over every sound, clutching her arm to her. Or what was left of it. A small stump oozed red liquid from the elbow and the woman pressed the end, a futile attempt to stop the bleeding.

Lily threw the severed limb away from her like trash and jolted upright. I watched in horror as the wrist and hand both crumbled into dust where they'd landed, becoming a puddle of gray beneath the shower of water. I looked up and realized Lily's eyes were locked on Harper's location. Her lilt was filled with command. "Move your ass out of our way."

She let out a loud oomph as a new combatant plowed her into the wall, their bodies diving through the sheetrock before

I saw those long boots shove her earlier dance partner with a double kick before she pounced into the hallway and gave me a quick glance. "You too."

"Not a chance." I wasn't sure if she even heard me as I re-aimed my gun. I put her chest in my sight and pulled the trigger. The kickback shifted my hands upwards a fraction, and I saw her face scrunch as she turned wholly away from me. She swung back, her blonde locks slashing the air in wet streaks. Rocks fell in my gut as confirmation looked me dead in the eye. The cold blue of her eyes was replaced with dark black ink. She flew backward, two bodies falling back, and I turned to Harper. But he wasn't there.

I turned, my heart thudding and my brain trying to return to a busy street corner. I shook my head. *Now is not the time to take a stroll down memory lane. Stay focused.* My eyes locked on Harper's heavy frame.

He was back at the bar, his jaw slack as he stared into the distance. A loud crash brought my attention back to the fight, and I turned. The tangle of bodies flailed, Lily's arms and legs shooting at her assailants without mercy. Her movements were without pause but they kept coming. The brisk motion of the three vampires made it impossible to get a sight on any of them.

"Shit." I lowered my gun a fraction, backing up as their movements brought them closer. I barely avoided the mass of limbs and grunts. Water splashed up at me in several hues as the cluster of bodies rolled past.

They landed with a heavy splash. The man on bottom, his arms stretched up as Lily clawed and bit at him. The skimpy woman had one hand wrapped around her neck. Her other hand pulled at her head, keeping Lily from her intended target. I gaped at the fingers holding the PI's head. Hadn't that arm been ripped off? Long fangs extended from the blonde's face, and Lily hissed as she grabbed the man's wrists and twisted, savagely.

The man grunted and Lily dropped downwards, twisting her body, and slamming the woman behind her onto the concrete dance floor. The woman let out a pained wheeze and Lily shot her elbow backward over and over until her hair was released. She rolled away and crouched, her hands diving into the long black boots still covering her legs. She pulled out a knife from each boot, both glimmering. Tiny specks of light danced over the silver shine, and I looked up in realization. I pointed my gun up and fired. One. Two. Three.

A loud snap stole the air a second before the crash. Hundreds of tiny little mirrors splintered across the ground as the disco ball dissolved over the male vampire; his body spasmed and went limp. Lily chose that moment to lunge, the knives gleaming in each hand as she landed on top of the woman. Her arms arched in several trails, red sprinkling her blouse and the woman twisting in apparent pain. Lily flipped one of the knives in her hand and plunged it sideways into the Asian woman's neck. The woman stilled but her eyes blinked in cold fury as red pooled into the puddle below them.

Lily sat back and gave me an annoyed look. She shouted, barely audible over the surrounding ruckus. "Ya *shot* me."

I pulled the hammer back and shouted back, "And I'll do it again if you don't get on the ground."

She smirked and opened her mouth to speak but a loud squeal echoed over every sound. We both snapped our heads up. Another squeal became redundant as an overhead spotlight plunged towards me.

The large fixture pinned me to the hard floor and pain burst from every nerve. I tried to scream, but my mouth filled with something thick and metallic. New little lights danced, and I vaguely wondered where the other disco ball was. I'd only seen the one. My body ran cold, and someone must've turned some of the lights off because the sides of my vision turned dark. I stared down the tunnel, a large metal grate the only thing I saw.

The grate lifted, and I felt a hollow space where my chest normally resided. My head lifted and a gold blob filled my vision. I tried to speak, but I only choked as that thick liquid spilled down my chin instead. A heavily accented voice shouted, and something shook me. Hard.

Something cold pressed against my mouth, liquid spilling in. I pulled back from the heavy taste of old pennies, but something pressed the back of my head closer to the faucet. "Drink, or you'll die!"

I swallowed to clear my throat; my vision cleared a little. The person was still fuzzy, but I could see deep colors where a nose and lips would normally reside. I drank again, wondering what the EMT was giving me. It tasted like shit but, God, it was working. Something in my body snapped, and I gasped. The steel grip latched my face back in place and the EMT ordered me again. "Drink goddammit!"

I swallowed again and my vision shifted, clearing in some ways, and turning fuzzy in others. I finally realized who was holding me. It wasn't an EMT. I lurched away from the vampire's arms, and she let me go this time. I looked down and my stomach fell away when I saw the red trickling from her wrist. I held a hand up to my mouth and stared at the ruby drops washing away in the sprinkler's relentless downpour.

I looked around wildly, my movements staggered. The pain was receding, but the fuzz in my vision was slowly being replaced by duplicates of everything around me. I swung forward, my limbs not quite reacting the way they should. I slid across the wet floor through empty air. Air rushed from my lungs as a boulder slammed into my gut. Something soothed over my back, and I heard her voice, sirens filling the background. "Shhhhh, it'll wear off."

Who the hell was playing drums? Didn't they know it hurt? Pain rushed through every fiber, and I reached for my skull. One arm made it. The other tugged away from me, refusing to comfort my aching head. I opened my eyes to a dimly lit room, gray dusting everything for the lack of light. Something under me shifted, and I felt a cool hand brushing over my back like I was a sick kid. "It's okay, it'll pass."

I snapped my head up at the accent. I pulled away, only to have my arm pull me back to the vampire. Her eyes were wide, and I would have called the look concern on anyone else. She reached towards my face, and I flinched.

"Stop squirmin'. I could've killed ya ten times in the last two minutes and ya wouldn't have been able to stop me." Her chiding voice filled my body with ice. She was right. I was a vampire's hostage, and I couldn't do squat about it. I opened my mouth to reply but something churned inside before I could speak. I leaned sideways, my guts spewing forward. She lunged out of the path but continued to stroke my back. "That's it. Let it out."

My stomach twisted and ringed itself out for what felt like hours. I dry heaved once more, the taste of metal coating my tongue. I gagged and spat before speaking. My speech was slurred, and I wasn't even sure what I was trying to say. "You...fed me...blooood."

She lifted me by my underarms and sat me against something. "Yep."

I scoffed and went to stand. My arm reminded me that it was still protesting all movement. I had to roll my head so I could figure out why it wasn't cooperating. "You...cuffed me!"

The words were little more than a growl, not the angry shout I'd intended. I glared into those sky eyes, and she placed a cool hand over my forehead. "The fever is almost over. I'll release ya when the blood's worn off."

"You." I stuck my hand in her face, the pad of my index finger pressed into her cheek. Cotton filled my mouth, and I tried to talk around it. "You...better not have change...me. If you did, I'll suck you dry...you fuckin' suck head."

She snorted. "Noted."

She stood and walked across the room. Something made a suction sound and then slammed. I reached for my ears, only one hand helping me to block the heavy echoes pounding in my skull. I slammed my eyes shut, but it didn't do anything to help. "Fuck!"

The surface beneath me shifted again and something cool was placed against my cheek. I relaxed and took the cool harmony in my hands. I pulled it away to examine it.

Was that a water bottle? I didn't care.

I held it against my other cheek, reveling in the feeling. Something cold touched my lips, but this time it splashed. I smacked her wrist away but it felt wrong. I looked down. Another bottle. It neared my mouth again, her lilt urging me. "Drink."

I was pretty sick of her saying that.

I swallowed to tell her where she could put the second bottle, but it felt like sandpaper working its way down my gullet. She pushed the bottle against my still-closed lips. "Come on, while you're still young."

I swallowed again and winced before opening my mouth slowly. I took a few gulps and the fire in my throat eased a fraction. The acrid taste of vomit washed back down, and I nearly puked again, the soothing water on my throat made me hold it back. She pulled away, and I coughed once as a few drops strayed into the wrong tube.

She stood and walked across the space. I looked around. My vision only showed me one of everything but it still gave a small shadow to anything in my sight. Of course, in this dark, everything was a shadow. But I could make out what everything was. Neat trick.

I was sitting on a bed, deep crimson and black spilling over the side with tiny drips, which echoed louder than they had any right to. The smell was horrible and my guts threatened to heave again. There were no windows. The wall and floors were barren concrete, with a drain in the middle of an otherwise empty floor. The only door was large and metal. To the right of it was a tiny screen of some kind. Next, I looked at my captor.

She was sitting on a large blue box, her eyes locked on the screen of her phone as it illuminated her face. The light stung a little, and I closed my eyes before looking back again. Her fingers flew across the touchscreen like a swarm of bees. Watching the motion made my stomach do an unpleasant jig. I looked away, letting my eyes stay closed this time. I curled up, surprised at how comfortable I was. I turned away from the pool of sick, as far as my cuffed arm would allow, and let the inside of my eyelids claim my weary body.

CHAPTER 10

LILY

H e woke twice more throughout the night. The smell of his body ejecting my blood filled the concrete cell and it took all of my energy to stay in the small space with him. But this was my mess; I would clean it up. He passed out again, and I picked up my phone from the cooler. "Sorry, I'm back."

"Next time kid, just hang up." Ivan's Russian accent was filled with disgust. "I'd rather not hear that again."

"I doubt ya will." I checked my screen to be certain before pressing the phone back to my ear. "The blood's had six hours to work through his system. He should be clear next time he wakes up."

"He certainly sounded coherent when he told you to fuck off." My adoptive sire let out a weary sigh. "Anyway, where were we?"

"Footage."

"Ah, yes." There was a quick snap in the background of the call. "Cyrus says he's having his team track one last cell phone down. Apparently, there's a video of you being smashed under the table right before you hear the police shouting. Doesn't show you doing anything supernatural, but still."

I nodded, even if he couldn't see it. "I agree, I'd rather not be exposed."

"So, where does that leave the cop?"

My eyes were locked on the Detective as he snored softly, his face mere inches from the chunks he'd just released. "I'll keep my promise."

"Heh?"

"I told him I would give him full disclosure."

"What!?"

I pulled the phone a foot away from my head, grimacing. Not that Ivan's reaction was any kind of surprise, but that didn't prevent my ears from ringing at his sudden change in volume. He shouted something else, and I held the phone away a bit longer until I finally heard him squawking at a more reasonable volume. "Kid? Kid?!"

"I gather ya don't like that plan much?"

"Good gathering!" Ivan's voice was still annoyed.

"Too bad, Boss." I looked at the man lying before me and pinched the bridge of my nose. "He can't be mesmerized."

"You just fed him blood. It'll take time for your suggestions to work."

"Even before that." I pulled my hand away and stared at the gray slab of ceiling overhead. "Ami tried to get him too. His partner took to it, he didn't."

"He's immune?" Ivan's voice filled with awe.

"So, it would seem." I blew out a breath. How the hell did I keep finding these folks? I'd been lucky before but I doubted it would go that well this time around. "The only way I'm keeping my secret is with him on my side."

"Or you could just lock him down there forever," Ivan offered. I knew he was joking. In part at least. "You do have a veritable dungeon in your basement."

"It's a rehab center. Besides, I can't take up Alex's work-space forever."

"It's not like he's in the middle of busy season," Ivan grumbled something else but it seemed like it was aimed elsewhere.

Probably one of his lieutenants checking in. "You sure about this kid?"

"Not at all, but I don't see another option." I hung up before Ivan could make any bright suggestions. I looked down at my outfit and scowled.

The skirt and blouse were ruined, red and black streaks turning both into some kind of Gothic Jackson Pollock deal. The pleats were practically torn from each other, making my plaid skirt into zombie apocalypse underwear. Several buttons were torn from my blouse and the lace camisole underneath looked like Wolverine had tried to feel me up, not that there was much to *feel*. I debated on changing for the third time when I heard soft squeaks across the little room.

I snapped my head up to find Detective Collins sitting up on the mattress, running a hand through his dark hair. He stopped almost instantly, shaking his hand. Tiny flecks of red and black sprinkled the bedspread and nearby wall. He sat up trying to scoot from the pool of sick and glared at me.

"I was really hoping that I'd wake up in a straitjacket."

I snorted and stood, grabbing his keys from the top of the cooler. "Why not just hope it was all a dream?"

"Nightmare," he corrected.

He locked his eyes with mine as he snatched the keychain I dangled before him. I'd realized his eyes were deep green sometime last night. Without the harsh lines of intoxication, they reminded me of fresh foliage at the beginning of spring. Or grass rolling in hills of a country much further away. I gave my head a shake and watched him flip through his keys before jamming a smaller one into the lock. A faint *click* echoed off the walls and his hand dropped to the mattress. His words were still slurred but they were much easier to understand this time. "You used my handcuffs?"

I raised an eyebrow, giving his messy state a meaningful glance. "Don't ya think ya have more pressing issues?"

"Suppose I do." He sat against the wall and swallowed, his eyes still locked on mine. "So, why am I still alive?"

"Why wouldn't ya be?" I tilted my head to one side.

"You're a vampire, you fed me your blood." He gave me a look like it was obvious. "Yet, I can hear my pulse in my own ears. It's deafening."

"Ah." I nodded. "That'll wear off slowly. Might take a week before your hearing isn't so sensitive."

"Why am I alive?" He repeated the words like I was dense.

I fought the urge to yell, knowing it would only hurt us both. "Because blood isn't enough to initiate the change. There has to be intent."

"So, what were you *intending* by feeding me that shit?" He motioned towards the puddle still dripping next to him.

"I was intendin' on savin' your life." I crossed my arms over my chest. "That light turned your insides into pudding. Even with the ambulance right outside, there was no saving ya without my blood."

"Bullshit!" He grabbed at his button-up shirt, or what was left of it. Half of his necktie was missing and there was a ragged hole starting at the bottom of his ribs, ending below his navel. Every inch of his front was stained red like a roasted pepper. His trousers had met a similar fate, barely covering the important bits with his blue boxers. He looked around and grabbed at the blanket, realizing his exposure for the first time.

"Nothing I haven't seen. We've been down here for several hours." I rolled my eyes though I kind of wanted to avert them.

"Hours?" His eyes darkened. "Harper, he must be—"

"Your partner is upstairs, crashed on my couch."

The cop's eyes became twin slits. "I want to see him."

"Don't ya want a shower first?" He gave me a look, and I returned it. "Seriously, it reeks in here, and we both look like we danced with a machete. I'm sure Detective Harper can wait for us to get cleaned up."

He took in a deep breath and looked like he instantly regretted it. His nose had to be just as hypersensitive as mine to the stink, and only one of us needed to breathe. He looked down at the blanket and back to me. "Do you have something I could wear?"

I eyed his body through the blanket, trying to take measurements. His knuckles turned white, clutching the white fabric over his body. I brought my eyes back to his face. "One of my roommates might have something, but you'll swim in it."

"As long as it covers me," he growled.

I turned and placed my hand on the scanner. A green stripe illuminated the space, its neon glow covering everything before it ducked behind my palm. Detective Collins groaned and the bedsprings squeaked with movement. He'd tossed the blanket over his head to block out the new offense. I swore. "Sorry, shut your eyes."

"Too late for that!" The blanket fell away. His hands were pressed over each socket as he complied, squeezing the lids like he was trying to melt them together. "God, what's wrong with me?"

"Light and sounds are going to be harsh for a few hours. Here." I grasped one of his hands, and he yanked away. I sighed. I was too fucking tired for this "There are stairs. Ya want to break your nose? I know chicks dig scars, but we usually like our faces symmetrical."

He clenched his jaw in a tight line. "Go get Harper."

"Really? Ya want him to see ya like this? You're covered in your own puke and blood, but not much else!"

"Better than holding your hand!"

I blew out another breath. "Fine, wait here."

CHAPTER II

GABE

S omething squealed, and I covered both of my ears, wishing I could just rip them off. That pain couldn't begin to cover the pressure building in my mind with every receding step as she left. I cautiously lifted one lid, slamming it shut as a golden beam scored new pain through my brain. Soft steps came back, heavy *thumps* following close behind. The drum of my own heart was still playing over it all. The soft steps stopped, but the thumps came closer and a rough hand gripped my shoulder. "Up and at 'em, buddy."

I gripped my head tighter as Harper's voice boomed. The vampire's lilt came into the room, softer than anything else surrounding me. Even the drips of vomit still spilling from the side of the bed.

"Ya need to whisper."

Harper patted my shoulder again, urging me forward without words. I grabbed his big hand and drew myself up, but my legs were wet spaghetti above my ankles. Harper caught me, his voice more reasonable this time. "I got you, Collins. I got you."

He tossed one of my arms over his large shoulders and pulled me alongside him. He ascended a step at a time, and I felt something move past us, a shadow crossing the red insides of my closed eyelids briefly. "Keep your eyes shut tight, Detective."

My vision turned orange briefly and something grated against the ground. Harper pulled me along a flat surface, heavy *thuds* turning softer. The vampire kept directing him, and we ascended again. "He can use my bathroom."

"What about you? Not to be unkind, but you look like hammered shit."

I heard a soft snort. "I'm not the one covered in vomit. Can ya get him into the tub while I find him somethin' else to wear?"

"Sure thing."

I heard something rustle before I leaned against a cool surface, the smell of oranges and soap bathing my senses. Blackness soaked my eyes again, and I hazarded a glance. We were in a tiny tiled room, a marble vanity serving as my seat. The door was closed, and Harper was leaning his large frame into a tub. I heard him pat softly several times before something gurgled in the walls, and I covered my ears again. The gurgle switched to a soft groan and water began splashing against the inside of the tub with rapid licks. He'd plugged the tub so the shower would slowly fill it.

I looked around again, realizing the room was still dark. "Why didn't you turn the lights on?"

"She said it would hurt your eyes."

"Great. You're trusting the word of a vampire."

"I had to see your torn body when she lifted that light off you. Then I watched her fix you. She could have left you there. She didn't." He scowled at me. "Yeah, I'm giving her the benefit of the doubt."

I drew my hands through my hair and groaned, remembering the slick mess that still coated one of my palms. The heavy strum of water rushing into the tub was still overwhelming and his breath was like a gust to my ears. "How am I supposed to work?"

"Whatever you're experiencing, she said it'll get better after you clean up and eat something." He stuck his hand into the steam of the shower, drawing it out and flicking the water back into the tub. It was then I realized I could see him, as clearly as I could see the white of the marble tub and the crack of gray light looming beneath the door.

Every frizzy hair of his beard and the badges on his leather jacket showed. I couldn't determine color, but the outlines were unmistakable. I stared, the wisps of steam clouding small details but not covering them. I looked into Harper's deep eyes and swallowed. "Can you see me?"

His face shifted in surprise. "You're kidding, right?"

I shook my head and waved my hand in front of him. His eyes stayed fixed on their position, and I realized he was looking at some point behind me. I swallowed. "I can see you perfectly."

His expression darkened. "You serious?"

I nodded, realizing the gesture was pointless only after he didn't say anything else. I looked at the steaming tub. "I think I can handle that by myself. Get out of here."

He turned and patted the wall until he found the doorknob. "Shout if you need me."

The crack of gray expanded momentarily as he left, and I leaned back against the counter, kicking off my shoes slowly, pressing my weight into the thick marble behind me as I did so. I followed a similar procedure for the rest of my clothes, sitting on the toilet to pull off my shredded dress pants.

I stuck my hand in the spray and pulled it back. Too hot. I turned it down and waited, rinsing the vomit from my hand while the water cooled. I stepped into the tub and gratefully sank to the bottom, letting the water cover my shoulders and neck. The warm spray loosened muscles I hadn't realized were tense, and I took in a deep breath and sat there until the water ran cold.

When I emerged from the shower, the shreds of my jacket and pants were gone, replaced with thick gray sweats and a matching shirt. My personal effects sat next to the new clothes, sans the ruined suit I'd been wearing. The vampire hadn't lied. Even with the drawstring pulled taught, the pants threatened to expose me. The sweatshirt hung low on me and it felt like I was wearing a small tent. I put on my dress shoes and socks, happy they'd survived.

I gave the gray crack of light a dubious look before stumbling once and grasping the handle. The soft glow still stung my eyes but it wasn't as potent as the first time. I walked forward, barely keeping myself upright without grabbing the nearby bedposts or desk as I made my way towards an illuminated rectangle at the other end of the room. I wobbled forward and grasped the doorknob, pulling it open to another section of gray illumination.

A long wooden banister shaped the second floor, leaving the main level open to my view from the top. Three doors popped along the sides of the large living room, a modern kitchen taking shape in the back corner. A huge sectional couch enclosed the sitting area for an even larger entertainment center. On the same wall as the large hutch, a huge arch revealed a tiled floor and the beginnings of a counter.

I gripped the banister for support and made my way towards a long staircase. Something savory filled my nose and my stomach tried to heave and growl simultaneously. I descended one step at a time, my limbs growing stiff, heading towards the vampire and Harper's voices, coming from the arch on the other side of the house. Harper's deep voice was low as he spoke. "How long will he be like that?"

"It varies, but the worst of the hangover should be gone before ya go."

"So, we get to leave?" I leaned against the arch and looked around the modern kitchen, silver gleaming dimly and threatening my eyes. A window revealed the barest glow of the low sun over Oregon hills, the light dimmed by heavy drapes. The vampire was sitting at a marble kitchen island, Harper kitty-corner from her. An old-fashioned sugar shaker and two coffee mugs sat before him. A broad man was at the stove, tongs in hand as bacon sizzled loudly in the frying pan.

The PI placed her own mug on the counter before her and shook her head. Her hair was wet, and her blonde tail swung heavily with the gesture. "Not until we reach an understandin.'"

"An understanding about what?" My voice was scratchy, and I coughed. Before I'd pulled my hand from my mouth, Harper was holding up one of the steaming mugs. I took it and swallowed gratefully. The warm liquid stung, but the pain eased quickly. I took in a deep breath after several gulps, my chest lifting and falling in heavy waves. Harper sat back and looked at me, waiting.

I smacked my lips and stuck out my tongue. "Needs cream."

"Here." The guy at the stove stuck his hand in the fridge and handed over a carton. He had a bushy little beard, nowhere near as long as Harper's. It was a deep brown that matched his eyes. I assumed the hair on top of his head matched, but could hardly tell. His black beanie covered all but a few little curls. He was wearing a simple button-up shirt, worn jeans, and striped socks. His face was round and seemed genuinely friendly despite the circumstances.

"Thanks." I poured in as much as the mug would allow before handing it back. He nodded and went back to his task. I walked over and took a dark bar stool next to Harper, putting me directly in front of her.

Her blue eyes were filled with steel as she spoke over her own mug. "We obviously have a problem."

"Give me a stake and I'll solve it." I fixed my eyes on her mug. The heavy aroma of coffee was mixing with something else, something thick.

She snorted and sipped at her mug, her lips coming back a slightly deeper shade of red. "Just try it. I dare ya."

I stiffened. "Could you at least not drink that in front of us?"

"Why?" She sat back and crossed her arms, giving me a direct stare. "Ya already know what I am."

"It's disgusting." I spat the words out and a heavy thump clashed into my side. "Oomph."

"She saved me the effort of attending your funeral." Harper glared at me, his elbow still at the ready. "Shut up and let the lady eat her breakfast."

"Thank you, Detective Harper." Lily raised her mug in a toast before drinking again.

The stocky man came away from the stove, a plate in hand that he set between me and Harper before taking the last stool. He reached over and grabbed two long pieces of bacon, crunching them in his teeth and smiling. "Have some. It's good."

I gaped. "You're human?"

He laughed and chewed some more before speaking. "Yeah, working on fixing that."

Great, a freaking Renfield had made me breakfast.

Harper grabbed a few slices and the crunches became numerous, barely manageable with the enhanced hearing.

"A man who actually knows how to cook bacon till it's crispy." Harper sighed in pure pleasure. "You're alright."

The man nodded before turning back to his chewing. I locked my eyes with her and took a sip of the hazelnut roast. "So, what kind of understanding do you want to reach?"

"I want ya to back off," she said it like she was asking us to pick the tab at a burger joint.

"Worried we'll bring your buddies down?" I scoffed and took a sip.

"Did ya miss the part where I was fightin' with those eejits? What part of this makes ya think we're buddies?"

"Birds of a feather," I drawled. Harper elbowed me again, and I shot him a look.

"You racist cock!" She stood, her slender hands slapping against the marble surface. The loud smack issued me another headache that rose with her voice. "We're not any more alike than you and the scum ya put in prison!"

"Yeah, I saw so many shades during the massacre." I jutted my chin out, pointing at her with the tip, desperately trying not to cradle my head. I would not appear weak. "All the colors of sadistic in one fun species."

Her body shook, and she glared at me. Her companion placed a tentative hand on her shoulder. "Rome wasn't built in a day."

She snorted and gave the man a disbelieving look. "Alex would have jumped across the table and strangled him for that."

"To be clear, I won't." Harper's deep voice rose. "I'm grateful for what you did and I'm willing to listen. But don't threaten his life."

Lily blew out a breath and leaned forward slowly, placing her hands closer to me on the surface. She ground the words through clenched teeth. "Has it ever occurred to ya how many vampires there probably are in the world?"

"Yeah." I leaned forward, covering the space between us. The twin clicks of the handcuffs echoed softly in the kitchen. "Too many."

She looked down slowly, amusement spreading on her face. She lifted her wrists in front of me, a small chain stretching between them and aluminum shining in the early morning light. She gave an exasperated sigh. "Really?"

"Special aluminum and steel, developed after the massacre. Haven't ever been able to test them, before now." I gave her a satisfied grin. "Lillian Edwards, you are under arrest. You have the right to shut—"

She snapped her wrists apart, metal links flying in every direction. Several *clinks* sounded against marble and wood surfaces before the pieces settled.

She locked her eyes with mine as she spoke, her tone falsely cheerful and volume grave-low. "Consider them tested."

CHAPTER 12

LILY

D etective Harper let out a surprised laugh that made his partner wince, even as they both stared in bewilderment. Metal wrapped around each of my tiny wrists, but the chain had practically dissolved under a simple tug. Detective Collins finally looked past my wrists, his green eyes wide as saucers.

"Ya mind unlockin' these?" I waggled my wrists for emphasis. "Ya put them on a bit tight."

He shook as he reached forward, a set of keys jingling in his hands. I rolled my eyes and snatched the keys before fanning them out to find the smaller and more unique one that would be for the handcuffs. It took a second to locate. Why the hell did this guy have so many keys?

I moved with deft hands and dropped the remnants of the police-issue cuffs onto the island with a solid clang. Detective Collins dropped his gaze and stared at the twin loops in disbelief. I rubbed my wrists for a moment before sitting back in my seat. Darren and Detective Harper both stared at us, silent witnesses to the show.

I arched a brow at the more annoying detective. "Try again?"

He swallowed a lump and looked up, his gaze filled with equal parts horror and wonder. "What do you want?"

"I already told ya. I want ya to stay out of my way."

"No deal." He shook his head, his still wet hair letting a few drops fly.

"Ya saw what I just did to your bracelets. Imagine what I can do to your spine." I smiled at him, trying to imagine a wolf considering an entertaining rabbit. There were benefits to being a natural predator, annoying as it may be. James Harper let out a low growl, and I glared at him. "We both know ya can't do shit about it, either."

The large man set his jaw, the scruffy one just shook his head again. "You won't. Break my spine I mean. You won't."

"Oh?" I let out a chuckle and crossed my arms. "I won't?"

"No." His voice was raspy again, and he took another sip of his coffee before speaking again. "According to my partner, you could have left me to die. Instead, you rescued me. I have no clue why, but you wouldn't bother if you were just going to kill me anyway."

"Shite. I was kind of hopin' ya wouldn't notice that."

"Detective, remember?" Confidence filled his tone, but it was somehow cautious.

Had that last part had been a guess? Fuck, I needed sleep. He was getting the better of me.

He lifted his chin. "I'm not backing down, vampire. This is my case."

I debated on telling him to stop me call me that, but he wasn't technically wrong, and we had bigger problems.

"No, it's not." I tried to keep my tone calm, but I wasn't sure how well I succeeded. I was so worn out. "It's mine. Ya can let it go cold or whatever. I'll handle it."

Detective Collins scoffed. "Forgive me if I don't trust you."

"And forgive me if I don't feel like babysittin' ya while I sort this nonsense out." Good grief this man was tiresome.

"What's going to stop us from telling our captain about you?"

Darren let out a little sigh. "Oh, boy."

I kept smiling and turned my face to Detective Harper.

"Would ya kindly tell your partner what species I am?"

The dark man's face took on a hint of purple, and he shook furiously as he tried to form the words. I felt a little bad watching him try to overcome my mental handiwork, when at last he puffed out, "She's human. The EMTs did a full workup after I took her statement."

Detective Collins snapped his attention to his partner, his mouth open in surprise. James Harper's jaw was set and the twinkle was lost from his eyes. Guilt twisted my stomach.

I hardly knew the man, and I couldn't take the risk. Still, I had never had someone so *aware* of me toying with their mind after the fact. It usually felt like a victimless crime.

"You're not the first human investigation to get too close. Ya certainly won't be the last." I gave the two a relaxed smile I didn't feel and leaned my chin on the heel of my hand. "*My* team was workin' hard while ya were coming down from the blood. Everyone has new memories. The club was burned to the ground, no casualties of course."

The scruffy detective looked at me, anger scrunching his features and pinching his lips tight between words. "Harper called in the vampires. There's no erasing that call."

"True." I fanned my fingers out in acknowledgment before placing my chin back in place. "The police know there were vampires at Holocene. Couldn't undo that, but they believe there were only *two* vampires on the scene. Both seem to have killed each other in a struggle."

Detective Collins leaned back in his chair, a stunned look on his face. "No way. People were filming the fight on their phones. I remember yelling at one of them."

"Ah, but none of the videos show *me* doing anythin' special." I smiled at him. "I think your yelling scared them off before they could catch anythin', in fact."

I raised my mug in cheers again, and he flinched away from me.

"So, why not just dry erase my memory? Or Harper's for that matter?" His eyes darkened with suspicion.

"I left Harper with his memories for your sake. He's been given a strong compulsion so he can't reveal what he knows. Still, ya can still talk to him and he'll believe ya. The rest of your team believes the version we gave them without question."

"You still didn't answer." His eyes became twin slits of curiosity. "Why'd you leave my brain alone?

I chewed my cheek, trying to think of any way I could avoid this question. Aside from outright lying, I couldn't think of anything. And I was too bloody tired to come up with a good fib. "You're immune."

The crunches from Darren's chewing slowed for a moment, but he kept his thoughts to himself.

"What?" The scruffy man looked baffled.

I shrugged, trying to act like it was nothing special. "It's rare but not unheard of. Now that I've given ya so much blood that immunity might be even stronger, but ya already repelled the will of two vampires."

"What do you mean *two*?" He leaned forward a fraction and his eyes looked like they were searching for something in me.

"The lingerie model." I waited for memory to strike, but his features remained confused. "The naked little Asian chick. She tried to compel ya to stand still and leave us alone. Instead, ya threatened to shoot her. Thanks for surprising her, by the way. Gave me a second to think of how to get out of her claws."

"Gee, you're welcome." He smiled and it sent chills down my back. No human had ever smiled like they were going to eat me.

"What?"

"You just told me you can't get rid of me."

"I told ya, ya can't expose me." I pointed a finger in the air, emphasizing my point. "No one at your precinct will take the idea of me being a vampire seriously."

"Still, you can't really make me back off. Not if you can't compel me and won't injure me." His grin became one of victory.

Darren said something about checking on Alex and trotted away. I squinted after him. Coward. Still, I had bigger problems.

I returned my attention to the man in front of me. "Your point?"

"Well, neither of us is getting our first choice." He leaned back and placed his arms across his chest in a leisurely way. "What's behind door number two?"

We stared at each other for a moment, probably both assessing the other with the new information. He was right, I couldn't get rid of him. I'd keep tripping over the little maggot and he'd probably get himself killed trying to one-up or out me.

A wicked idea molded in my brain. The little cabbage did have some handy resources. And if I knew where he was going, I would hardly be tripping over him. Hell, I might even be able to get this case over with quicker. Get the business back up before I even had to see Ritti.

I chuckled at my own insanity. "I might grow to like ya."

His reassured smile collapsed. "Please don't."

"Now, now." I lifted my mug up, sipping at the now cool liquid. I suppressed a grimace. Maria really needed to lay off the nighttime Kit Kat bars. "Is that any way to start a new partnership?"

James Harper's mouth dropped open, letting out a startled bark that might have been a laugh. Detective Collins just stared ahead for a second, his jaw clenched. "You're serious?"

I shrugged and sipped again. "I don't see another option. Like ya said, we can't really get rid of each other. We'll just get in each other's way otherwise."

Plus, he might prove useful. But I decided to keep that to myself.

Detective Harper did laugh this time, slapping his partner on the back with a solid thump. "No way I'm playing for this one. She's all yours, buddy."

Detective Collins glowered at me another moment, and I ticked up an eyebrow in challenge. He ground his teeth and stuck out a hand, jabbing the air with his sudden movement.

"If I find out you're the murderer or the dealer, I will put you down."

I eyed the outstretched hand for just a moment before placing my hand in his.

"Deal."

His warmth crushed my hand with a single, hard shake.

"You did what again?" Ivan's Russian accent was harsh with annoyance, and I sat in the large chair, trying to hold still. His steps were heavy on the wood floor, despite the expensive throw-rugs he used for his office. I let my eyes swivel back and forth as my adoptive sire jerked from one side to the next.

The fire loomed behind him, turning his already dusky skin to ash in the shadows. He stopped and glowered down at me. His face was disproportionate in places, his nose and ears not quite fitting with his chin or lips. His long black hair hung in waves to shape a strong jaw. Most people would be intimidated when he aimed that look at them.

I shrugged. "Better to work with him than spend all my time tripping over him."

"Lily." Ivan flopped into the dark chair behind his heavy desk and pinched the bridge of his nose. "We just captured two of the dealers."

"And…" I drew out the word, trying to see how that affected my point.

"Had you succeeded in going unnoticed or let them continue to do business, that wouldn't matter." Ivan held up his large hand as my mouth dropped to protest. "I am not criticizing, just reviewing the facts. This investigation has the potential for us to figure out where the red cocaine chain starts and stops. I don't need to tell you how huge that would be for our cause and capturing two of the flunkies in this whole thing is going to change the reaction of whoever is running the show."

"Yes." I nodded sharply. "And now, I might have access to the resources of the VPB. Do you not see the potential here?"

Ivan mussed his hair and leaned forward, his elbow resting on legs the size of tree trunks. "Kid, how can you trust this guy?"

"I don't. And he trusts me even less." I chuckled. "Hell, he threatened to stake me over breakfast."

Ivan's eyes widened, and he threw his head back in a long laugh. "Let me know if he tries it. The look on his face would be *priceless*."

"I know." I lifted my lips in a grin. "Still, better to leave him assumin' that'll work, in case he gets antsy later."

"I hope you know what you're doing." Ivan's eye ground into me, concern contorting his features.

"Don't we all?" I gave Ivan what I hoped was a reassuring smile before letting it fall. "But that's not the only reason I came."

One of Ivan's eyebrows peaked with interest. "Oh?"

"The male vamp, he mentioned something that I didn't get a chance to question before Ami interrupted us. I was wondering if Cyrus had heard anything."

Ivan pulled out his phone and dialed, his eyes distant as he waited for the other side to pick up.

"Cyrus, can you take ten to update us? Lily may have a new lead for you anyway." He paused, responding to the other end after a beat. "Yes, she's here in my office."

He hung up after a moment of listening and nodded. "He'll be up in a moment."

I fought the urge to grumble. I'd been hoping to avoid Ivan's second in command. I was still annoyed by his handling of Ami when he'd taken her in. A knock sounded behind me, and I heard the heavy oak door graze the thick rug as it opened, heavy steps coming closer. I turned and gave the approaching vampire a quick nod.

"Cyrus." I filled the tone with a chill, hoping he'd take the hint and leave me be this time.

Cyrus was even paler than me, or maybe his thick black hair made it appear so. His shoulder-length Mohawk was pulled back from his sculpted face and broad shoulders, the black stubble of his temples almost concealing the lines of his tattoos before the dark swirls of a Norse dragon curled around his neck and ears.

His black T-shirt was covered in streaks of ash and the numerous large rings on his hands were decorated with fresh blood in their crevices. I grimaced, and not entirely because of the potent smell. Cyrus nodded in return, his wolf-gray eyes locked on me. The tiny gold flecks of his gaze sparkled with mischief.

"Lily."

He stood and nodded his head to Ivan, who looked more than a little annoyed at coming second in the acknowledgments. The petty part of me wanted to tell him he could have first and last as far as I was concerned, but I bit the comment back. Never knew if I might need Cyrus' help later. The warden was handy in a tight spot when Ivan didn't have him assigned to dungeon duty. Ivan gave Cyrus a measured look and motioned to the second seat across his large desk.

Cyrus sat, a languid motion that made his well-toned body ripple beneath the T-shirt. He propped his chin on the heel of one hand as he spoke, his eyes back on me. "I heard you had a lead."

His accent was thick and elongated but still rough around the edges.

"Yeah, somethin' about a college. Sounds like more sales are going on there, but I didn't have a chance to figure out which campus." I gave Cyrus a dark look. "I was too busy being beaten by that girl ya were feelin' up last night."

"My hand slipped." Cyrus grinned, confidence oozing through his teeth. "It's not my fault her skirt was so short."

"Bet it wouldn't have slipped in front of the queen." I arched a brow in challenge. "Maybe I should visit her on my way out. It's been a while since we talked."

Cyrus rolled his eyes. "You two aren't exactly close. I'm not worried about you braiding each other's hair and gossiping."

"Children." Ivan's tone was granite. I snapped my attention to him, shame smothering some of my irritation. Cyrus always knew exactly where to stick that hot poker. Ivan gave us each a look before turning his attention back to Cyrus. "Did the guy say anything about a college while you were interrogating him?"

Cyrus shook his head, his long braid shifting in the motion. "No, but give me twenty minutes, and I'll see what I can do."

"Text me the answer." I stood, grabbing my leather jacket off the back of the chair and my helmet from the ground.

Cyrus let out a sound that was half-snort and half-chuckle at the sight of the extra fiberglass shapes that graced the top of my helmet. "Only you would wear something that ridiculous looking."

"Watch it, Cyrus," Ivan warned, his smile wry. "Kitty's got claws."

"Meow," I said it in a bland tone and gripped the knob to leave. "Let me know what ya find out. See ya, Boss."

CHAPTER 13

GABE

"**Y**ou've got to be shitting me!" I hissed, staring at the screen like it might change its answer. Harper rolled his chair over and snorted.

"Background check didn't get her, 'ey?"

"No." I scrolled to the top, clicking the mouse button harder than strictly necessary. "I mean, I knew she had to have at least some paperwork, being a licensed PI and all. But she's got everything. Even a birth certificate!"

"Maybe she's a new..." Harper looked like something had literally stolen his tongue for a moment before he just shook his head. "Maybe she's new. How old does the certificate say she is?"

"Twenty-six, immigrated from Ireland just over ten years ago with her family."

"She's got parents?"

"According to this, her mom and dad died in a car wreck shortly after she turned eighteen. Left her the house outside town. But it's too convenient, like someone wrote this whole story." I sat back from my desk and sank my teeth into the second Egg McMuffin.

Annoyingly, the vamp had been right. The protein was quickly correcting most of the loopy feelings and my legs were working again. Sounds were still louder than they should be, and I was forced to wear my sunglasses on an overcast day, but that was fading with each bite.

Harper looked at my ravenous state and shook his head. "She said to eat it, not breathe it, pal."

I gave him a dark look and swallowed the last bite before reaching into the paper bag for another. "Tell you what, when you get poisoned by that thing you can eat however you want."

"Hey, keep it down." Harper looked around the bullpen to see if anyone had heard me. If they had, they weren't reacting. Harper twisted his lips in an annoyed frown and glared at me. "You know, for a guy who just got a second chance at life, you're being a real asshole. Did it ever occur to you to thank her for saving your ass? Or to *try* the bacon?"

I shrugged, ripping the paper away from my third greasy sandwich. "It's not like the bacon was specially laid out for us. Her little Renfield made it."

"Yeah, he did." Harper glowered at me. "After she woke him up and *begged* him to. Just for you. She said it would help clear your head before we left. But you'd rather stumble into a McDonald's with your wobbly pride and threaten the person who just saved your ass."

It was certainly odd that she'd begged the guy, but something else Harper said caught me off guard.

"*Person?*" My jaw hung slightly open, a small piece of the egg falling into my lap. I looked around and hissed out my reply. "She's a vampire. We hunt them. It's kind of our job."

"No, our job is to investigate illegal vampire activity." Harper rolled back to his desk. "Last I checked, self-defense is not illegal."

"Their *existence* is illegal. What the hell did she do to your brain? I mean, I knew she scrambled it last night, but this..." I looked him over. "This isn't you."

"It is." Harper gave me a sympathetic sideways glance. "I know you lost a lot during the massacre—"

"Don't."

Harper tapped the arms of his chair a few times then nodded. "Fine. Just try to consider not being such a dick when you two meet later tonight."

I suppressed an annoyed sound and looked for a new topic of conversation. "Why hasn't Murphy called us in? The captain usually wants an update first thing."

"I told him we didn't have anything new and it would be better to let us work. I didn't think your new wardrobe would impress him."

"What, sweatpants aren't in this season?"

"Collins, you've never worn anything less than a button-up and slacks. Not in the entire time I've known you." Harper gave the sweatsuit a humorous glance. "You show up wearing that, the captain will demand a psych eval."

"I could probably use one." I chewed and swallowed, putting the rest of the half-finished breakfast sandwich back in the bag. I wanted more, but my stomach was starting to reject the excess grease. "I must be losing my mind, working with her."

Even if it did give me more time to pin her down.

"Have you decided where you're going to meet her?"

"Oh, yeah." I smiled in vicious satisfaction. "I know just the place."

———◆———

I leaned against the copper statue, orange and yellow leaves skittering past my feet with the rush of children running. I had my face buried in a novel, but I hadn't turned the page in half an hour. I really did need a shrink. Here I was, getting ready to meet a vampire. Public location or not, this had to be the first sign of insanity.

I let out an annoyed breath and surveyed the crowd again. Several people surrounded me. A few of them blonde. None of them her. A set of giggles drew my eyes to the entrance of a *Claire's*. Several girls trotted out wearing tiaras that shimmered in the golden afternoon light. They hoisted their cell phones, aiming at each other as they pronounced their enjoyment for the entire outlet mall to hear. I smiled and tried to return my attention back to *Odd Thomas*. It didn't work.

Five minutes later, I was still reading the same line when I looked for her again. Still no one. I stood and walked around the monument; a thick slab displaying the hundreds of names lost two years ago. I could find one name on that list blindfolded, but I wasn't here for him today. I was looking for the thing that had killed him.

I was pulling her business card from my pocket and calling her when a mess of blonde curls caught my eye. It was pale and fluffy, sprouting from the back of a woman's head in a long tail. It swayed in the wind slowly as the owner peered in the window of a jewelry store.

The low sun reflected off the glass, and I couldn't tell it if was her. I checked my watch. 6:15 PM. She was fifteen minutes late; surely even she wouldn't be window shopping while the agreed meeting place was directly behind her.

The woman tilted her head to gaze at the shop display from another angle and the elf-point of her nose showed itself.

My blood curdled in my veins. I'd been waiting patiently and she had literally been distracted by something shiny. I started forward, ready to chew her out.

Sure, she'd broken my cuffs this morning, but we were in public now. She wouldn't expose herself. I could give her an honest piece of my mind.

I kept my eyes locked on her face as I shuffled through shoppers and teenagers alike. A few feet from the storefront, the glint of the sun became less bright on the window, and I could see her reflection, a pale shadow over a display of men's watches.

Her eyes were larger than usual and, even in the glass, they seemed heavy somehow. Something flickered in the glass, maybe a pedestrian running for something, and she started, shaking her head, and rubbing her eyes, still not noticing my reflection behind her in the glass.

She looked again at the display and groaned towards the heavens, "Great, the little gobshite already hates me."

I finally stood next to her. "You're late."

She jumped a little and opened her mouth, letting it hang for a moment for before biting her lower lip and straightening her spine. "And you're fuckin' rude."

I crossed my arms. "Not as rude as being late when you're standing a foot away from our meeting place."

She snorted and walked past me, making a b-line for the benches. Only then did I notice the twin paper cups in her hands.

"And you stopped for coffee?" I followed behind her.

"Yep, but it's all mine now," She tossed the comment over her shoulder before making a big show of drinking from one of the cups.

"Seriously?" I sat hard on the bench and glared. "You were late so you could buy coffee and window shop?"

I mean, I knew she wasn't excited to work with me either but this was just unreal.

"I got the coffee as a peace offering!" She finished the coffee first cup and slammed the still full one on the bench. It popped, the contents splashing up, and she swore. People around us, parents especially, glared. Probably getting annoyed by the mess and foul language.

The vampire was still mopping up the mess with flimsy napkins, barely containing the spill when she growled, "You're lucky I even showed, you gigantic asshole."

It was my turn to snort.

"What? I thought you'd simply remember the directions easy enough. After all, you were here just two years ago. The event was quite memorable."

Her gaze grew icy, and she tossed the napkin into the spill. "Fuck this, I don't know why I thought ya could be reasonable."

She stormed away. I looked between the mess and her receding back before clambering after her.

"Hey, we had a deal," I reached out and placed a hand on her shoulder.

She spun, grabbed my arm like she meant to twist it, and stopped just short of the deed. Someone nearby let out a surprised gasp but no one else seemed to notice the exchange. Meanwhile, we stared each other down, measuring one another and trying to force the other to blink first.

"I only agreed to *team up* so I wouldn't be tripping over ya every five seconds."

My BS detector lit up, but I wasn't certain why.

"Yeah? And what do think will happen if you leave now?" I didn't really want to work with her but keep your friends close and your enemies closer. She'd slip up. I'd be able to catch her and take her in. I couldn't do that if she was at a distance.

We glared at each other a moment longer before she spat another curse out, dropped the hand, and crossed her arms over the tattered tank top. "Seems we need to set some boundaries with the partnership."

"This is not a partnership!" I spat every word in her face, stupid human instinct taking over. "What Harper and I have, that's a partnership. You're just a parasite I have to—"

She moved faster than I could process. One minute she was a foot away, the next her pointy nose was almost touching mine, like someone had hit the fast-forward button on my life. With the sudden jerk in movement, I heard my police cuffs snapping this morning.

She could kill me, here and now, and be gone before I even dropped the ground.

"Thought that might get your attention. Now—" she backed away, slowly and at a more reasonable pace. It looked creepy after the sudden jerk before, "you and I have to deal with each other, thanks to your annoying little immunity. Granted, your unique strength could come in handy, but if we're going to be stuck together, then we need to set some rules."

"Fine, like what?"

"Like, no more inviting me to sites of the massacre." She walked around me, back towards the messy bench, and scooped the coffee off the surface with her hands, flinging droplets into the ground. "Believe it or not, I come durin' the memorial services. That's bad enough, thank you very much."

I glared at the back of her head, tempted to tell her what bad really was. I decided it was pointless; she wouldn't care. "Fine, what else do you want?"

A few people were watching us, but they didn't stop to gawk. We must look like a couple having a spat. The idea made my stomach churn.

"How about a thank you?" She shook her hand free of the coffee and sat hard on the bench, her arms crossed over her chest.

I ground my teeth, Harper's earlier words echoing in my head. I looked around and walked closer so I could say it only to her. "Fine, thank you for saving my life. Even if I have no clue why you did it."

"I suppose that's the best ya can do." She rolled her eyes and shook her head. "Your terms?"

I blinked in surprise. "Mine?"

"Ya have mine, though I'm sure that list will grow." She waved me forward impatiently. "Let's hear it."

I gave her a hard look as I sat back on the bench, the now drying spill separating us. "No more hiding details of your investigation from me or Harper. And no more messing with his head."

"I shouldn't have to do any more of that, but I can't promise. All I can say is, he will have his memories intact unless he asks me to do otherwise. Good enough?"

"No, I mean it. Do, not scramble his brains again. And the investigation?"

"Seriously?" She arched a single brow. "His own wishes mean so little to ya?"

"Don't do it."

"Fine." She raised her hands in resignation.

I didn't believe her, but I was planning on keeping Harper far away from her anyway. After his earlier words about self-defense, I couldn't let her near him again. "And the investigation?"

"I figured that rather went without saying. Share and share-alike."

Yeah, sure.

Still, I nodded like I was agreeing and searched my brain for anything else I wanted to add.

She looked at the thin puddle of brown and let out a sigh, "Coffee?"

"Huh?"

CHAPTER 14

LILY

Old memories still tried to climb back to the surface as I stood and walked around the memorial, letting my gaze wander over the watches once more. I bet Isaac would have liked the gold one. I had a feeling he'd hate the digital ones. Then, again, I'd never know.

The detective let out a rude sound and walked past me to the nearest coffee store. I shook my head of the past and followed after the scruffy asshole.

I should have taken Alex's advice and blown him off. Coming to the memorial always stirred shit up that was better left alone. I wasn't sure why. It wasn't like I'd lost anyone here. Maybe one mob's actions simply reminded me of the others. I didn't know.

The rich aroma of espresso and caramel invaded my senses as I stepped into the coffee house, nearly bumping into the detective.

"You're buying."

"To hell, I am." I crossed my arms. "I bought the first two, it's your turn."

"Not like I got any," he pointed out as we shuffled with the line.

I tried to focus on the grinding noise of coffee being pulverized or the high squeal of the frother, trying to raise their perspective volume in my head and drown out the obnoxious man in front of me. Sadly, the noise did little to change his face as he continued to scowl at me.

Why, oh *why*, did this prick have to be immune? A simple glance, and I could have been rid of him, but *no*...

I glared up at the ceiling once before rolling my eyes and returning my attention back to him. He was flinching at the coffee store's noises, and I had to suppress a smile. Good, the prick deserved a little pain for inviting me here.

"Fine, what do ya want?" I could just add it to my growing list of expenses. This eejit and Ritti deserved each other.

He ordered black coffee with a shit ton of cream and went to find a table. When I turned to find him, he secured the tiniest table in the farthest corner. The store was packed to the brim, but this table was near the loo, so people seemed to be giving it space.

"So, feel any better?" I tried to keep my tone level as I set his new coffee before him, but a little sarcasm slipped in.

"Define better," he grunted low as he twirled the paper cup. "I mean, yeah sound and light are only about twice as bad instead of ten times. Beyond that, it's pretty much the same as this morning. Not sure why anyone would use that shit recreationally if this is the hangover."

"Why do ya think the vamps are mixing it with cocaine?" I sat and took a small sip of my own. "After all, one kilo of regular cocaine usually brings in...what, about thirty thousand dollars?"

"I'm not in narcotics." His tone was dry, and I waved him off.

"Don't have to be if ya just do a little homework. Anyway, we've gotten reports of the vampire variety getting double easily. Plus, the cocaine dilutes some of the blood's effects, less blood to get a similar high. Less cocaine needed, as the blood amps it up. See?"

"Who's we?" Detective Collins watched me like I was some kind of snake and I shook my head. He pulled a novel from one of his coat pockets and slapped it onto the table surface before glowering at the cup. It was going to be a long night.

"Ya have your contacts. I have mine." I took another sip.

He gave me a dark look.

"I agreed to share the case with ya. Seeing as neither of us is aiming to become Facebook friends, I'm not inclined to share outside those parameters."

"Fine."

A silent hole filled our tiny space.

"I might have a lead." I hoped the topic of work would dissolve some of this tension. His eyes flicked up from the coffee and he waited. "Ya remember the guy I was talkin' to before the fight?"

He nodded, and I went on, "Well, he mentioned something about a campus getting Cheri Coke sales beforehand. It sounds like whoever is runnin' the drugs is operatin' it like some sort of pyramid scheme. Anyway, I had one of my colleagues ask him more forcefully—"

"You did what?" Detective Collins' eyebrows drove into his dark hair.

"Ya heard me." He gave me a grim look, and I blew out another annoyed breath. "What do ya care? It's not like you're attached to him."

Yes, we'd tortured the asshole. Yes, I thought that was sick, but I hadn't really had a say in the matter. Still, I wasn't sure why he'd give a shit. It was just a vampire to him.

"Fine." He ground his teeth and sipped at his coffee, the sneer deepening as he swallowed. "What'd you find out?"

"Sounds like the dealer is at Warner Pacific University. Given how close that campus is to Rockwood, I'm bettin' the dealer is the same guy from the party."

"Not a bad place to start." His head teetered on his shoulders in thought and his tone lost a little of the bite. He still eyed the coffee in annoyance.

"Oh, for Pete's sake." I rolled my eyes and leaned in closed. "It's not like it's contaminated because I held the fuckin' cup, ya know."

His cheeks reddened, and he purposefully took a larger gulp. I wasn't sure who he tried to fool.

"Are ya always so stubborn?" I shook my head as I whispered.

"Are you always so pale?" His tone mocked mine, and I snorted, trying to suppress a surprised laugh.

"Yeah, tends to come with the territory."

"So, why didn't I notice it when we met?" He placed his cup on the table and tapped the exterior with his fingers like he was playing invisible piano keys. "The club I get, that lighting was all over the place. But our precinct is brighter than daylight."

I gave him a half-smile of appreciation. Annoying or not, at least he wasn't a complete idiot. "Rub on tan. I had to practically peel my skin to get that crap off, but it makes blendin' in a lot easier if I'm in a crowd."

"So, why not just leave it on?" He gave the other coffee patrons a meaningful glance.

"I wasn't tryin' to blend in last night." I smiled, and he actually winced.

He considered me for a moment longer, his nose scrunched. "So, what do you want to do about the college?"

"I was thinkin' I'd talk to the dean tomorrow, see what they know. The dealer is being smart about how they're doing business. I haven't found any victims linked to that location yet, and I was lookin' all day."

"That reminds me." His tone downshifted further into a business tone and his finger-tapping became less rapid. "How'd you know to check the club?"

I sat back and sipped on my own cup, licking my lips before lowering it to reveal my mouth. "How did you?"

He looked like he was chewing on an idea before he nodded and spoke. "Lead from the party. Rich kid who didn't want his dad cutting him off or something."

I ran my tongue over the back of my teeth and laughed a little. "The kid with the magic marker all over his face?"

He looked a little surprised but nodded.

I smiled. "He was on my original list of victims, but he was passed out when I found him at the party. I didn't get a chance to talk to him."

"So." He leaned forward, his elbows propped against the surface of the table. "How did you know to go to Holocene?"

"Seven people have shown up in hospital records recently. Three of them treated by an associate of mine. I got a hold of the records and all three had notes about the stamp Holocene uses for admission." I held up my left hand, the large blue H still contrasting against my skin.

"Your friend have any more information?"

"She's not my friend," I corrected. "But yeah, she said there were five additional cases she treated in the last couple of weeks. She was able to keep those off the records. I'm still tryin' to find those."

"Why not just ask your contact?"

"Did I mention she's not my friend?" I gave him a grim smile. "I'd rather not twist her arm."

I winced at the same time as him. No doubt we were both thinking about the severed limb I had just ripped from Ami the night before.

"Okay." He grimaced again and nodded once, making me wonder if he'd taken me literally. "What time are we heading to the college?"

"Who said anythin' about *we*?" I glared at him.

"You did." Triumph filled his green eyes, and he imitated my accent, poorly, "Share and share-alike."

That was not what I'd intended. I'd been hoping to send him into an electronic trail while I did the sleuthing on my end. I had to reign this in, fast.

"I'll give ya everythin' I find. Hell, I'll give ya the hospital records right now. Ya can run those through official channels and add them to the case before the media gets a hold of them."

"I'll take those, too." His grin deepened, and he held up his cup in cheers, mocking my posture from this morning. "But I'm going to that campus. With or without you."

I tilted my head back and groaned. "Ya know, if ya liked the taste so much, I could just give ya a sample. No need to run into danger again."

I really didn't need him cramping me.

He scrunched his brows together, trying to puzzle out my meaning maybe, before his face reddened and bunched unnaturally. The smile was gone and his face was filled with a deadly promise as he hissed, "Don't you ever feed me that shit again."

"Then try not havin' any more near-death experiences," I whispered back. "That's going to be hard to do if you're facing off against a vampire. I can't promise ya won't need it again."

"I'll manage." He placed his cup on the table surface and leaned forward. "When do you want to meet?

Yup, he was always this stubborn.

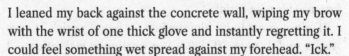

I leaned my back against the concrete wall, wiping my brow with the wrist of one thick glove and instantly regretting it. I could feel something wet spread against my forehead. "Ick."

"Get back to work." Alex shook his head down at me, his ears wobbling a little with the gesture. I scowled and debated tossing the red-soaked sponge at him.

"Don't push your luck. I could just walk out of here."

"Not likely." His dark eyes gave the mess a meaningful glance. "Don't think Darren will hack any more hospital records if you renege on our deal."

I sighed, stepped towards the day-old blood, and knelt back on the ground. I scrubbed at the floor, pushing the puddle towards the drain in the middle of the concrete cell. The smell of soap and rot filled the room. I winced in disgust when I came across a tiny pile of ash soaked in the blood. "What the hell was that?"

"His ear." Alex directed the blood with a garden hose as he spoke. It turned a few shades lighter as it rushed towards the drain. "He tried to block out the noise and pulled it right off."

I dry heaved a bit and decided I was glad I didn't need to breathe. I was used to Alex telling me what some of his clients did during the transition, but seeing the results was another matter. "Remind me why I agreed to this."

"Because I have to replace a whole mattress set thanks to your little detox session." Alex sneered. "I can still smell the vomit in that cell, even after you bleached it."

"Sorry, I had to give him about a pint just to keep him alive."

Alex knelt to scrub away some of what I'd missed. The hose gushed, a stream of new water between us. "He seemed like a jackass."

"Hard not to agree there."

"And really." Alex looked up, anger filling his face. "Inviting you to the original site of the massacre? That's a dick move."

"No arguments here." I stood, shaking my rubber gloves off.

"I vote you let him die if he gets hurt again. And not just because his vomit stinks."

"I'm not going to let him die just for being a prick." I gave Alex a rueful smile. "If that was a worthy-enough offense, I would have taken Cyrus' head long ago."

"Hey, the cop said he didn't want your blood again. You'd just be honoring his wishes."

I snorted. "And you're all about honoring people's wishes."

Alex stood and eyed the floor before walking into the tiny concrete hallway. The spigot squeaked as he turned the handle and the water went from a thick gush to a steady trickle as he returned. "Hey, it'll be his last. Those are supposed to be important, right?"

I grinned up at my best friend and shook my head, feeling the bandanna over my hair loosen a little. "Any other thoughts?"

"Yeah." Alex gave me a serious look. "You should really tell him stakes don't work before he does something stupid and gets himself hurt."

I groaned. "I'm not really a fan of telling him how to properly kill me."

"Yeah, well are you a fan of dying? Jackass or not, if this guy is acting as your backup, you should at least give him some direction. Speaking of which—" Alex gave me a baleful look, "would you be more careful? That last fight you had pulled pretty hard. The tether almost had me out the door before Darren stopped me."

"Sorry." I massaged the chilly spot just above my breast bone out of habit. Where Alex's tether had attempted to pull him to me in my moment of crisis, mine was numb and cold from centuries of disuse. "I'll try to stay out of trouble."

"Nah, I'd never ask that. I am talking to you." Alex picked up the bucket and sponges, heading back into the hallway. I snorted and peeled off my gloves, tossing them into the bucket with a soft splash. We ascended the stairs and a few muffled cries rose from one of the other cells. I turned and nodded towards the steel door. "How's that one doin'?"

"Pretty good." Alex looked proud. "She'll probably be back at Court by Monday."

"Impressive." I nodded approval. "Ya took twice as long."

Alex gave me a light punch to the shoulder. "My transition also wasn't as well managed."

I laughed and placed my hand flat on the palm scanner at the top of the stairs. A green bar of light appeared at the top of the tiny screen before disappearing beneath my hand. The door unlocked with a soft click, and I pushed it open, squeezing through our pantry and back into the house.

CHAPTER 15

GABE

I plopped the writing tablet on my desk and sat down to enter my password. The screen loaded as I pulled out the scrap of paper Lily had given me from my pocket.

I brought up the police database right as Harper sat on the corner of my desk. "Hey, partner. Captain wants us in for an update."

I nodded and locked my screen before standing, stuffing the scrap of paper back into my pocket. "How was your night?"

"I was going to ask the same thing." Harper gave me a sly smile. "Your new playmate show up?"

"Yes." I rolled my eyes. "Though, she got rather offended by the location I suggested."

"Shocking." Harper chuckled. At my look, he shook his head and started walking towards the back of the building. "You didn't exactly give her a neutral location."

I made a noncommittal grunt and knocked gently against the glass of the captain's door.

"Come in." His response was quick, and I heard him tell someone he'd have to call them back. I opened the door and walked into the captain's office. The linoleum was covered with a cheap rug, making our footfalls quieter. Sean Murphy scribbled something on a sticky note and set his cell phone down before looking up. "Ah, Collins. Harper. Have a seat."

His deep voice resonated in the small space, and I took one of the wooden chairs seated across from him. Harper closed the door and took the other. Behind the captain, a large cherrywood shelf was littered with awards. Some from the police academy and some from high school football. The shelf matched his large L-shaped desk. His computer sat on the part of the desk flanking his blue walls. His wife smiled her million-dollar grin from a ten-dollar frame. She was the only truly personal touch to the room.

Captain Murphy smiled, his features chiseled, and his grin perfect despite being in his mid-forties. He sat straight, making his square shoulders and thick arms seem even more formidable. He pushed some of his dark hair away from his forehead and leaned forward. "How are we doing on the St. Claire kid?"

"Not great." Harper sighed. "I checked the 911 calls. The voices were all different and the calls came from different numbers. I'm having someone down in tech run traces now. Maybe we'll get lucky and someone used a personal phone."

"What about the old bat you interviewed the first day?"

"Nothing." Harper and I said it in unison, and I waved him forward. He nodded and started speaking. "I ran a check on her. Nothing out of the ordinary in her background. Lives alone. She mentioned children, but I didn't find any. Otherwise, nothing really stuck out."

"But you said her interview was odd." The captain sat back and steepled his fingers together.

"Yeah, it was," I acknowledged. "She said she heard one argument, but she didn't hear the sirens of our police cruisers. Plus, she didn't seem that upset that her lack of action might have cost someone their life."

"Thoughts?"

"We think she has basically numbed herself to the violence of the Rockwood area." Harper shrugged. "We all know it's common. She probably just tuned into the fight because it was more interesting than late-night TV."

"Okay." The captain nodded sharply. "Anything else from the mother?"

"She did call me yesterday," I interjected. "She found a stash of vampire novels and movies in her basement. I'm going to pick those up from her later tomorrow."

"Why tomorrow?"

I shrugged. "She had a work thing and couldn't let me in before then. She didn't want to be seen coming here with them."

Captain Murphy nodded and stroked his smooth chin. "You think there might be a clue in the contraband?"

"I think it's worth looking through. Either way, we don't want it ending up in public hands."

"Anything on the Cheri Coke front?" The captain's blue eyes darted to the side of the building that faced the street. "The media vultures are hounding me more for the drugs than the dead kid."

"Did you see some of the theories on the news this morning?" Harper chuckled mildly.

"I'd rather see our own." The captain's deep voice held an edge, and Harper's smile dropped.

"Well," I started, trying to pull Harper's foot from his mouth. "I'm going to check out hospital records, see if there are other cases of the drug."

"Okay, keep me in the loop." The captain nodded. "You're still the lead on both cases."

We both bobbed our heads once and stood to leave.

"Collins, hold up." Captain Murphy's words halted my progress. A lump formed in my throat. God, I hoped he didn't have anything that would require me to lie to him. I nodded at Harper, and he shut the door while I sat back down.

"What's up?"

"I hear you broke it off with Michelle?" Captain Murphy gave me a conspiratorial smile. I let out a long laugh. I hadn't been expecting that. I probably should have been surprised it took this long for him to hear.

"Yeah, like two months ago. Why?"

"Dare I ask what happened?"

"Depends." I nodded my head at the picture of his wife, now able to see her long auburn hair flowing over her shoulders in thick waves. "Her sister going to hear the report?"

"I can't lie to Barbara." He shrugged his large shoulders. "You know that."

"Then let's just say the ending fight was noted by my neighbors and it wasn't the first time."

"Ha!" Captain Murphy slapped his desk with a laugh. Triumph lit in his eyes. "I told Barbara not to try matchmaking. She'll be sad to hear it, though. She really wants Michelle to find a good guy."

"Tell her I said thanks for the compliment." I smiled and made to stand again. "Anything else?"

"Nah." He waved a big hand, dismissing me while he reached for the phone. Probably to tell his wife he'd told her so.

Harper was waiting outside the office. I shut the door again, and we walked back to our desks. He gave me a curious look.

"Trouble?"

"Just dating advice."

"Oh, figured out you and Michelle broke up?"

"Surprised it took this long. That woman's pride kept her from even telling her own sister." I shook my head in mild disbelief.

"So, what made you think to check the hospitals?"

"I didn't." I fished the scrap out of my pocket and handed it to Harper. "Got some new info during my meeting with the PI last night."

Three names, including the kid Harper had questioned, were written in blue. In black, Lily had scribbled the name of the hospital and the nurse she was checking into. Harper whistled.

"That's not a bad start."

"Yeah, but we'll need to steer clear of that last name for a little bit." I pointed at Anna Martín's name and gave Harper a meaningful glance. He looked confused for a moment, then nodded.

"Ah, another one. Gotcha." He handed the slip back, and I stuffed it back into my jacket.

"How are you so cool about this?" I all but hissed it, looking around to make sure no one was listening. "I mean, what did she do to your head?"

"Later, buddy." He shook his head.

I blew out a breath and nodded as I settled back into my computer chair and re-entered my password. I smoothed the tiny paper out and typed the second name into our database.

<hr />

I'd barely engaged the brake pedal when Lily climbed into my passenger seat and slammed the door. She held a small bag that jingled in one hand and her helmet in the other. "Adrian St. Claire."

"Hello to you, too." I blinked at her, taking in her apparel. Even at the mall, I was too busy arguing to really notice what she was wearing. This was the first time I was seeing her without a costume. It was a little underwhelming. True, I hadn't expected her to walk around in a cape or wear one of those long dresses that looked like it was composed of a corset and spider webs. But after the plaid skirt in the club and goth getup before that, her everyday clothes were surprisingly...ordinary.

Her skinny jeans were either ripped for fashion or had seen better days. Based on the state of her dark tank top, I was figuring the second. The shirt was frayed at the hem with several stretched sections along the bottom, like the fabric had been pulled on repeatedly.

The only thing that looked well cared for in her wardrobe was the motorcycle gear. Her jacket had some areas of wear and use, but it practically shined. Same thing with her boots, a few scuffs from where she might have kicked something with her toes, but otherwise clean and polished. The smell of leather was starting to overpower the pine tree air freshener of my vehicle, but it wasn't unpleasant.

I was also a little stunned watching her flounce about in the five o'clock sun without so much as wincing. I'd wondered about that when she suggested time, but her skin didn't hold any telltale shines of burn. I didn't even see any signs of makeup, Goth or otherwise. The only concession she seemed to make for the bright day was revealed in the slight sheen of sunscreen on her cheeks and nose.

She waved away the sarcastic greeting, the little clutch sounding its bells and drawing me from my examination. "Adrian was your victim from Rockwood?"

"Yeah." I put the car in park and killed the engine. "How'd you find out?"

"I do watch the news." She arched a golden brow at me. "Your case ties right in with the drugs. The media is having a field day."

Guess the vultures were smelling more meat than I realized.

"Okay, aside from the drugs on Adrian, what does that have to do with what we're working on?" I didn't really like the idea of giving her anything on that angle.

"Adrian was on my original list of people showing up in the hospital. He was patient zero."

I looked at her, only a little surprised. "I didn't find him in the hospital records you gave me."

"Ya wouldn't. He was dropped off at a different location, one I hadn't really looked into yet. God, I am so dense!" She palmed her forehead. "Why didn't I think about your murder case?"

I looked out the windshield, trying to think. The large visitor parking sign directly in front of me gave me no inspiration. "Okay, so Adrian was the first case you had of the Cheri Coke popping up in Portland."

"First case of it popping up on the *human* record," she corrected. "The drug has been around for a little less than a year but it's stayed off your radar this whole time. But suddenly, we've got a vampire murder and kids popping up across Portland with the evidence literally all over their faces."

"So what, dangerous vampire drug didn't make you guys think you should warn us?"

She snorted, an annoyed sound. "Would ya've listened?"

"Yes!"

"You're so full of shit." Her voice was calmer than mine. "Ya never would've trusted us if we'd told ya. Better if we could stop the trade before ya even realized it existed. That way, your kind doesn't get all worked up."

"Oh, and you've done a bang-up job of that!"

"I don't see your species winnin' any awards for being perfect. In fact, your very job rather indicates otherwise, doesn't it?" I chewed on my cheek, trying to come up with a retort. She kept talking, "How did ya find Adrian?"

I shook my head, a little surprised by her change back to the original topic. Still, at least it was work-related and not a species-ethics debate. "Huh?"

"I mean, how did ya know where to find the body?" She said each word distinctly, and I frowned at her. "Ya didn't just drive around and stumble on a corpse, did you?"

"Kind of, yeah." I relayed the basic details of the 911 calls and what uniforms had been found. None of it was outside standard police procedure so she shouldn't gain too much out of it, but maybe she'd offer me some insight.

"I want to hear those calls," she said instantly.

"No!" I snapped it out and glared at her. "Those are police evidence."

"Fine, then I'm not givin' ya any more of my leads." She leaned against the passenger door and crossed her arms. "Hope ya found those hospital records handy."

My scowl deepened. I had actually. Harper was calling in the other two kids for interviews while I dealt with this. She tapped her long fingers against the leather of her jacket, her eyes a silent challenge. I fought the urge to punch the steering wheel and swore. "Fine. I'll bring them next time we meet."

I'd have to screen them first for anything special she could use, but I hadn't told her how many there were.

"Good." She nodded and turned her attention back to the building. "So, how do ya want to handle this?"

"What do you mean?"

"Well, if I was by myself, I'd just BS my way into the Dean's office and get what I want in five minutes. But with you being here, and wantin' legitimate leads..."

She let the sentence dangle, and I realized she was asking if I wanted to use my badge and make this an official part of the investigation. The consideration surprised me and my only response was to shake my head. "No, we can do this your way."

I didn't have anything tying this to my investigation anyway. Better to watch her and learn what I could.

She shrugged and opened her door, tugging her tank top, as though to cover herself, as she stepped into the street. I stepped out and used the fob to lock the car twice for good measure. I took a moment to look at the motorcycle I'd parked next to, not really having the chance before she'd ambushed me. I didn't know squat about bikes, despite Harper's lecturing over the years. Still, the machine looked nice.

It was midnight blue. Lined with large saddlebags and a double seat of some kind, all the leather was black and shiny despite some obvious wear. She walked towards one of the large saddlebags and loaded her helmet in. I almost snorted when extra fiberglass formed cat ears on her headgear. God, did she even know how to act like a vampire?

"I can see why Harper was so enamored with your bike." I jutted my chin at the Harley as she walked back to me on the sidewalk.

"Yeah, she's my baby." She smiled fondly at the bike before turning back to me. "Your partner's Kawasaki sounds pretty sweet, though."

"Wouldn't know." I shrugged. "I just know Harper has spent way more money on that thing than he should."

"Ya don't ride?" She folded the little bag I'd seen earlier. It was still making that noise as she zipped it into her jacket pocket. She turned and walked towards the campus.

"Nah." I stepped next to her, speeding up to match her brisk pace. Silence fell between us for a moment. I looked over and found she was smiling as she walked. "What?"

"You just had an actual conversation with me." She gave me a quick glance. "I may need to mark the day on my calendar."

I blinked and realized she was right. I shook my head, reminding myself to get some sleep tonight. My little *Interview with the Vampire* last night had worn me out. I wasn't thinking straight. I walked a few steps ahead of her and heard a soft chuckle behind me as I neared the large building ahead.

It didn't take us long to find the dean's office, though we'd had to follow a few different signs to get there. A couple wrong turns and one mesmerized secretary later, the woman opened her office door to us. She was long, in every sense of the word. She shut the door before shaking each of our hands. "Mavis said you had some questions for me..."

The woman's slender face went a little slack, and I gave Lily a dark look. "You couldn't even let her sit down?"

Lily turned back to me, her eyes twin holes that swallowed all the color. "Why would it matter? She's not going to remember this conversation in five minutes."

I scoffed and turned back to the woman. True, it had made getting in here without flashing my badge fairly simple. Still, the ease of which she controlled these people made my stomach twist. I cleared my throat. "Do you know of any dealers on campus?"

The woman just stared at Lily, who snickered a little before I redirected my eyes back to her. She tried to school her expression and failed a few times. "Sorry, she just needs some direction."

She repeated the question and the woman answered mechanically. "There are a few dealers on campus."

The dean listed off several names, and I sputtered for her to slow down. Lily repeated the command I pulled out my pen and paper to take notes as she spoke. Three names. "Ask her if she's got anyone she knows is dealing Cheri Coke."

Lily rolled those black orbs, turning her attention back to the woman, "You will answer the man's questions as though they were my own. Do ya understand?"

The woman nodded slowly, and Lily waved a hand invitation. I asked the question and the dean shook her head with the same lethargic pace. I tapped my pen against my pad in thought but Lily stepped up. "What about any cocaine dealers?"

I gave her an approving nod. "Makes sense."

Lily gave me a small smile as the woman responded again. "There is one person we suspect of dealing hard drugs on campus. Kimberly Ashland."

I felt my brows twist together. That name wasn't familiar to me. "What can you tell us about Kimberly?"

"She's almost failing most of her classes but she's intent on living on campus. We've tried to have her investigated a couple of times, but everyone always says she's clean. Still, there are rumors."

"What kind of rumors?" Lily tilted her head in thought.

"That she's got some new trendy drug." The dean shrugged, her shoulders peaking sharply in her jacket. "No one can prove anything, so I can't kick her out."

"Can you look up Kimberly's dorm number and class schedule?" I felt the wheels twisting in my mind. "Please print us a copy."

I don't know why I bothered adding please, it just didn't feel right ordering her around. The dean walked around her desk to a small computer terminal. She tapped away for a few minutes before a printer in the corner pulsed and ground with work. The dean pulled the sheet away and handed it over to Lily.

The vampire scanned the page before looking at me. "Anything else?"

"I think that's it." I shook my head and turned my attention back to the dean. "Thank you for..."

I stopped speaking at the still loose expression of the woman. Lily snickered again and stepped forward. "When we leave, you will not remember this conversation. If anyone asks about meetin' us, you'll say it was nothing and redirect the conversation. Do ya understand?"

The woman nodded, and Lily's eyes slowly filled with their typical sky color. We went back the way we came, Lily engrossed in the paper the dean had handed her. Still, with her eyes fixed on the sheet, her movements in the crowd were like water rolling around stones. She never even bumped one of the people we walked past.

CHAPTER 16

LILY

The padlock clicked, and I swung the metal loop out, a tiny triumph bubbling in me. "Ha!"

Collins put the binoculars down and looked down at my task, twisting his lips in annoyance. He'd seemed surprised to see what I'd brought to pass the time. Now, he just seemed irritated as I closed the lock and looked through my tools. "So, you can pick locks?"

"Yeah." I smiled proudly at him, and his scowl melted a little before freezing back in place.

"And yet you decided to *break* my police-issue cuffs why?"

"Ya weren't taking me seriously." I actually hadn't even thought about just picking those bloody handcuffs yesterday, but he didn't need to know that. I shrugged and began scanning my lap for a new tool. I picked up a paperclip, debating between it and the screwdriver. Opting for the paperclip, I jammed it into the locking mechanism and twisted. "What'd ya tell your work about that anyway?"

"That I must have lost them during the club fire. They didn't even question it, just grumbled and got me a new set." Collins scoffed.

The padlock clicked open again, and I clapped with the enthusiasm of a cheerleader at homecoming.

That small smile crept on his lips before he schooled the expression. "You're pretty good. Where'd you even learn to do a thing like that?"

"YouTube," I said while picking a new padlock out. At his silence, I looked up. His expression was equal parts accusation and shock; I responded more defensively than I'd meant. "What? Even vampires can get bored."

He continued to stare in disbelief, blinking several times and holding the binoculars away from his face. "You used YouTube to learn how to pick locks?"

"Hey, we don't all use the internet for kitty videos and Twitter."

"It wasn't an insult," Collins said, like he was upset that he hadn't managed the task. "I was just surprised."

"It seemed like a handy trick to know; something I could do while still keepin' my eyes on the target. Speakin' of which." I lifted a butter knife and pointed at the building ahead of us. "I let ya read your book in peace when it was my turn. Pay attention."

He grumbled something unintelligible and pointed his eyes back to the brick building in question. The large dorm loomed in the darkness. Tiny dots of light from the occasional window and lampposts revealed the deep red of some bricks, but most of the color was swallowed by the night. We hadn't seen anyone new on the path for a little over an hour, but Kimberly was about to get out of one of her night classes.

Her room was supposed to be on the third floor, this side of the building. We'd debated just waiting in the hallway for her, but decided it'd be best if as few as possible saw us. So, we traded turns watching her dorm window for light or the door for her approach. So far, nada.

Collins shook his head but kept his eyes fixed ahead. "So, you what, watch cheating spouses and see what you can jam into a lock for a few hours?"

"I also investigate insurance fraud and the occasional missing person, but I try to stay away from anythin' that might force me to contact the police." The padlock clicked again, and I picked a new tool. "So, yeah, infidelity is kind of my bread and butter."

"Like you use butter," he grumbled before speaking up again. "Can I ask you something?"

"Ya just did." I smiled mischievously at him.

"Ha, ha." His tone was deadpan. "Why are you a private investigator?"

"Why are you a cop?" I wanted to slap myself for even asking. Everybody knew that Vampire Crimes only took officers who requested the assignment. I'd probably just pried open the biggest can of worms ever.

"Why would you care?"

"Why would you?" I arched a brow at him, silently hoping he'd just drop the subject. I really didn't need to hear more about how much he didn't like my kind. Especially after an afternoon of reasonable, if not begrudging, respect.

Gabe looked into his lap, green eyes turning dark in thought. He seemed to be debating something. He chose words slowly, and I wondered if he was deciding whether or not he should answer me. "*Where's the Big Bad Wolf?*"

"Huh?" I was certain I'd misheard.

"It's a kid's book my mom gave me when I was little. Detective Doggedly trying to catch the Big Bad Wolf before he eats the three little pigs."

"Ya became a cop because of Detective Doggedly?" I tried really hard to keep my tone level but a snicker escaped me. It was cute, and that just didn't mesh with this raging asshole.

"No, but it was the first book I remember reading." He glared at me, and I dropped my smile. "It was also the first thing I remember getting from my mother."

I swallowed and tried to piece together what he was saying. "So, what, you became a detective for your mum?"

Shit, that wouldn't translate well in this conversation. Especially considering how things had ended with my folks.

"No, if I was doing things for her I would have become an English teacher. She probably would have liked that." He smiled fondly. "But I remember thinking that Detective Doggedly was like a real-life superhero. And then, I just kept reading. Hardy Boys and so on. I can't think of a time I didn't want to be a detective."

A tiny pang hit my heart, and I struggled to shove it aside. My family had been gone for over a century.

"So, there's a sense of duty?"

"Yeah, I guess so." Gabe nodded, mild surprise in his features before he scowled at me again. "So, what about you?"

"I like solving the puzzles and sortin' things out. I love that humanity can still surprise me after two centuries of being on this ball of mud."

A white lie, but it's not like he really cared anyway. Really, I wasn't even sure why he'd answered me.

"That makes no sense. You always run the risk of bumping into law enforcement. You already said this isn't the first investigation that's gotten you close to the police. There have got to be other puzzles you could solve."

"There are, but..." I might have to give him a little bit more. Otherwise, he'd just have one more reason not to trust me. "I can make a difference. It's not a big one, not one that will go down in history. But it gives me a purpose, and I like that." I let silence fill the car and looked out the windshield.

It was hard not to think about the other reasons. Like not being able to really rely on the Court for steady income. Or only really having a specific set of skills after they'd taken me in, then only still have those when I left. But all the shit that came with a story that would *not* help us get along.

A soft chuckle broke my musing, and I turned back to my companion. Gabe's eyes were back on the building and his body was shuddering with low laughter.

"Something ya find amusin'?"

"Nothing." He brought his other hand up to the binoculars and leaned forward a bit. I retorted something, but he cut my sentence short. "Shut up!"

"Excuse you; do we need to discuss manners again?" And here I'd thought we'd been making some progress.

"No, shut up and look." He shoved the binoculars at me. I didn't take them but looked in the direction of the college campus and squinted at the open arch of the dormitory entrance.

A slender girl walked up the beaten path. She was about my height with hair that had to take a pound of spray just to hold the shape. Her large glasses shone in the light of each street lamp she passed under as she followed the cracked sidewalk. A huge pack was slung over one shoulder. Big enough to hold several books.

I flipped through the file the dean gave us, looking for the school ID photo. A large smile spread across my lips. "Bingo."

"Wait." He looked in disbelief at the binoculars still in his hands. "You can see her from *here*?"

"Did ya see me usin' those when it was my turn? Being undead does have some perks." I tapped the side of my skull, indicating my eyes. "We better use your badge this time. I don't want to get caught on some kid's camera phone mesmerizin' her."

I got out of the passenger side of his old sedan and waited for him to take the lead. He locked the car from the inside this time, probably to avoid the beeps that would accompany using the fob. He walked a few steps ahead and reached into his coat pocket.

Kimberly Ashland was still walking at her steady pace as we slowly approached. I realized she was swiveling her head, somewhat wildly. Granted, it was ten at night, and I could bench-press the girl. Most women would be smart to be vigilant in that situation, but most people who were smart enough to do that were also smart enough to avoid walking alone in the dark.

The ones who were confident enough to walk by themselves usually stood straight and had a taser or mace ready to go. Kimberly's hands were in her pockets; she could have a weapon ready, but her posture was all wrong. She was hunched over, her shoulders almost higher than her ears. Her body language screamed 'target'.

Collins must have picked up on it, too; his pace slowed, and he gave me a sideways glance. I nodded. We'd come this far. If she wasn't involved, I could always erase the memory of scaring her. Maybe I'd even instill some decent safety tips for later.

"Excuse me, ma'am. Detective Collins, Portland VPB." Gabe stepped onto the sidewalk and paused, holding his badge up in the street lamp. I stood next to him. He'd stopped with a few feet between us and Kimberly, like he tried not to scare her. He bobbed his head in my direction. "This is my associate, Lillian Edwards."

At my name, the girl's eyes shot to me, and she stiffened. Gabe's own stance became rock solid. Kimberly looked like a trap ready to spring. I tried to look reassuring, wondering what the hell we'd said to set her off.

Kimberly bolted; her large bag rose and fell against her back as she ran as fast as her legs could carry her.

That bag looked heavy and this girl was a toothpick. Yet she was moving with the swiftness of a rabbit, though her jerky movements were more than clumsy. They were awkward and hindering her quick speed. Collins swore and ran after the girl, his swift and practiced movements slowly closing the gap while I continued to watch.

The girl's impressive speed made no sense. Not only was Kimberly tiny, but her skin had almost as little color as mine. Unless she ran indoors on a treadmill, she wasn't practiced at it. Given the state of her scrawny legs and her less-than-Olympian form, I doubted she had a gym membership.

"She's getting away!" Collins shouted over his shoulder, and a few lights in overhead dorms flicked on. Shit, we'd drawn attention. Oh well, nothing we could do about that now.

I snorted and walked towards the running pair. "No, she's just givin' me new information."

Even if my suspicions were correct, he'd catch up. After all, Collins had the same advantage and practice chasing a target. He grunted something that I didn't understand but had a pretty good guess it wasn't flattering. Seeing I wasn't rushing after them, he ran harder, his shoes making hard slaps against the asphalt that echoed against the brick building once before dying on the cold autumn night.

Collins told the girl to stop one more time, before plowing into her and tumbling out of the light of the lamps. It didn't take me long to catch up to the pair, even at my steady stride. She clawed and kicked before he pinned her down, holding her arms behind her back and seating himself just over her legs to prevent further thrashing. Her large glasses had survived the tumble and shown under the streetlamps, making her appear like a big, scrawny bug.

Dead leaves and dormant grass crunched under my boots as I walked over, bending my head low and taking a long whiff. Bingo.

"Soup's not on!" Collins hissed, slightly out of breath and swatting my shoulder.

"Oh, shut up!" I looked up at the lit dorm windows and winced. A few curious heads were silhouetted against the windows, most of them with tousled hair that suggested our little show might have woken them. Still, I didn't see the tiny lights of cameras or black rectangles that might be cell phones recording us. Maybe the universe had decided to cooperate. Yeah, and maybe I'd start wearing body glitter when I went out during the day.

Sighing with annoyance, I lifted the struggling girl to her feet, forcing Collins to move off her in the process. She was staring at him, wide-eyed and clearly confused behind those owlish glasses. She probably hadn't expected him to catch up. With his dark skin and heavy breathing, he all but shouted *human*. She didn't realize Popeye had been eating his greens. Even after the drunken episode, my blood left residual effects for speed and stamina in him, making it all too easy to catch our willowy prey. I held her shoulders firmly and pointed her body towards the detective. "Sniff."

He looked at me like I was deranged, and I rolled my eyes. "Your sense of smell can't be back to factory settings yet. Sniff, right next to her neck."

He grimaced but stepped forward and sniffed tentatively before stepping back, a scowl prominent in his features. His eyes became twin slits as he inhaled again, a little closer this time. "She smells like that puddle I vomited."

"Precisely." I nodded. "We've caught ourselves a Renfield."

We walked through the dormitory halls, my arm draped over Kimberly in a friendly gesture. At least, it looked friendly if you didn't realize I could crush her neck in an instant. Gabe walked on the other side of her, several expressions warring in his eyes, though his features stayed relatively controlled. The girl led us towards her room. Windows filled the stairwell with several evacuation plans plastered on the adjoining walls. More windows covered each end of the hallway as we exited onto the third floor.

Luckily, only a few people were in the halls. Most of them were carrying towels and toiletries, probably heading to a community bathroom. Kimberly waved at the people passing us, a few of them asking if she had anything new in stock. She wisely said she was out. Some had asked about Collins and me or the little show outside. She said we were just clients or the show outside had been a drunken game of tag. They all eyed the detective's khakis and jacket with confusion, but let it go otherwise. Guess my jeans and motorcycle gear looked more appropriate for partying.

She stopped at a door and fished in her pockets before producing a key ring that was filled with little cartoon trinkets. She flipped through the few actual keys on it, each a different shade of neon. She finally chose a green one and stuck it in her lock, slowly opening the door.

She reached to the right and flicked her arm up, forcing fluorescent light to fill the little room. I sneered. The room looked like one of those Japanese cartoons had puked all over it. The twin bed was covered in a big Hello Kitty blanket, a desk with several varieties of sparkly gel pens flanking it. A tiny mini-fridge that was covered in bright magnets sat to the side of the desk. The room didn't hold much else. Just some cork boards on the walls that were littered with postcards and pictures of more cartoon characters and a small closet with no door and clothes all over the floor.

Collins entered first and began checking crevices and the closet for surprises before nodding at me. I nudged Kimberly forward and shut the door behind us.

"So, Kim..." I gave the girl a hungry look and flashed my teeth. "Care to share who's been feedin' ya?"

"Fuck you. You'll just kill me anyway." Kimberly straightened her spine and gave me a sassy look. It didn't carry into her eyes. "I'd rather die than give anything to your precious Court."

"Court?" Collins gave me a confused look.

Shit, I hadn't given him much detail on vampire culture. Okay, I hadn't given him any. I should really fix that. He already had his head packed with all sorts of rubbish. I didn't need any of the bad guys giving him the wrong idea. But it would have to wait until later. I shook my head.

"Later." I pointed at our little friend. "When we don't have company."

"Fine." He searched the room, producing a pair of latex gloves from his pocket before opening the first desk drawer. Kimberly's eyes followed his movements intently. Especially when he sifted through her various CDs and pens. I snapped my fingers in front of her eyes and smiled again.

"Ya think I'm going to kill ya? If ya don't tell me what I want to know, I'll just hand ya over to my *precious Court* and emphasize how little ya helped."

"You wouldn't." Her face went pale, but she tried to stand still, her eyes still watching his motions. "They won't bother with a pathetic little calf like me."

I stiffened at her word choice. Collins' eyes caught the motion, and he paused in the middle of checking the final drawer. Dammit, I didn't need this right now.

"What?"

"Later." I gave him a pleading look. "I promise."

"Oh, you didn't tell him, did you?" Kimberly smiled, her pink lipstick shining with the gesture. "How funny, you forced a human to help but you didn't even tell him the truth."

"What truth?" Detective Collins glared twin holes into me, and I sighed. Okay, guess that little lesson would be happening sooner rather than later.

"There are different types of vampires," I said slowly, picking my words carefully.

"Yeah, I remember your little speech. What's she talking about?"

"I'm talking about what happens when the vampires take over the swine of humanity." Kimberly grinned and turned her body to face him.

Collins' eyes widened, and he glared at me. I barely registered the bag of red powder dangling from his gloved hand.

CHAPTER 17

GABE

I kept my eyes on the vampire ahead of me. She let out a long breath and looked up at the ceiling like she was asking it something.

"Ya want to even hear the rest, or is your mind already made up?" Her eyes were still directed upwards as she spoke.

"Depends."

"She's speaking for a limited number of us." Lily gave Kimberly a dark look, but the student didn't lose her maniacal grin. That smile was the first expression that took over the girl's whole face. Her earlier bravado had looked more than a little forced. Lily looked like she wanted to snap the girl in half. "Apparently, our little Renfield is more involved than I thought."

"Involved in what?" I bit the words out.

"I told you," Kimberly the words left a definitive *duh* implied. "We're putting the humans under the vampire's rule, where they belong."

"Not what," Lily ground the word like gravel. "Who."

"Fine. Who?" I was getting frustrated and it showed in my tone.

"Elias." They answered simultaneously but their tones were polar. Kimberly's was one of hope and awe, while Lily sounded disgusted by even letting the name slip across her tongue.

"Who is Elias?"

"Elias is my master. Unlike yours—" Kimberly bobbed her head at Lily, "mine tells me everything. He gives me blood to make me strong and—"

"Wait, Elias gave ya blood?" Lily flattened the girl against the wall. "Do ya know where he is?"

"Of course, *Elias* didn't give me blood," Kimberly said the name with the same infatuation many girls gave rock stars. "But he makes sure I get it, so none of you can control me."

"Eejit." Lily let go of the girl and gave her a look one might bestow on old mold. "You're already being controlled."

"Not like him." Kimberly pointed a finger at me. "After all your big talk, you're controlling this cop like a zombie."

Lily snorted and gave me a direct look, her eyes ink black. "Come here and lick my boot."

"Bite me," I shot back, then inwardly cursed myself for the poor word choice.

"No thanks." Lily turned her attention back to the girl, a sly smile on her lips. "What was that about me controllin' the nice police officer?"

"Wait, when you sniffed me earlier." Kimberly's eyes were all for me. Her frail hand shot to her neck and her mouth hung open. "She *fed* you?"

Interesting. It didn't even occur to the girl that I was simply immune to Lily's gaze, she just assumed that being fed the vampire blood did the trick. Well, no reason to give her additional information.

"Not my choice." I grimaced, no acting required. "I assure you."

"But you work to take down vampires. Everyone knows what the VPB stands for!" Kimberly's eyes became saucers, and she stared at me like I was some holy relic. "The Court gave *you* the gift?"

"Gift? What gift?" I'd up-chucked everything I'd had in the last two weeks when Lily had given me her blood. I suppose the extra hearing and acute sight might be handy, but right now they were more annoying. The scraping of every pen over paper in the bullpen was audible whenever I needed to go in. Kimberly continued to look at me like I had a mystic idol over my head.

"The blood years." The student's tone was slow and reverent.

At those words, Lily winced, and I gave her a hard look. "*Blood* years?"

"Yeah." Lily used her free hand to rub the back of her neck and gave Kimberly an annoyed little glare. "Feedin' ya that much blood, it probably added about twenty-five or thirty years to your lifespan. Assumin' ya die of old age."

"What?" I looked at the brunette in front of her. Kimberly's continued look of wonder confirmed the truth in Lily's words. I looked back at the vampire, my irritation building higher. "And you were going to tell me this when exactly?"

"When ya stop lookin' at my chest like a fun place to stab!" She snapped it out and crossed her arms. Kimberly sagged away from the wall and let out a little breath as the vampire let her go. "Ya obviously don't trust me. Forgive me if I was worried ya might take the news poorly."

"We're clearing the air when we get out of here, vampire." I shook my head in annoyance. "Let's deal with her and get going. Kimberly Ashland, you are under arrest. You have the right to remain—"

"You're fuckin' jokin', right?" Lily gave me a look of disbelief.

"Look." I held up one of the bags of red powder I'd found in the third drawer. "I've got her on possession."

I'd have to work to get a good reason as to why I was here in the first place, making sure to give myself some probable cause for being up here, but that wouldn't be impossible. She had run when I tried to simply question her. I might be able to build off that, if I only found a good reason to explain being at the campus in the first place.

"I don't care if ya caught her durin' a bloody sting!" Lily growled. "You're not takin' her in."

"To hell, I'm not!"

"Don't ya get it?" Lily gave the girl a serious look. "She's had vampire blood. She can't be mesmerized."

"Exactly, she's not going to bend to your whim like the dean did. She needs to be interrogated."

"Not in a place with cameras, she doesn't." Lily gritted her teeth. "Not with your kiddy gloves."

"Hell. No." I felt the blood rush out of my face. "You want to torture her?"

"Do you see an alternative where we get the information we need?"

"She has rights!"

"She gave those rights up the minute she willfully entered my world!" Lily's arm shot out, and I realized it was blocking the path Kimberly had been slowly making during our bickering. Those blue eyes stayed locked on mine. "Vampire law is incredibly simple. She broke it. She's mine."

"She broke human law too. Seeing as her blood isn't undead, she's mine."

Lily rolled her eyes. "Do I need to remind ya that I can literally pick her up and run out of here?"

"Don't let her take me!" The brunette squawked, her face filled with terror. She rushed forward, her wrists held out to me. Lily snorted and the girl kept talking. "Arrest me. Arrest the shit out of me!"

I smiled triumphantly over her shoulder while I reached for my cuffs. Lily rolled her blue eyes in what was quickly becoming a familiar look. "We can talk about this more when we get out to the car. Let's just finish up."

I nodded and opened the zipper of Kimberly's backpack. Heavy books took the majority of the bag, almost covering a large back pocket. I sneered at the other five bags of Cheri Coke stuffed into the pocket. I piled three more from the desk on top and closed the pack again. Lily held out a hand. "Got any more gloves?"

I reached into my pocket, drew out a second set, and offered them. She took them, drawing them over her slender hands smoothly.

"I'll check the rest of the room."

Before I could argue, the mattress lifted and fell back in place without a sound. As did the bed frame. Then the desk and mini-fridge. The hangers in the closet clicked as the clothes swung one by one from left to right before Lily stood before me again. Okay, maybe being undead did have some perks. The whole spectacle had taken less than five minutes, and I gaped at her. She held up a large shopping bag and smiled gleefully. "Burner phones."

"Phones? Plural?" I looked in the bag. Sure enough, several pink flip-phones lay at the bottom, some of them flashing the late hour back at me. *They still make those things?*

"Bet these have something very interestin' in their history." She held the bag back and gave me a devilish look. "Too bad ya don't get any."

I opened my mouth to retort but a loud rumbling stopped me. I looked up at the ceiling, trying to remember how thick the clouds had been earlier. But the rumbling wasn't from overhead. It was from below. The building didn't tremble like an earthquake. Still, the slow pounding grew thicker, louder, and more rapid.

I snapped my attention back when I heard Lily curse. Her head was turned towards the door and her voice was low. "Take the girl and run."

"What is it?"

"My boss." It wasn't Lily that responded, but Kimberly. Her smile was wide, and she watched the door like a fangirl waiting for the band.

The sound of thunder grew before I could ask anything further. Lily turned towards the door, her fists up. Short screams rose, and the hair on the back of my neck followed suit. The door splintered open in a large crash.

A short man with a round belly barreled forward, pushing Lily into the back wall. They crashed against the desk with a loud clatter, pens and papers scattering everywhere. He punched, and Lily kicked, both of them frantic. "Get her out of here!"

I nodded and ran out, taking Kimberly roughly by the elbow. I propelled the girl forward until we entered the hall. She whirled, ramming the heel of her hand upwards and almost breaking my nose. I swore at the new sensation and pushed the girl away. She tried to punch, her movement fast, but awkward with the cuffs. The few people in the hall screamed in panic, and I yelled, my response to the screams automatic. "Police! Everyone out!"

Kimberly ran forward, her knees shooting up in clumsy attempts to catch my groin. I swiped my arm to one side, blocking both blows with the movement before I shot the other arm out and pinned the girl to the wall. She couldn't weigh much, but I still had to press hard to keep her in place. "Stop struggling or I will use force."

"It won't matter." The girl chuckled. "Joey's coming for me!"

I grabbed the girl's elbow again and guided her towards the stairs, pulling the fire alarm with my free hand as I passed it. The loud alarm blared, between loud shrills I heard footsteps as the hall filled with confused students in their pajamas. I repeated my police directive, barely audible over the shrill alarm. I needed to get the civilians clear of the brawl.

The swarm of people rushed past us, a few trying to ask Kimberly what was going on.

"Hello, alarm! Get the fuck out of here!" I barked at them. One of them made a wisecrack about police brutality but they shuffled towards the stairwell.

I directed my suspect down the stairs, trying to force her calmly towards the car. I moved awkwardly against the exploding crowd, keeping my grip strong so I wouldn't lose her in the jostling of people in PJs.

"Finish her Joey!" Kimberly was still laughing, yelling back over her shoulder. "Kill the bitch!"

I counted every blessing as we passed the signs for the first floor, and I kept pushing forward. Campus security was out in the autumn evening, directing the students to move away from the building and meet in their positions. They were probably acting on one of the evacuation plans we'd seen posted in the dorms, helping to account for anyone missing.

I saw my car parked close to the path and continued to pull the struggling Kimberly towards the vehicle. That is, I did until she screamed for something other than Joey. "Help, help! I'm being kidnapped."

It took three cries for help before a man came running after us. He looked to be in his early twenties, a blue security uniform overwhelmed by a small orange vest that reflected what little light there was on the campus sidewalk. He had one hand positioned over a stun gun at his belt and the other held up in a barring gesture. "Sir! Sir! Let the girl go!"

"Detective Collins, Portland VPB." I held my badge up with my free hand, barely keeping the other one locked on Kimberly's elbow as she yelled and pulled. "This woman is under arrest for conspiring with a vampire and possession of an illegal substance."

A few gasps sounded in the people around me. The guy edged forward, and Kimberly continued to yell. He held up a small flashlight to review my credentials. A small crowd watched the exchange, some in uniform and some in a variety of street clothes and nightclothes. Some holding up phones.

Shit. I already wasn't certain what I was going to tell my captain about Kimberly's arrest. None of my own leads could have brought me up this way. Now I had to contend with the internet. The security officer in the vest looked back to my face, his brows furrowed together. "What's a Fang Cop doing here?"

"There's a vampire in there." I shot my thumb over my shoulder to indicate the building. Kimberly finally stopped yelling, seeing that her victim routine wasn't working.

"You sure?" The campus security stared at the building in horrified wonder.

"Pretty certain." I nodded. "My associate is back there trying to take it out."

"She's a vampire too!" Kimberly pushed at me furiously, and I had to tighten my grip on her, my skin turning red at the new pressure. Jesus. The scrawny little thing had some muscle behind her. "He's working with them. He wants to silence me. Don't let him take me!"

"They'll say anything when they've been caught." I put on an annoyed expression and rolled my eyes. "Look, tell your men to keep an eye out for a blonde with an Irish accent. She's with me. I'll go put this troublemaker in my car."

"George!" The security officer yelled the single name, and a tall man poked his head out of the crowd surrounding us. Presumably, this was George.

"I'm going to escort the detective and Kimberly. You take over the crowd control. The rest of you!" The security officer in charge raised his volume and pitched a level of command into his tone. "Show's over! Get back to your evacuation sites, check to see who is missing! Go, go, go!"

The man in charge came forward and motioned with a hand. "Lead the way, Detective."

I pushed more easily through the crowd, being able to announce who we were. I fished in my pockets and found the keys to my Toyota. The light blinked in and out as the car unlocked before I placed Kimberly in the backseat. She growled something nasty at us when I slammed the door in her face. Strong or not, she wasn't getting past the car's child locks. I'd had bodybuilders try and fail. I clicked the fob twice and heard the car beep a few times.

"Gabe." I stuck a hand out to the security guard.

"Michael." The security officer took my hand, giving me a single shake before turning back to the evacuating dorm before us. "Aren't you worried about your partner? Dealing with a vamp on her own?"

"I didn't say she was my partner," I corrected and looked at the building. The only noise coming from it was the alarm. A small foreboding built in me. Where the hell was she? I'd seen Lily fight. She'd seemed capable at the club. And that was two against one. My mind snarked, *But you were distracting one of them.*

"So, you're not worried?" Michael prodded.

"I didn't say that either."

CHAPTER 18

LILY

"**G**et her out of here!" I snapped the order out, right as Joey plowed his fist into my gut. The punch sent me backward over the tiny desk. A corner shoved its way into my spine, and I gasped in pain.

Joey's knuckles cracked against my chin. I ground my boot into his instep. He grunted, and I rammed the heel of my hand into his nose. The cartilage sank with a satisfying crunch. He stumbled backward, gripping his face. Shit, guess I hadn't pushed his nose in far enough. His brain was still intact.

Alarms rang in the building, and I fought the urge to cover my ears against the onslaught. I spun and sent a foot into Joey's chest, pushing the tubby man back a step. His head shone in the hallway light as he smashed against the wall. I surged forward. People crowded the hall and ran away, cries of fear mixing in the air. Shit. I couldn't do anything vampiric until they left. I was going to kill whoever pulled that fucking alarm.

Joey came up and punched rapidly. His fists flew past my head as I dodged, and I felt something snag my hair right before he twisted, slamming my head into the wall. Drywall blew apart and bits of the wall raked my face as he slammed my head repeatedly, using the base of my ponytail like a handle. Blood streamed down my face, mixing with the drywall to blur my vision. I scratched his hand futilely as I fought to think. Vampire or not, even I could be knocked out if he kept this up. Or worse.

I kicked wildly until my foot connected with something. Joey grunted and slowed his attack for a moment. I kicked again and missed as he pulled my head back for another strike. He pulled it back too far; I could see what I'd kicked through smears of blood and dust.

His knee tried to twist back in place. I kicked again, my boot meeting the half-healed joint. It popped further out of place, and he roared in pain. I pushed away. He still held my hair. A huge chunk ripped out as I yanked myself away and I yowled in pain.

The people were finally out of my way. But that fucking alarm would summon someone soon. Now or never.

I charged forward, my natural speed taking over, the solid thumps of my feet pounding over the still-shrilling alarm. I jumped, straddling Joey and forcing him to the ground. I smiled savagely. "My turn."

I grabbed his head with both hands, slamming it against the floor. Over and over. Carpet or no, it wasn't soft. A divot formed in the multicolored rug. Concrete was soon revealed, tiny specks of gray and red flying away with every smash. I pulled my fist back and punched his skull. Hard.

Heavy steps sounded behind me and I swore. I gripped Joey's neck tight as I turned to black eye the asshole into leaving. Gabe cleared the staircase, his gun clear of the holster. The shock distracted me. Just for a second. A second too long.

Joey flipped us over and began pummeling my face. I fought the urge to shield my face and bent my knees, reaching desperately for my boots. Joey saw the motion and grabbed the leg. He twisted the bone with a sharp thrust. Pain rocketed through every nerve. A loud snap announced the bone-shattering. I screamed and punched whatever I could.

"Let her up or I'll shoot!" Gabe's voice barely registered over the alarms.

Joey didn't even acknowledge the shout. He reached into his coat and produced his own gun. He pointed the muzzle at my heart and pulled the trigger. I screamed again and again. He shot me several more times, new holes ripping through the tissue each time. He pressed the scalding muzzle to my skull.

Joey smiled wickedly. "Beat this, bitch!"

The gun fired. Twice. A shot sliced past my temple and blood-spattered my skin. I looked up. Joey's shoulder was bleeding heavily. More shots rang, and I finally understood. Gabe had shot him, dislodging his arm from its former position. Gabe had just saved my life. He'd also just royally pissed a vampire off.

Joey turned, his attention focused on the new target. I punched upwards. My blow barely connected with the flabby vampire's chin.

"Over here, asshole."

Joey turned, his rage apparent. I rammed my fist upwards as I screamed in blind fury. I wrapped my legs around his body and rolled. The motion sent him off me. Just barely. I reached into my boots. The hilt of one knife greeted my palm like an old friend.

"Get the fuck out of here!"

"Not a chance." Gabe ran to stand next to me. He spread his legs in the standard stance for gun use.

We didn't have time to argue. Joey sat up and started firing in our direction. Bang. Bang. Bang. Gabe growled out a curse. Pain sliced through several sections of my leg. I growled and lunged for the other vampire. I wrapped my hands around his throat and ground my good knee into his groin. Over and over. Joey flailed and jerked away from me, his face turning purple. I gripped his skull, plunging the knife into his ear and twisting.

Joey fell to the floor, screaming. He clutched his head and reached for the blade. I kicked him in the head over and over.

His hand crunched beneath my boot. I didn't care that my vision was blurring. I didn't care about the scorching pain in my chest and leg.

Really, were the bullets still in there? Pop-out already.

Joey's screams stopped. His body went limp. I kept kicking, screaming with all the pent-up rage. A strong hand landed on my shoulder, and I braced to elbow the owner in the face.

"Lily!" It was Gabe. I dropped the elbow. From his tone, he'd called my name a few times.

"Present," I ground the word out before softly kicking my attacker again and slumping against the wall. The corpse was already turning gray, then black. The clothes smoldered on the hot pile of ash that was quickly replacing the body. I groaned, wincing as the adrenaline wore off. "What the hell are ya doin' here?"

"You didn't come out." Gabe stared at the smoldering remains of our attacker and gulped. "Is that normal?"

"Internal cremation. Happens in the instant of vampire death. How else do ya think we kept our actual existence a secret for so long?" I reached into my pocket and grasped my phone. I gasped from the immense pain the little motion elicited.

Gabe's head snapped to take me in. With my missing hair, bleeding bullet wounds, and smashed-up scalp, I'm sure I was a sight.

"Jesus, are you okay?"

I gave him a sly smile through the pain. "I believe that's the nicest thing you've said to—"

Agony flashed through every nerve. I dropped to the floor. Foam and blood flooded my mouth. I spasmed uncontrollably. Shit, now I understood why my body hadn't pushed the bullets out yet.

Silver.

CHAPTER 19

GABE

"Lily?" I knelt in front of her, my hands out to help. But I wasn't sure what to do. "Lily!?"

She pushed her words through the relentless maroon foam. They were garbled but understandable. "Call...Ivan..."

I watched her thrash on the ground, ash stirring in the air as she kicked into the other vampire's corpse. Her words finally clicked, and I floundered to find her phone in the mess. It was covered in blood and soot. I had to wipe the residue away with my shirt before I could unlock the screen. Thank God. She didn't have a password on the contraption. My hands shook as my eyes darted between the quivering form of the woman in front of me and the tiny screen in my hands.

"Ivan. Ivan." I chanted the name like prayer as I opened her dial function and punched in the four tiny letters. Only one entry with that name. I smashed my thumb against the green phone icon and gulped as a single ring broke off.

"Kid? What's that noise?" The voice was heavy and filled with worry.

"My name is Detective Collins," I said, my eyes widening at the sight of her continued convulsions.

"What'd you do to her?" The harsh accent growled.

"Nothing!" I stuttered. "We were fighting a vamp and now she's having some kind of seizure. There's foam coming from her mouth!"

"Did she get stabbed with anything?" The harsh voice became cold and level, still with an edge to it. I looked at the still squirming form of Lily and shook my head before remembering to speak.

"No, but he shot her in the heart several times."

"Goddammit, kid! Where are you?"

I told him.

"Stay with her! We'll be there in ten minutes. Don't let anyone near her."

The line disconnected, and I stared at the phone like it had new answers. I heard the heavy storm of steps below and the alarm silence in time to a new announcement. "Police! Is anyone in here?"

"Shit!" I looked at Lily's shuddering body and back to the stairwell. The heavy stomps grew louder, and I stood, grabbing her by the underarms. She screamed, the sound dampened by the goo that continued to pour from her mouth. I dropped her out of a moment of bad instinct. She let out a garbled howl as she smacked against the floor. I cursed myself, picking her back up and drawing her into the first open room I saw.

"Did you hear something?" The voice echoed in the stairwell.

I laid Lily on the ground and closed the dorm door. My hand shuddered and I jumped before I realized it was her phone, still clutched in my palm. A picture of a scrawny guy flashed on the screen, the name Alex lighting up in big block letters.

Was this her backup? I slid the call button, unsure of what else to do. "Hello?"

"Where is she?" The raspy voice on the other end was filled with agony. I sputtered out a response, keeping my volume low as I explained the situation.

"Go through her phone book, look for the contact names Ivan—"

"Already done. He says he's on the way. But there are cops in the building."

"Don't let any of them near her!"

"So, I've heard," I hissed the reply right before hanging up and pocketing the phone. If he had something useful to say, he'd call back. Right now, I needed to concentrate. I placed an ear to the door and listened.

"I got the third floor." Harper's familiar voice echoed through the hall. I nearly sagged in relief. I cracked the door and watched the staircase for his broad form.

"Psst."

Harper's face filled with relief and he sauntered over to me, looking quizzically at the unruly pile of ash as he stepped around it. He closed the door and stared at Lily as she jerked on the floor. "Holy shit. What's wrong with her?"

"I don't know. She got shot in the heart while she was fighting another vamp. Guessing it wasn't enough to kill her but it did some damage."

"Is she going to be okay?"

"She's got someone coming for her. But we need to keep people away from her until then."

"That might be hard." Harper blew out a breath. "Half the department is here. The security called saying you were here reporting a vampire sighting and possible officer down."

"Fuck," I spat the word out and gave Lily's quivering body a worried glance. "Hope her team can be just as creative this time."

"They were pretty efficient last time, but they didn't have a crowd of onlookers with cell phones at the ready. Those college kids are worse than the media right now."

"Fuck," I groaned again, for lack of anything better to say. "Tell the team that this level is clear. That'll buy us some time, at least."

"What about you?"

A heavy thump sounded against the dorm door, and we both flinched.

"I'll figure it out, just go. Oh, and there's a suspect in my car. Kimberly Ashland." I handed him the keys. "One of campus security is watching her. She's got the evidence in her back- pack. Still needs her Miranda Rights."

Harper pocketed the keys and cracked the door open. Shock registered in his dark features, and he gave me a con- fused look. "I think this might be for you, pal."

"Huh?" I looked around the edge of the door and stepped back. It wasn't anyone from vampire crimes.

A short man with a braided beard knocked me out of his path. His hair whipped my face as he knelt next to Lily's prone form. She groaned again as he lifted her.

"Oh, it's just a little silver," he whispered. "You can take it."

He turned back to us and looked between our faces before speaking.

"Which of you is Collins?" His voice was military in its precision. It didn't sound like the man on the phone. The accent was rough rather than dark. Who was this guy?

I pointed at myself. He nodded and looked at Harper. "Are you Detective Harper then?"

Harper nodded. The man's eyes became twin pools of black.

"You will never speak of seeing Detective Collins or any vampires this evening. Do you understand?"

Harper nodded mechanically, his jaw slack. The vampire turned his black gaze back to me and bobbed his head sharply. "Let's go."

Harper still stared into space as I followed the man carrying Lily.

"Hey! We had a deal, no messing with Harper's brains!"

"Did she really make that offer?" The man shook his head and continued walking at the same pace I would normally sprint. Footsteps sounded below us, and I saw him heading towards the second stairwell.

I'd have to argue about the arrangement later.

"That won't work. The VPB is already downstairs."

"I noticed." The newcomer walked right past the stairs. He stopped at one of the windows lining the end of the hallway. I looked past his shoulder. The exterior lawn was vacant, but for one van and a large man standing below. The chiseled man turned back to me. "Stay here. I'll be right back."

He hopped down, landing with a soft *thud* three stories below us. He handed Lily over to the larger man, who turned back to the van and slowly loaded her in. The supermodel lunged and landed silently on the windowsill again. He stepped in and gave me a look. "How do you prefer to be carried?"

"I don't," I said instantly, and he gave me a dark look.

"Fair enough."

I saw his fist fly just before my world went black.

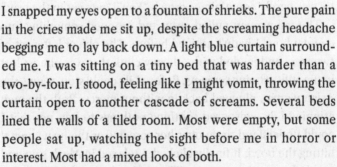

I snapped my eyes open to a fountain of shrieks. The pure pain in the cries made me sit up, despite the screaming headache begging me to lay back down. A light blue curtain surrounded me. I was sitting on a tiny bed that was harder than a two-by-four. I stood, feeling like I might vomit, throwing the curtain open to another cascade of screams. Several beds lined the walls of a tiled room. Most were empty, but some people sat up, watching the sight before me in horror or interest. Most had a mixed look of both.

Lily was lying on the bed nearest to me, crying in anguish over and over again. The guy with the braid was holding her shoulders down as she writhed, the big guy holding her down by her knees. Her movements weren't those of the earlier seizures, more like she tried to pull away from something. If seeing her held down hadn't been bad enough, her current state was enough to make me want to jump to her aide.

Lily's leather jacket and tank top were both in shreds, her bra the only practical thing covering her above the waist. The parts of the shirt that remained were so stained; they were a deep red instead of the gray I remembered. Most of her hair was loose from its usual tail; the lower half stained a bright ruby.

A tall woman dug into Lily's chest like she was searching for lost treasure. Her eastern features were mostly covered in a surgical mask, and she wore a long lab coat that was more red than white.

Lily's rib cage strained against her chest, making her look more skeleton than woman as she arched and writhed. She shrieked again, her mouth extending to an impossible length. The cry echoed against the tiles, sounding like thousands of cries instead of one.

I lunged forward instinctively, but someone caught me.

"Back off!" I raised my fist and almost immediately dropped it.

It was the guy from the phone. Alex? His voice was low, like he was barely containing a growl. "You'll only get in the way."

The tall woman pulled away and dropped something into a metal bowl I hadn't noticed before. The object left a set of tweezers and landed with a heavy clink that was almost lost in the still-echoing screams. Before Lily could stop crying, the Asian woman plunged back in without mercy. Both the men gripping Lily whispered soothing nothings to her, not that I could understand them over her screams or the heavy metal hitting the bowl. It finally clicked. I relaxed in Alex's grip and nodded my understanding. "They're removing the bullets."

"Yeah." The scrawny man let me go and sat next to me on the bed. "Or the pieces of them anyway. I guess they shattered going through her ribs."

"Why don't they sedate her?" I winced at another loud shriek.

"Can't." Alex snorted. "There's not a lot of ways to knock one of us out, short of beating our brains in. But she'd wake up the minute they started up again."

"Okay, Lily." The doctor wiped her brow, smearing red from her gloves. Her voice was soft, almost impossible to hear through the medical mask. "We're done with your heart. Now the leg."

"Almost there, kid." The large man released a leg as he spoke, his harsh accent low with concern.

I gulped and looked at the man next to me. "Why is her face still bleeding?"

Sure, her face had been in rough shape when I'd come to help her, but it was mostly solid now. The pointed nose and sharp cheekbones back in place. Yet, streams of red flowed down in her face in every direction as she struggled.

Alex swallowed a hard lump. "She's crying."

"Those are *tears*?" I gawked. Sure enough, the rivers of red all came from one central location, streaming faster and faster with every scream.

"Blood to water ratio." The man's tone was numb as he recited the fact.

Lily screamed again and the shrill echo of pain broke my horror at her tears.

I looked away and watched my companion instead. His eyes were dark pools of pain, and he had his hand clutched over his heart. He was definitely close to Lily; could be a boyfriend.

I looked back to Lily as she continued to cry out twice more. The doctor pronounced her deed done and the two men let Lily go. The woman pulled her mask off and walked over to me. She bent down and shined a light in my eyes without any preamble. Her copper eyes locked on mine as she spoke. "Does your head hurt?"

"A vampire sucker-punched my skull, what do you think?" I pulled my head out of her light. It was making the ache worse.

"Any nausea?"

I shook my head, even though it made me want to upchuck. No way I was admitting weakness in their presence.

"What about that scratch on your arm?"

"Huh?" I looked at one shoulder, then the other, finally spotting a shallow gash. That's right, Joey's wild shooting had managed to snag me once. "It's just a bullet graze, I've had worse."

"You should take some vampire blood." The woman stood and stuck her penlight back into a pocket. She reached back and pulled something from her hair. It fell from a bun, a long deep wave of black. "It would clear the graze and all the bruises. You could have a concussion, but blood would help if you did."

"I'll let it heal naturally, thanks." I grimaced and scraped my teeth over my tongue in memory. I'd had a concussion before. I could manage until I saw a human doctor.

"Have it your way." She shrugged. "Make sure to have someone watch you for a bit. You don't want to pass out again."

Without another word, she walked away, her shoes padding against the tile quickly as she examined other patients. I turned my attention back to the bed nearest mine. They'd covered Lily with a white sheet that was already turning crimson. The big man was stroking her cheek while he barked an order, "Cyrus, get her something to eat and something to wear."

"Got it." Cyrus nodded sharply and turned to leave, tossing a comment over his shoulder, "The whelp is awake."

"So he is." The large man's head snapped up and eyes the color of whiskey landed on me. He stood and walked over. Alex straightened a little next to me.

"Alex, go see to her." The large man nodded at Lily's prone form. She curled beneath the thin sheets and moaned softly.

"Wish I could say it was nice to meet you." Alex stood and walked away, turning to me. "Thanks."

I felt my brows furrow together but didn't get a chance to ask for what. A dusky hand was pushed in front of me, claiming my attention a second before the thick accent. "Ivan."

"I kind of guessed." I grasped the cold hand and looked directly into those eyes. "Gabe."

"I kind of guessed," Ivan imitated and released my hand. "You might have saved her."

"I just followed instructions." I shrugged. "She's the one that told me to call you."

"Still, from what she tells me, you just threatened to kill her yesterday morning. Why the change of heart?"

I opened my mouth to respond and closed it. I hadn't even thought about that. I'd just reacted. I opened my mouth again. Closed it again. I finally just shook my head. "I have no clue."

"Well, at least you're honest." Ivan shrugged and walked away. "You should probably check in with your superiors. If they're anything like me, they're having kittens."

My eyes widened, and I hunted through my jacket pockets for my phone. I found the device in my left pocket and pulled it out. I clicked the side button and was instantly confused by the picture of a zombie bear that filled my screen.

What the hell?

It hadn't even asked for my password. Then I realized it wasn't my phone, it was hers. Several text messages stood opaque over the little bear, most of them asking if she was alright. I looked at the other hospital bed. She was sobbing now and the two men were crowding around her in silent comfort.

I placed the phone on the bed and searched for my own. When I unlocked the screen, I had several of my own messages. Only two asking if I was okay. Most just wanted to know where I was and why I hadn't reported in yet. I tapped my phone against my forehead in thought. What could I even say?

Sorry, guys, my vampire partner needed medical attention.

Yeah, that wouldn't work. And how had she survived that anyway? Wasn't the heart what you used to put a vampire down? Then again, she hadn't stabbed that other man in the heart. She drilled her knife into his ear and kept kicking until the guy disintegrated. I shook my head free of the thought, filing away it as one more thing I'd ask her later.

I decided to wait to call until I had a half-decent excuse, returning the phone to my pocket. I ran my hands through my hair and blew out a breath, my eyes landing on the still whimpering form ahead of me. Alex held one hand tightly and Ivan sat on the other side of the bed silently. The guy with the braid came back, a stack of folded clothes in his arms and a young woman following close behind.

The woman was a waif of a person, her baggy clothes making her appear even frailer than her petite stature. She trotted over to the bed and sat on the edge. I expected her to start saying something comforting to Lily.

Instead, the waif pulled the loose neck of her hoodie away, exposing her shoulder. My gut did a sick little twist, but I kept my thoughts to myself, watching silently as the two men lifted Lily to the tiny woman. Lily licked her lips slowly and opened her mouth. Her canines grew, extending to resemble something in a snake's mouth before she sank both fangs into the woman's neck.

The woman gasped but it didn't seem to be in pain. Loud gulps reverberated against the tiled space with each swallow.

I looked around, but no one was watching. Dig bullets out her chest, that was worth a look. But a woman bites someone else, that was completely normal. What rabbit hole had I fallen down?

Alex let go of Lily's hand and strolled over, his hands buried in his pockets as he sat next to me and watched Lily take her meal. "Freaks you out?"

"That obvious?" I gulped and tried to look away. I couldn't. It was oddly fascinating. Lily drank in hard swallows and the girl moaned in rapture like someone had given her something delicious. The irony was palpable.

"Don't worry about it." He shrugged, his eyes still fixed on her. "I imagine it's a little awkward for a gazelle to sit next to a lion."

I didn't get the chance to respond.

"Stop, kid." Ivan watched Lily drink intently, his hands positioned like he was ready to grab her at a moment's notice.

Lily finally sat back, leaning against the wall, and licking her lips off a few stray drops. Her voice was breathy and faint. "Thanks."

The girl nodded absently and the vampire with the braid dropped the clothes on the bed before escorting her out. The girl wobbled a little as she walked, but he kept her upright. Lily took in a deep breath, the motion pulling my eyes to her chest as it rose and fell. The gaping wound slowly seemed to stitch itself together a centimeter at a time. She took in another breath and fell back down into the sheets, her head sinking into the pillow. Alex pulled out his phone and checked the time.

"Shit, it's getting early." He looked up at the larger man. "You got her Ivan?"

"Go take care of your client. She'll be okay." Ivan nodded and Alex padded away, stopping at the door.

"Detective Collins."

"Yeah?" My head snapped up, and my eyes fell into his obsidian gaze.

"Thanks again. That woman gave me the best parts of my childhood." With that, he left.

CHAPTER 20

LILY

S tones dug their way through the flesh of my bare feet, turning into tiny needles. I could smell the smoke, even taste it, clear across the town.

Please don't let it be too late.

The horizon glowed, a warm orange that mocked me against the starry sky. The cracks grew louder as wood and mortar burned, turning our home to rubble and ash. Even over the roar of the fire and groan of the building collapsing, I could hear the town. They cheered and hollered, the idea of capture turning them into wild beasts.

Frozen glass slammed through my chest, the icy pain crumpling my knees just as I could feel the warm glow of fire on my skin. I clutched my chest, the chemise tearing beneath my new strength. The cold agony lashed through my chest again, and I screamed, my voice a chorus with his in the night. It was too late. I'd killed him. He saved me, saved my whole family, and I had murdered him.

Someone cried out in triumph, and I screamed his name. An apology and a plea all in one pathetic verse. Again and again, until my throat was raw and my eyes dry.

"Isaac!"

I bolted upright. Cold sweat plastered my hair to my lips and eyelashes, making it harder to breathe. Or blink. Where a village on the edge of famine once was, now ceramic tile and sterile beds took over. Where the curl of smoke had filled my nostrils, antiseptic and old blood clogged the air.

I let out a breath and closed my eyes. "Just a dream."

Something shifted next to me, and I opened my eyes, expecting to find Alex or Ivan. Green eyes drew me away from the memory, confusion taking over.

"Are you okay?" Gabe's gaze was filled with concern and uncertainty. "Do I need to call someone back for you?"

I shook my head, checking for anyone else in the room. "No, I'm fine."

There were a few patients, some looking at me. They had the decency to look embarrassed as I caught them gawking. Oh well, I looked like a loon. Nothing to be done about that.

I took in the detective and winced. He had a huge bruise on one temple and another forming to the left of his nose. There was a tear in one of his sleeves, covered in red. Probably from Joey's shitty aim. His green eyes were filled with red, the veins of his sclera popping out.

"What are ya doin' here?"

He snorted. "Well, your friend had to go home. Something to do with a client."

"Heh?" I fought to make sense of his words. "Friend?"

"Yeah, the lanky guy. Alex, right?" He shrugged. "Anyway, the big guy, Ivan? He said he had to check in with another team but he'd be back later. He also said something about recon assignments and you needing a new definition."

I chuckled. Ivan was probably going to tear me a new one for this later.

"He did say to tell you that you need to stop getting hurt on the job."

"Ya share that opinion?" I arched a brow at Gabe playfully.

"Why would I?" His face scrunched in confusion. That's right, I was just a filthy vampire to him. I'd almost forgotten. Still, I knew what it was like dealing with someone with a high level of silver in their body. Been there, done that.

"It's not like that could have been an easy experience for ya. Havin' to deal with me seizing all over the floor and being dragged here."

"I won't pretend I liked it, but..." He looked like he was searching for the word, his eyes scanning the air back and forth. After a moment he drew up his shirt, stopping just under his ribs. His stomach wasn't rock-solid or flabby, but somewhere in between, and it took me a second to realize what he was showing me. Interrupting smooth flesh was a set of shiny, puckered scars.

The first was a circle, twice as big as my thumb and jagged. It was accompanied by two similar ones a bit higher.

"I got these when I was off duty once. Kid holding up a convenience store didn't take me seriously when I told him to put the gun down. We get wounded in the line of duty." He dropped his shirt back in place, and I lifted my gaze back to his eyes.

"Fair enough." I nodded, a little surprised at his reasoning. Maybe he was starting to see me as more than a monster. And maybe I'd turn into a wolf and howl at the moon. Still, one could hope. He had come back for me, after all. Which begged the question. "Ya still haven't answered me. Why are *you* still here? And why the hell did ya come back?"

"I thought you might need help. Seeing as that guy was plugging your chest with bullet after bullet when I shot him, I don't think a thank you is out of the question."

Shit, that was right. Joey had been pumping rounds into me when Gabe had shot him. True, if Gabe hadn't distracted me in the first place, I might not have needed the help but still...

"Fine, thank you. Ya still haven't answered what you're still doing here. I doubt ya were ringin' your hands with worry."

"Matter of fact, I was worried. It took them a while to get all those rounds out of you and you were screaming so loud it could wake the dead. As for still being here, I didn't have anything else to do." He shrugged. "Other than avoid my superiors and try to come up with a half-ass excuse as to where I've disappeared to."

"Oh, shit!" I smacked the palm of my hand against my forehead. "Your job. What are ya goin' to tell them?"

"No idea." He shrugged again. "I thought about it all night, but nothing seems reasonable. Of course, that doesn't stop people from asking."

He twisted the phone in his hand, the screen lighting up with a new notification as the device chimed.

I winced. "Shit, we need to come up with somethin' quick."

"We? Who said anything about *we?*" His tone was mocking.

"Ha, ha." I rolled my eyes and sat up.

His eyes drifted down in surprise, and I followed the gesture, snatching the sheet back in place. Gabe's face flushed, and he turned his back to me. Guess I'd ruined my outfit during the fight. At least it only fell past my breasts. They were in a bra. He didn't see anything.

"The guy with the braid dropped off some clothes." He pointed to the foot of the bed. Sure enough, a gray T-shirt, black hoodie, and jeans sat next to my feet.

"Can ya, um, close the curtain?"

He did, but he stayed on the inside, his back still turned to me. Guess he felt safer on this side of the fabric. Seeing as we were in a Vampire Court, it was hard to blame him. I wondered if he knew where he was. I checked to make sure the detective really had his eyes averted before dropping the sheet and snatching the short stack of clothes.

"Seriously, we need to think of somethin' fast. Can't have ya losin' your job." I dropped the remnants of my jacket and tank top to the floor, a sad sigh escaping me. Dammit, I'd really liked that jacket. I pulled the top over me, grateful my bra was still intact. No way I would have worn another chick's but going without was a bit awkward. It had already taken me forever to get used to not having to wear a corset.

"It's my problem, I'll deal with it," Gabe shifted as he spoke.

"Stop being stubborn and let me help ya." I surveyed my trousers and decided they were also a lost cause. One pant leg was shredded; the red staining the ripped fabric was only icing on the morbid cake. If I left wearing them, they'd just draw attention to me. My hair had a lot of blood in it too, but most people would assume that was some sort of dye. I'd clean it at home. My roommates had to be freaking out.

"I'm not being stubborn." Gabe's rounded on me, right as I'd pushed the trousers to my knees.

"Hey, not a free show!" I tore the trousers off and threw the shreds at his face.

He coughed out an apology and turned his back to me again. His neck was the color of an eggplant and my cheeks stung with the desire to blush. I grabbed the clean jeans and yanked them on. They were a bit snug, but at least they covered my ass. I gave his hunched shoulders a measured look before I spoke.

"Safe."

He slowly turned back to me, the shredded jeans dangling over one shoulder. He gripped the fabric and tossed it into the pile of my other ruined clothing. "Can someone give me a ride to the precinct? I gave Harper my keys to take in Kimberly and—"

"Shit!" I shot out of bed and hunted for my boots. Under the bed. All but one knife.

"Hey come on! You were just shot in the heart! Lay back down."

"Stop acting like I'm a bloody human. I'm fine." I rummaged through my jacket pockets, looking for my phone and keys. Found my keys and the bag of flip phones. Where was my phone?

It took me a moment to notice the phone hanging in my peripheral. I snatched it out of Gabe's hands and pocketed it before standing. "Thanks!"

"You should really put a lock on your screen. Anyone could mess with it."

"Ya went through my phone?!" I shook the thought away. Whatever, not important right now. "With everythin' else going on, I'd almost forgotten Kimberly. How long has your department had her?"

"I don't know." He shrugged. "I guess about ten hours, but God knows how long it took to take witness statements last night."

"Okay, well we need to sort that out, too. Ya said Harper took her in. Do ya think he questioned her?"

"No clue." He shrugged, and I gave him an annoyed look. "Hey, your little-braided friend knocked me out cold. Besides, I haven't even called Harper yet. I didn't want to implicate him through phone records."

"Fine." I nodded sharply. I'd have to talk to Cyrus later. At least now I knew what had caused that goose egg on the side of Gabe's face. "We need to get ya an alibi first, then we can figure out what happened with Kimberly."

"Oh, you've got one lying around?" Gabe crossed his arms and gave me a speculative look. I smiled and gave the bruise on his temple a wicked glance.

"I do, but you're not going to like it." I was about to explain when a cough interrupted us outside the curtain. We both looked over. A silhouette turned the light blue of the curtain a richer shade. The shadow was about Gabe's height but far slenderer.

"Edwards, are you ready?"

Gabe looked at me in confusion, and I groaned. I knew that voice.

I walked around him and drew the privacy curtain open. My stomach sank as I confirmed the newcomer's identity. "Hey Melody."

The warden grimaced at me and crossed her arms, covering her usual collage of tribal necklaces. Her dreadlocks were thick and decorated in an array of collared strings and ribbons, the original ebony peeking through individual pieces to contrast with her tawny skin.

Shit. I guess I wouldn't make it out before seeing Ritti.

"Hope you're ready to meet royalty."

Melody smiled wickedly and nodded once before turning to leave the hospital wing. I walked after her, Gabe scrambling after us for a few steps. It took a moment before I realized why he was struggling to keep up. Right, not a vampire.

"Ahem." I waited for her to stop and bobbed my head at Gabe. "Only polite to go the pace of our guest."

"Of course." She looked mildly irritated at the mistake, bowing her head to Gabe once. "My apologies, Detective Collins."

"No problem," Gabe stuttered and bowed his head in return, awkwardly. The woman returned to walking, and he gave me a hard look. "What do you mean royalty?"

"Silly human." I smiled playfully, though I didn't feel it. "Politics aren't just for you."

CHAPTER 21

GABE

Lily smoothed her borrowed clothes as we walked into the hallway. My jaw dropped. The hall was almost as wide as my apartment. The entire floor was covered in a rich hardwood. Each door we passed looked like it was made of thick oak. An elegant rug ran down the center of the floor, several jeweled patterns merging into one collage. The walls were all trimmed with fancy molding and light sconces that probably cost more than my apartment. I whistled.

"This place must cost a fortune."

"I suppose it does." Lily looked distracted as she checked out our surroundings. "Rumor has it the queen met Jane Austen during a stint in Europe. I guess she grew pretty attached to the era, though who knows if that's true."

I gaped, but she didn't seem to notice. I'd never thought about the walking history these creatures possessed. Jesus, my dad would have been drooling at the chance to talk to any one of them. The thought made me swallow a new lump, and I fought to focus again.

"Is that who we're going to meet? Your queen?"

"Yeah." Her face tensed and her tone was clipped.

"What does she want with me?"

"My guess, to figure out if you're a threat to security." She tried to smile, but it wasn't even deep enough to dimple her cheeks. "It's not exactly common for us to work with humans like this. I'm kind of surprised she didn't summon us both before now."

"Like I would have come." I snorted. The vampire ahead stopped, twirling on her heel, and glared at me.

"*You* will not disrespect my queen!" Her accented voice didn't raise, but the anger was clear in her features. Lily stepped between us, her tone exhausted.

"Melody, he is *not* a member of our court. Like it or not, the queen cannot make demands of him, and he has the right to refuse any invitation." Lily let the sentence hang before turning back to me.

I chewed on my cheek in thought before looking directly into those sky eyes.

Was she really giving me the option to leave? Granted I had no clue where the door was and this house was huge. Plus, the wavering pools of blue didn't offer reassurance.

They begged for help. I was weaker than her, in a house full of vampires, and she looked like I was her last hope. How could that be? We barely knew each other.

I nodded once, and Lily turned back to the other woman. Melody scowled at Lily for a moment longer before turning back to her path. Lily gave me a warning glance when I opened my mouth, and I clamped it shut. The questions could wait.

We climbed several flights of stairs, the woman ahead of us confidently choosing which hallways to go down and which turns to make. Lily followed, watching the woman's steps like a hawk. I got the feeling she wasn't entirely sure where we were heading.

Several people we passed scowled openly at her, nodding politely at our escort or eyeing me with curiosity. She didn't respond to any of it, just continued trying to smooth the wrinkles from her clothes.

We finally came to a door flanked by four men, two on each side of the hall. Each had a gun on his belt and a steadfast stare that would make those English guards with the looming hats envious. The other woman and Lily nodded to each other as we entered. I bobbed my head awkwardly and walked through the double doors.

The room ahead was like a small sitting room, furnished in a way that suited the rest of the house. A long lounge sofa sat across from a matching chair of the same deep emerald fabric. A rich-colored coffee table divided the space and a large circular rug covered the wooden floors with more jewel tones. The room was flanked by two more sets of double doors. A large screen took up one wall and a fireplace took another.

"Sit." Our escort gestured to the large lounge couch. Lily sat, her hands twirling in her lap. I followed suit, sitting as far away from her as the furniture would allow. The escort turned and knocked on the nearest set of double doors.

"Come in."

Lily tensed at the voice. I couldn't understand why. It was like audible honey, smooth and sweet. It had a slight Middle-Eastern accent. It was the kind of voice that could end a war by just saying *please*.

Not more than five minutes later, a woman came into the room and Lily rose, her eyes directly ahead, her hands twisting in knots before her. I was too stunned to stand. Even with her heels, the woman couldn't be more than five feet tall. It didn't matter. She glided over the floor, the back of her sharp shoes not even clicking on the wood. Her copper gaze met Lily's and the woman bowed her head. Lily bobbed her head in return and sat back down, hard like she was ready to fall over.

The shorter woman looked amused as her eyes roamed my face. What, was I supposed to bow? They couldn't seriously expect that. Like Lily said, I wasn't one of this woman's subjects. Then again, they could also kill me easily enough, and I didn't know what might provoke them.

I should have turned the offer down.

The woman took the chair across from us and lazily draped one leg over the other. Calling the fluid motion crossing them just didn't do it justice. This woman was grace. It wasn't just her looks, though she was stunning. It was her whole presentation. Put her in a potato sack, and she'd be just as powerful. Though I doubted I'd ever see her wear that.

The vampire queen wore a silver strapless sheath, the aforementioned heels a deep wine color that contrasted the dress but mimicked the color she'd used on her lips. Her thick raven hair was cut in a short bob and the only other hint of makeup on her cinnamon skin was a thick eyeliner that turned your attention straight to those copper eyes.

"I do not think Lily is going to infect you, Detective Collins." The queen smiled indulgently at the empty space between us. "Nor will she bite, unless you ask."

"Thanks, but I'm not on the menu." I bristled at the mental image her words had conjured.

Lily shot me a warning glance before sputtering out, "I'm sorry, your majesty. I didn't have the chance to let him know about our customs."

"No need to apologize, Lily. You're quite right, *he* is not one of my subjects. Though I have a vested interest in him, I will not expect him to hold himself like I do you or Ivan." The queen's voice iced over at the mention of Lily and her boss.

The vampire next to me gulped and nodded. "Thank ya, Majesty. He uses snark like armor."

"Like you're one to talk," I grumbled.

"Can we please *not* do this now?"

I turned to snap at her, but the look on her face halted my words. Replacing that bravado, her eyes shimmered, and she chewed on her bottom lip slowly.

Was she *scared*? She'd given me assurances I would be safe, but she looked terrified.

"I can see why you chose to work with him, my dear. He is very entertaining." The queen laughed, her voice turning to soft wind chimes. She held out one hand towards me, her smile disarming. "My subjects know me as Ritti. Your kind remembers me as Nefertiti."

"Bullshit." The word slipped out before I could help myself. Part of me wished I lived in a comic book so I could shove the talk bubble back in. Lily groaned.

"Now, now Lily. Even you can admit that is quite the pill to swallow."

"I feel like I handled the news better." Lily glared at me in my peripheral vision, but I kept my eyes straight ahead.

"Indeed." The queen smiled indulgently at me. "Well, enough chatter. I'm sure Detective Collins is anxious to know why I summoned the two of you."

At this, I sat up. The queen sat even straighter and brought her gaze directly to my eyes. Slowly, the copper swallowed by her pupil like her eyes had formed black holes that sucked out all the color. I felt a wave of fuzz entering my mind when she spoke. "Gabriel, you never met a vampire. You don't remember ever talking to a vampire or discovering any vampire secrets, do you?"

"I do not remember any vampire secrets," I said mechanically as I stared ahead, my jaw heavy and slack.

Lily gasped next to me. As she did, the queen leaned forward. She eyed me for a long moment. Then, she stuck a long finger directly in my eye. I yowled and sat back in surprise.

"What was that for?" I held my hand over my eye out of some stupid instinct.

"I didn't know if it really took, but only a human faking mind control would pull back after a simple eye poke." The queen sat in her chair, looking imperious and a little smug. "Took me over a century to think of that trick."

"Gabe, why the fuck would ya do that?" Lily rounded on me, panic making her voice raise and her accent thickening. It took me a second to figure out what she was saying.

"Because I wasn't sure what she was up to. For all I know, it's either get my memories erased or die!"

"Do all humans think of us so?" The queen looked amused. Lily shrugged noncommittally. The queen turned back to me. "I have no intention of killing you, Detective. Though, you do pose a unique risk, especially now. One I only became aware of today."

Lily hunched at these words, picking at the skin around a thumbnail with great and sudden interest.

"So what, then?" I turned to face the queen.

"In the hopes our secrecy could be kept intact, I feel we need to reach some form of arrangement. From what my captain tells me, you two have been stuck in a situation where you are forced to deal with each other. I also understand your actions may have even saved my subject's life tonight. However, from the Great Pyramid you are placing between the two of you on that couch, you still don't trust her."

"Hard for a gazelle to trust a lion." Alex's words flowed from my mouth before I could contain them. The queen smiled.

"I suppose I can see that point of view. But a gazelle should hardly fear a tiny tick."

"Tick?" I gave her and Lily speculative glances. "You're rather large for me to think of you as parasites."

"Is it not true, though?" The queen tilted her head in thought. "We do not need to kill you to thrive. We only need to take a little off the top."

"Your big coming-out party two years back begs to differ." Again, I wanted to shove the words back down and choke on them. I was going to get myself killed at this rate.

Why the hell was I picking a fight with this woman? After seeing what Lily could do, I knew this wasn't the time or place. But...the vortex of images that threatened my mind when I thought of that day seemed to be out for retribution. Right here, right now.

"You're very outspoken, aren't you?" The queen's lips quirked up.

No response came to mind, so I tried to look confident.

"Believe it or not, most of us were happier in the dark." The queen eyed Lily for a second before continuing. "Our lives were complicated, but hiding was easier than this. Still, someone kept making trouble over the last few decades."

"Elias?" I guessed, remembering Kimberly's earlier words.

"Ah, so Lily has told you." Those eyes turned to slits and returned to Lily.

Lily looked scared as she opened her mouth to explain.

"No." I shook my head. "I heard about him earlier from the Renfield."

"Did you now?" The queen continued to eye her subject with suspicion just a second longer before turning back to me. "Elias kept claiming that humanity was no better than cattle and should be afforded as much in the way of rights."

"What?" I wasn't sure why. Kimberly had basically said as much, but something about the way the queen said it froze my innards.

"We turned down several of his propositions, and I thought that was the end of the matter. Looking back, I should have realized, history is littered with stories of the oppressed rising to power through violence."

"Oppressed?" I shook my head. "You guys can't be justifying this under some Civil Rights notion. You let this maniac kill *how* many?"

"Do we hold every awful thing one human has done against your race?" Lily's voice was bitter, even brittle. "High time ya stopped holding Elias's actions against mine."

"Oh please!" Some indignity leaked into my tone. Lily, I could spar with. "It wasn't just one vampire tearing people apart that night. There were at least thirty at the mall alone! So don't go blaming it all on one guy."

Lily held her hand in front of my face, ticking off a list on her fingers as she spoke.

"The Crusades. The KKK. The Nazis. That doesn't even begin to cover all the wars your kind has gone to over religion and land. I'm still not hearing your kind clamoring for a mass extinction over their mistakes!"

"You're telling me that night was some sort of vampire group terrorist attack?" I scoffed.

"Exactly," the queen interjected. Her voice was silk, gliding over my fury. I turned my attention back to her. "Why do you think there were so many stories of people saying they'd been saved by vampires that same night?"

It was true, several of the vampire-sympathy groups constantly cited claims from victims of the massacre. Claims from survivors saying they'd been saved by other vampires. The majority of the population had figured it was either PTSD, shock, or general fruitcakes making the claims. Then again, I hadn't seen anyone with fangs trying to save us.

But if they were telling me the truth, then some of those claims actually made sense. Something must have registered on my face. The queen nodded like she could read my thoughts.

"We did try to stop it," the queen continued. "Elias's people planned carefully and caught us off-guard. We got the West Coast under control right as they hit the mountains, and suddenly the bloodbath began all over again. We tried to get ahead of them, but their choice of cities and locations was random at best. We simply couldn't predict where they would strike."

Lily sank into the lounge chair next to me and put her face in her hands. Her body shook so hard that I felt the fabric shudder beneath me. At first, I thought she was crying. Then I saw her hands.

She had balled them into fists, the knuckles white against her pale skin. Her entire body was shaking, not just her shoulders. She was fighting for control. Realization clicked, a puzzle piece falling into place.

"You were there." I looked towards her face, still covered by her long fingers.

"Yeah." She looked up at me, her mouth a thin line. "I made it to the mall right after the EMTs and fire department. I watched for four hours, while they tried to sort out which limb belonged where. I finally realized there was nothing I could do and went home."

I blinked, unsure what to say. I'd been in the middle of that mess. I knew firsthand what it had looked like. Even from a distance, it would have been grizzly. I looked away before I could give anything away.

"What is the point to all of this?" I looked back to the queen.

"The point—" she sat forward, "is what you will do with our secrets."

"Your girl here has me in a pretty good knot. I can't even suggest she's a vampire without risking a trip to the nuthouse."

"Yes. A clever ploy." Queen Ritti gave her subject the same smile my mom used to give me when I tried to get away with something. "Sadly, it does not solve the long-term issue. What will you do when this case is over?"

I was taken aback. I hadn't thought that far ahead. Too much had been going on. And with Lily's computer records being so thorough, I really didn't think there was much I could do until I got proof.

"I take it you hadn't considered that." The queen tilted her head in thought. I shook my head, and she continued, "Might I propose a continuing trade?"

CHAPTER 22

LILY

The look on Gabe's face would have been comical if not for my own confusion. "A trade?"

"Yes, Lile."

I winced.

She called me by my original name, pronouncing it Lee-leh. Yeah, I was up shit-creek. Ritti's tone didn't betray a thing, but she was definitely pissed. "Since you and Ivan felt it best to involve this human in our affairs, I see no other alternative. He should earn something for the trouble of keeping our secret. Especially if you consider his occupation."

I stared in disbelief. Gabe's face held a similar bewilderment until her last words.

"I don't want your money." He gave our lavish surroundings a quick glance.

"That's good, I wasn't thinking of a cash payment." Ritti leaned back in her chair, her posture regal as ever. "While your department's solve rate is incredibly high, that's mostly due to weeding out the fakes. My research tells me your solve rate for actual vampire cases is very low. Not even double digits."

"We're still learning." Gabe's tone was smooth, but the words had a bite. Probably didn't appreciate having a vampire pointing that out.

"True, and you're still sorting legend from reality." Ritti gave him an amused look. "After all, how many novels contradict each other? How many myths do you have to sort through while dealing with all the human violence that pretends to be ours?"

"Your point?" His tone dropped a little, barely polite that time. I really hoped he didn't cross the line again.

"What if I offered my Court's ongoing resources to assist with your vampire cases?"

"What?" Gabe's eyes widened slightly, and his tone lost all the chill and anger.

"In exchange for your silence, we will help you take down the vampires you come across in your work." Ritti looked like she was moving a chess piece into the perfect position.

"So what, you would give me a liaison or something?" Gabe leaned forward.

I stared in horror. Oh, shit. Oooooh, shit. The queen smiled at me, and I swallowed.

"You seem to already have one. Why bother assigning someone else?"

I suppressed a groan. Check. Mate. Well, that was only fifty years coming.

"Lily?" Gabe looked at me, understanding dawning on his features. "I thought she had a business."

"I do." I ran a hand down my face. "This isn't optional, is it, Majesty?"

"Seeing as I wasn't consulted or advised of your dual investigation." Ritti shook her head. I suppressed a second groan as she continued. "Detective Collins, do we have a deal?"

Gabe looked across the coffee table, the silence stretching as he thought, his eyes shifting back and forth like he was reading the air. Finally, he spoke, "Why are you offering me this? What's in it for you?"

"I've already said. I want our secrets kept."

"You know when Lily first realized she couldn't toy with my memory, she threatened to break my spine if I didn't stay out of her way."

"Did she?" Ritti tilted her head in interest. I was mostly wondering where this was going.

"Yeah. I knew it was a line, just her way of trying to scare me off. You're right, I don't trust Lily, not entirely. But no one saves a man's life just to snap their spine the next day. No one practical anyway."

"I would agree." Ritti nodded in thoughtful interest.

"And no one trying to hide offers a liaison to their enemy."

"Ah..." Ritti smiled in apparent satisfaction. "The point emerges."

"Yeah. So, again, I ask why are you offering this to me?"

Ritti tilted her head this way and that before nodding once and smiling wider. "You're clever. I like clever."

"Thanks." Gabe nodded, a little impatience filtering the single word.

Ritti considered him again before nodding once.

"My kind tried to go back to the dark after the massacres. Old habits and such." Ritti's eyes grew sad. "Unfortunately, we have not captured our enemy yet and our reluctance to come into the light has given Elias control over the public view. Meanwhile, humans are insistent on involving themselves in our affairs. I believe this arrangement may be a useful first step to changing that narrative and making the involvement safer for everyone."

"So, essentially, you're hoping that giving humans a little contact with vampires might help us see another side to you."

"Precisely."

Gabe gave a low whistle "You've got your work cut out for you."

"I'm certain." Ritti let a smile take over her features, but it didn't reach her eyes.

"How long do I have to think about this?"

"You need time?" Ritti blinked a few times.

"I hardly know her." Gabe crooked a thumb at me. "And five minutes into meeting me, you decided to poke me in the eye. Yeah, I need time."

Ritti looked thoughtful before nodding.

"Very well, I shall give you until the end of the case you are currently working on. Consider it your trial run."

———◆———

I turned off Interstate Five, happy to feel my motorcycle flow over the road beneath me. The Court had dropped Gabe off at the ER, calling ahead first to make sure Anna was on duty. She'd growled something about me owing her a favor. Gabe had grumbled a bit, too, though his reason was sound.

After all, I'd just left him in the clutches of a vampire I didn't even trust. Still, Anna could fix the records the fastest. Hopefully, his bosses bought the story. Of course, Gabe had some demands about questions and answers later this evening, but I'd been expecting that. Especially given the offer Ritti had just made him. He'd probably have even more if Anna gave him her two cents.

The morning road glinted in the early sun as I exchanged asphalt for dirt, the city landscape slowly turning into dry autumn fields that rose and fell with the crest of each hill. The morning light was high in the sky, and I craved my old leather jacket more than ever; the late-September wind bit my skin through the hoodie. Ivan said he would replace the jacket as an expense for the case. I wasn't certain if the queen was going to let that fly, but figured I'd let him give it a shot.

I pulled up our gravel driveway, reaching into my saddlebag for the garage remote and my cell phone. I hoped Ivan got my new jacket sooner rather than later. I already missed my zipper pockets. The overhead door hummed and squealed lightly as it shifted upwards, and I rolled the bike forward, taking up the second half of the garage and setting the kickstand in place. The door to the house swung open right as I removed my kitty helmet, Maria and Darren rushing out.

They practically bounced in agitation as I killed the bike and dismounted, finally letting them envelop me in a tight hug. Maria pulled away first, her face barren of the usual cosmetics as she smirked at me. "I'm eating ghost peppers for a whole week if you ever do that again!"

"Threat received." I smacked my lips, remembering the fire of her last batch of curry. I turned my attention to Darren, his big arms still slung around me. "How is he?"

"He's managing. I guess your cop friend picked up the phone when you were out, gave him an update."

I nearly backed up in surprise. Gabe had told Alex how I was? That was news. I mean, I figured he'd called Ivan like I asked. Waking up with the doc digging the bullets out had kind of been a giveaway. Didn't think he'd updated my best friend on the situation. Huh, I'd have to look into that. I smiled weakly and twirled for my friends, allowing them to see I was whole. "Well, I'm good as new. You've threatened me. Have all the procedures been met?"

"Only once you get the blood out of your hair." Maria glared, but the corner of her mouth twitched. "Get out of my sight, before I beat you."

"You sound like your mum more every day." I snorted and walked past the two of them, hanging my helmet next to the spare on our garage wall.

I walked upstairs, not bumping into Alex. Not surprising. His client was about to go back to Court. He had to be triple-checking himself to make sure she was really ready. I'm sure he'd have an opinion later though.

I pulled my phone from my pocket and thumbed through the history. Most of my messages were from the very people who'd accosted me in the garage, threatening to kill me if I didn't come home. I snorted and kept scrolling. Sure enough, shortly after one outgoing call to Ivan, there was an incoming call from Alex that had lasted just under two minutes. I guess Gabe had picked up. Good thing, Alex probably would have fallen apart if he hadn't answered. After that, there was a fairly recent call and a voicemail. Both from Peter Andrews.

Huh, that was weird. Not that the other PI and I never chatted, but we weren't friends either. We only bugged each other when our caseload got too heavy or we needed a little help on a stakeout. Given how much we referred clients back and forth, we usually cut one-another a deal when things required us to be in two places at one time. Peter had to have heard my out-of-town voicemail. Yet, there it was. The tiny blinking phone icon indicated I had a new voicemail.

I looked at the bathroom and then at the red-soaked tips of my hair, grimacing. If not for all the ick glued to my body, I would have dived right in for a full bath with big bubbles, but I didn't feel like soaking in the filth. Still, I really, really needed a shower. I tossed my phone on the bed and stripped out of the borrowed clothes.

If Peter needed help on a case, I'd just be turning him down anyway. He could wait until I felt a little less like trampled shit. It took thirty minutes of scalding water and relentless shampoo use before my hair was free of the red. By then, I was surprised I had any skin left on my body. I exited the shower and wrapped myself in one of our large towels before flouncing back into my bedroom.

My phone was blinking with another missed call. And another voicemail. Okay, maybe Peter really needed something. Shit, hope it wasn't pressing. I just didn't have time for this right now. I opened my contact list and hit the green phone icon to dial Peter's number.

It took three rings before he answered, his gruff voice reminding me of a bulldog.

"Edwards, where you been?"

"Sorry Peter, I've got a weird case that has me pretty tied up." I laid down on my bed, the pillows practically begging me to hang up the phone. I settled for closing my eyes as I spoke. "What's up?"

"That's what I wanted to ask." He pulled the phone away from his face and mumbled something without preamble. Probably to his secretary, from the rigid tone of his voice. I rolled my eyes and waited for him to return. "What is with your friend? Does he think he's being funny?"

"What friend?" I fought an urgent yawn.

"The one leaving voicemails about having fun at the party. About hoping he can find a new dance partner soon."

"Huh?" My eyes popped open.

"Yeah, some kid keeps calling. He said he tried you first but you wouldn't pick up."

Possible. I still got all sorts of calls whenever I took time away from the business. I didn't answer unless I knew the number. I had to delete at least one voicemail a week from some cabbage who didn't bother listening to my message before the beep.

But I hadn't gotten any dance partner voicemails. Was it possible that someone from Thomas' team was taunting me? He and I had been dancing, so it could be a hint. But if they were, why use Peter for the relay? It would just slow the message down.

"Did they leave a number?"

"Yeah." Peter rattled off the ten digits, and I scrambled across my room, the towel falling to the ground. He didn't like to repeat himself.

I practically landed against my desk and snagged a pen out of the cup. I couldn't find a pad of paper fast enough, so I scrawled the digits on my palm. I blew on the ink to help it dry before reading the number back.

"That it?"

"Yeah, tell him to stop bugging me, will ya?" Peter drew the phone away and spoke to his secretary again before turning his attention back to our conversation. "I don't have enough time to be your message service. You missed a lot of good cases these last couple days."

"I bet." I grinned. He always said that when I took time off. Then again, he liked every job. "Thanks for the call Peter. I'll take care of it."

"Bye, Edwards." The line disconnected.

I walked back across the room and retrieved my towel as I stared at the digits I'd scrawled on my hand. I sat on the bed and dialed the ten digits into my phone. Before dialing, my phone located one missed call from the number. Two nights ago. Huh, guess they had tried me first. But why not leave a voicemail?

I hit the green phone icon and pressed the phone to my ear. It rang a few times and went to voicemail. I didn't bother listening, just hung up and redialed. Same thing. The voice on the other end wasn't familiar but that wasn't surprising. It was oddly cheery.

A woman's high voice asked me to leave a message after the beep. The voicemail sounded somewhat tinny. Like it wasn't an electronic recording. Maybe a tape. I looked at my phone in bewilderment. Nope, the ten digits on my hand matched those on the screen. I'd dialed right. I brought the phone back to my ear just in time for the beep. I tapped into my inner sorority sister as I left the message. After all, it could just be some mix-up.

"Hi, this is Lily." I smacked my lips like I was chewing gum. "My friend said ya left a message about dancin'. Just callin' to say I'm down when ya are. Okay, bye!"

I hit the end button and stared at the screen a moment longer. Hopefully, I'd just responded to a wrong number. Probably not, but any moron could read through my poorly veiled threat. I added the new number to my phone and assigned a custom ringtone. Didn't want to miss them again.

"Bring it on."

CHAPTER 23

GABE

The scent of antiseptic and bleach filled the little room. The hospital gown didn't do anything to cover me, and I was grateful for the thin blanket they'd provided. Outside the room, I could hear conversations and footsteps echoing lightly in the hallway. Occasionally, the wall clock *tick tick ticked* overhead, but the nurse's shoes slapping against the tile and the steady *beap beap beap* of the heart monitor she'd attached to me overrode the sound.

The clamp pinched my finger, and I wondered if she'd tightened it. The nurse tapped the inside of my elbow with deft fingers before jamming the needle into a large vein and taping it in place.

"Ouch." I glared at the short woman. Anna had Hispanic features and olive skin, a perpetual scowl taking residence on her lovely face ever since Lily had dropped me off.

"Aw, poor baby. Do you need a lollipop?" She glared while she hung the IV bag. "It's not bad enough I'm faking hospital records. Now I have to listen to you whine."

"Sorry to inconvenience you." I sat back against the raised bed. She rolled her eyes and crossed her arms over teal scrubs covered in little blue and green flowers that looked like a fifth-grader had drawn them. Her copper eyes pinned me with a stare my mother used to give me when I stole her books. It wasn't as effective coming from the little vampire.

"You're just lucky that Lily agreed she owes me a favor. Granted, the last favor I cashed in from her bit me right in the ass." My brows furrowed together, and she let out a humorless giggle. "Oh, she didn't tell you? Shocking. She's usually such an open book."

"Yeah, I've noticed she keeps things close to her chest." I gave Anna a speculative look. Maybe I could learn something before Lily and I had our little pow-wow tonight. Might be useful to go in armed. "What can you tell me about her?"

"Lily likes to stick people in a position where they're reliant on her, so she can control them." She growled the statement out.

"What do you mean?"

"Take me for example." She threw her hands out with a flourish like she was some kind of exhibit. "Lily and I used to be friends. I thought she was the best person to have on your side."

"So, what happened?"

"Simple, I didn't want to live at Court anymore. You been there?"

I nodded, remembering the huge Georgian-style mansion that had looked like it had been pulled straight from a novel or movie. Without Lily and the escort guiding me through the maze, I would have gotten lost on my way out.

"Well," Anna continued. "Have you seen a feeding there?"

The loud gulps from memory suddenly became present with the other racket in the room. The frail woman's moans overlapping everything. I nodded.

"Sick, right? They practically turn those people into addicts, with nowhere to go. They have them feed two or three vampires a day sometimes, then have the doctor fill them with fluids and iron." Anna flicked the banana bag she'd hung for emphasis. "I didn't like it and decided to move out. Just wanted to be on my own."

"And?" I prodded.

"The Court investigates everyone who petitions to live alone. Checks to see if they need a live-in-donor from the Court. I thought I had it in the bag when they assigned Lily. I mean, she's my friend. She knows me, right?"

I nodded, not sure where this was going.

"Well, she went through my history with a fine-tooth comb. She found one tiny little discrepancy. It was years ago. And no one got hurt, but she still turned it in. I was denied my donor. And now, everyone at Court knows about it, so I can't live there either."

"So, what do you do for food?" I wasn't sure I wanted to answer.

"I have to sneak blood from coma patients." She grimaced. "Instead of living with a willing donor and only having one person I depend on."

I grimaced but filed the idea in my head for later. Maybe I could find evidence of this. "So, how does Lily have you dependent on her?"

"They assign the same investigator when you petition again. I'm about a year from being eligible to request a donor again. Means I'm stuck playing nice with her until my request is processed." She gave me an annoyed look. "Essentially, Lily can ask me to do whatever she wants and bug me anytime she wants, because she's the one that tells the Court if they should let me have a donor."

Okay, now I got why she might be annoyed. The rest of her story had a lot of self-pity to it, and I wasn't sure how valuable it was. But if Lily was holding the upcoming review over this vampire's head for favors, that was definitely going to cause some frustration.

"I mean, come on!" Anna gave me a heavy look. "Surely you're not helping her with whatever got you going on by choice."

My blood froze. I'd thought the idea of working together was the lesser of all evils. But what if Lily had manipulated me into helping her? She had Harper's brain and my entire precinct believing she was just a normal woman. Nothing to see here, move along folks. Then again, why not just make Harper help her? And why save my life?

Had she saved my life? I only had Harper's word on that. I remembered the lighting fixture plummeting towards me. She said she'd fed me the blood to save my life. Harper even claimed that was the case, but she could have scrambled his brains for that too. Now I was stuck working with her, reliant on her trading with me. Then there was the queen's generous offer to make Lily keep working with me. What if they were playing me?

"See. I told you." Anna snickered and looked up at the clock. "Your cop buddies should be here pretty soon. I've got the computers showing you two were brought in by an anonymous party just after midnight and that you had a serious concussion. They didn't seem terribly pleased that it had taken us this long to call them."

"Yeah, they wouldn't." I scooted down on the bed. "Thanks, I guess."

"Like I really had a choice." Anna snorted and turned on her heel, her shoe emitting a soft squeak as she left.

Harper and Captain Murphy looked none too happy as they crossed the threshold of my hospital room. Concern filled Harper's eyes, and irritation filled the captain's.

"Hey partner, gotcha something." Harper shook a tiny stuffed gorilla, about the size of his fist and holding a fake balloon begging me to get well soon. I rolled my eyes and took the animal.

"God, how much did you overpay for this?"

"Got it for free, just swiped it from some kid's room on the way up." He smiled, his long beard shifting with the gesture. I rolled my eyes and let out an amused chuckle before looking at Sean Murphy. He stood ramrod straight and took in my appearance before speaking.

"Nurse who called us said you were out cold until a little bit ago."

"I guess so." I reached up and rubbed the back of my skull, carefully avoiding the large lump on the side. I may as well go with the lie we'd agreed on. I still didn't know her side of that little story. If Lily was playing me, I would sort it out later. But the paper trail had already been laid for this.

"What do you remember from last night? We found some videos of you talking about a blonde who was dealing with a vampire inside the dorm."

Yeah, a blonde I was going to be drilling for information tonight.

"Yeah, that PI we met at the party and the club called. She'd found a Renfield during her investigation and thought I might want to bring her in. What happened with Kimberly anyway? Any good information?"

"The only thing we got was a broken window." Harper gave me a sympathetic look. "The back window of your car was shattered when I found it."

"What?" I sat up straighter. "She got out?"

"More like someone broke her out. The window was broken inwards and a security officer had his throat ripped out."

I gulped, Michael's young face flashing in my mind. Granted, I wasn't much older but still. I'd left him guarding my suspect, thinking it was a safe enough gig while I went to help Lily. Instead, it had cost him his life.

"Damn." I pushed my hands through my hair, wincing as I passed over the bruise.

"That about sums it up. Dan already verified it was a vampire attack." Captain Murphy gave me an uncompromising look. "Why didn't you call in? Let us know where you were going?"

"I was right next to the college, great Chinese place near there. Anyway, I was less than five minutes out when she called. I didn't think to slow down. I was excited to finally have a new break in the Cheri Coke case. I know the press has been riding you."

"Yeah, now they're in an uproar." Captain Murphy pinched his nose. "Okay, so you arrested the girl, why'd you leave the PI to deal with the vampire? PI or no, she's a civilian."

"I had the suspect when it attacked. She ran after the vamp before I could stop her. The security officer offered to watch Kimberly and call the VPB for me. I went back in to help Lily."

"Lily? That's the PI?" Captain Murphy looked between Harper and me. We both nodded. "Okay, so you go back to help the PI, then what?"

"We had to pursue the vamp outside the building, through the south side. We ran after him and traced him off-campus. We made it into the campus gardens, and he ambushed us. Knocked me out cold. I guess he got her, too."

"Where's the PI now?" Captain Murphy's face was filled with interest. And suspicion.

"Nurse said she was brought in with me, but her injuries were less severe, and she checked out a few hours before I woke up. But she left me this." I reached to the plastic bedside table, depositing Harper's toy and holding up a little business card for the captain. He took it and read it out loud.

"Strictly Confidential Investigations." He rattled off the address and phone number before looking back at me. "So what? We could have looked this up online."

"Turn it over." I made a slow twirling motion with my forefinger.

Harper crowded next to the captain, and they read together in silence. Harper looked up first, intrigue on his face.

"She asked you to tell the captain that she'll come in whenever he's ready."

"Yup." I nodded. "Apparently, they didn't find my badge. Lily's the one that told them they should call the VPB."

"Yeah, the nurse said something about that when I yelled at her for not calling me earlier." Captain Murphy pocketed the card and glowered at me. "First your cuffs, now your badge. This is becoming a problem, Collins."

"I have my badge. They just didn't check my inner coat pocket. I always put it in there when I'm running. Makes it hard to lose."

"Freaking hospital can't look for extra pockets?" The captain grimaced. "When are they discharging you? Are you clear for duty?"

"They said it was just a minor concussion. They're releasing me later today. Said I should take it easy for two or three days then I can go back to normal."

"To be clear, there will be an investigation, Collins." Sean Murphy looked disappointed, and I wanted to sink into the faux bed of the hospital. "You broke protocol, losing a suspect, and costing a civilian their life."

He shook his head before adding, almost like an afterthought. "Almost two."

CHAPTER 24

LILY

Captain Murphy looked like an overgrown jock who had never stopped the upkeep, probably because he didn't know how. His demeanor said he was a man that liked routine. As did his line of questioning.

"You didn't think that you were maybe getting in the way? Chasing a vampire next to a trained police officer?" He was tapping a pen against his notepad, his eyes trying to pin me down. I kept my arms crossed. I'd decided against propping my legs on the metal table this time. I didn't think he would appreciate it. I had barely gotten an hour's nap when the captain had *invited* me to come in and give my statement.

I really hadn't wanted to come back in. But once Gabe told me about his admission of an Irish blonde being on the scene in front of several cell phone users, my fate had been kind of sealed. Since my injuries were already healed, I'd had Maria apply a little makeup around my eyes, using YouTube to direct her on costume makeup for a thick bruise that stretched from one eye to my temple, adding another under my chin. She'd done a pretty good job, blending the mixture of red and purple with just a hint of black.

After that, I'd had Alex wrap several layers of gauze and ace bandages over each wrist and palm. I was just grateful circulation wasn't an issue. He knew how to wrap it tightly. Must come from treating humans through the transition into a vampire. We'd even speckled a little tomato juice under the gauze, the effect peeking through the bandages in tiny droplets and smears.

"I can't say I was really thinkin' about it. I had a vampire threatenin' people around me. They weren't armed, and we were. I just didn't want to risk someone innocent getting hurt."

"How noble." The captain's tone was insincere as he made his notes. "And you say you stumbled across the girl on your case?"

I gave the camera in the upper corner a baleful look. If not for that recording, I could have just black-eyed this cabbage and been on my way an hour ago.

"I've already answered that. Twice. I tracked her down through social media and a few clients at the club that burned down. They all said Kimberly was a good place for a Cheri Coke hookup. Since Cheri Coke was at the party and the club, I figured I might be able to ask this girl if she'd been dealing to my client's kid."

"We'll need the name of this client to confirm your information." That captain slid a writing tablet and pen over to me.

"Not a problem!"

Luckily, I'd kind of planned for that. Hopefully, Ivan's people had held up their end and gotten my last client set up with a new memory. Nothing fancy, just something that would go with our little cover-up. I didn't have enough time to forge the paperwork, but the fib wouldn't hurt the guy.

I clicked the button on the end of the pen and scribbled out Mr. Andrews' name and cell phone number. When I was finished, I slid the paper back across the table. "Would ya also like to see the contract he signed with me?"

"Yes, that would be most helpful. Whenever you can get it to us."

I reached into my pocket and unfolded the sheet of paper I printed earlier today. Thank God I kept copies of my contracts on the laptop. I slid it across the table and suppressed a smile. I hadn't included the second page, showing the conclusion of our business.

"Ya can keep that, it's a copy of the original."

Captain Murphy looked down his perfect nose at me before lifting the paper and reading carefully. I waited until his eyes left the paper.

"Anythin' else?" I gave him my most award-winning smile.

"No, Miss Edwards. You're free to go. I'm sure I don't need to tell you—"

"Don't leave town?" I arched an amused brow.

"Precisely." Captain Murphy stood and extended his hand to me. I held both my hands up for show, wiggling the fingers.

"You'll understand if I don't take ya up on that offer."

"Of course." Captain Murphy drew his hand away and held his arm out in an open invitation to leave. I got up and gingerly opened the door, wincing a little as my supposedly injured hand closed around the knob. The captain stepped forward, an apology in his features that didn't reach his eyes. "Sorry Miss Edwards. Let me get that for you."

"Thank you." I smiled in gratitude, hoping I was a better actress than the captain. Son of a bitch had been watching to see if my hands were really messed up.

He suspected something. I suppressed the urge to groan on my way out. I'd known I couldn't pop up three times without police wanting to take a harder look at me. Still didn't mean I fancied coming in.

This case was starting to be a real pain in the ass.

I walked through the linoleum halls of the precinct and turned towards the main entrance. I grabbed the hood of my sweatshirt and drew it over my head before pushing against the metal bar to open the glass door. The police station seemed silent when compared with the bustle outside.

The parking lot was practically clear, but the public sidewalk was littered with reporters and protesters. Each took their prospective side of the pavement, badgering anyone that walked by.

Several signs displayed a set of fangs surrounded by a large cartoon heart and peace signs, *Support V.A.P.E.* under most of the illustrations. I couldn't remember what the acronym stood for, only that VAPE was considered the most organized vampire rights group on the West Coast. I chuckled at the sight. Sure, the signs were dorky, but I kind of liked them. Too bad I couldn't pick up one of the T-shirts. I strode forward, keeping my head low as I walked towards the crowd.

The camera crews shouted their questions at the demonstrators, the cacophony scrambling the words together. I surveyed the rest of the signs in the crowd. Not even one person was protesting giving vampires their rights. Because it wasn't even a concern. I was still assigned to a race that held a never-ending bounty over our heads, just for existing. Nobody was concerned that would change anytime soon.

I reached my bike and pulled the helmet from my saddle-bag, securing it over my head with a sigh. I revved the engine once and pulled the bike out of the parking lot.

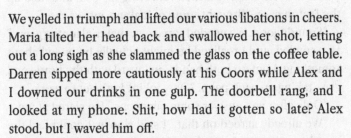

We yelled in triumph and lifted our various libations in cheers. Maria tilted her head back and swallowed her shot, letting out a long sigh as she slammed the glass on the coffee table. Darren sipped more cautiously at his Coors while Alex and I downed our drinks in one gulp. The doorbell rang, and I looked at my phone. Shit, how had it gotten so late? Alex stood, but I waved him off.

"It's the detective. He's comin' over for a little Q&A session."

I padded over to the door in my slippers and swung the door open. Sure enough, Gabe stood there. His bruises looked even darker with the sour look on his face. I opened the screen door and ushered him in wordlessly. He put a laptop case down and removed his coat, stopping in the middle of the gesture. His eyes were glued to the screen.

"You're shitting me."

"What, not a fan?" I blinked at the movie. The male was climbing a tree, his girlfriend clinging to his back and smiling. Gabe turned back to me and glared.

"It's illegal to even own this!"

"I know." I smiled. "But so is my very existence."

"It's a game." Darren raised his can in salutations. "We take a drink every time they get the mythology wrong. Those stupid sparkles have cost us at least five already."

"We used to drink for every time Edward looks constipated," Maria offered. "But there were too many debates about which scenes qualified. We ended up drinking almost every time he came on screen. And while those two can't get drunk, Darren and I still can."

Gabe still stood, his coat halfway on his arms. I laughed.

"I'm surprised ya even recognized it." I walked towards the living area and grabbed my bottle of whiskey and glass from the coffee table.

"I saw it in a pile of contraband that Adrian's mom gave me yesterday." He finally finished removing his coat and held up the laptop case. "Brought some of it along, just in case."

"Sounds good. We needed some new material for the game." He scowled, and I realized he might actually be pissed about something. I put up both hands, awkward with the bottle and glass taking up each palm. "Only jokin'. Let's get to work."

"Only after you answer some questions." He glared at me.

"We already agreed on that," I said slowly. I could feel the people on the couch watching our exchange. Gabe's tone had been less than enthusiastic.

"Yeah, we did. But the first question I have is one I need a really good answer to before I hand this over." He held up the case.

"And that is?" I wanted to groan. It was like talking to him on day one.

"How do I know I can trust you, vampire?" The movie behind me stopped playing. Guess the game was over.

"And what reason have I given you to distrust me?" I arched my brow.

"All I have is the word of my friend, whose brain you screwed with, that you saved my life. Then there's you, who can apparently survive when someone empties a magazine into your heart. I still figure you really can't hypnotize me. God knows you've had enough chances. But how do I know my injuries were really that severe? How do I know you're really helping me?"

"Are ya fucking kiddin' me?" I blew out a breath and gave him a level look. "Do ya even remember the *giant* hole in your shirt?"

"Yeah, it's the only tangible evidence I have. You and your kind burned down the club. And what about Anna? She says you have her bending over backward just so you don't screw her over on her certification for a donor."

"Is that what this is about?!" Alex was barreling across the room before I realized it. "You're getting in her face because of something *Anna* told you?"

Technically, Alex was the one getting in someone's face. He's practically shoved his right into Gabe's. To his credit, the scruffy man didn't cower away.

"I wasn't talking to—"

"Do you know how much hell she's getting from Court, because of you?" Alex pinned his fists to his sides, clenching and unclenching them rapidly. "And now you're taking the word of that fucking rapist over the woman who *saved* your ass!"

Oh. Shit.

"Trouble? What's he talking about?" Gabe looked around to me. "Is this about that offer from your queen?"

Oh, shit. I *so* was not ready for this can of worms.

"Um..." I glanced down at Darren, nodding at his partner.

Darren nodded and got up, putting his big hands on my friend's shoulders. "It's Lily's business, let her handle it."

"Hey!" Gabe's tone was calmer, but he still looked like a trap ready to spring. "I asked you a question!"

Alex growled, literally growled at him before Darren drew him away. Yeah, Alex could have pulled away easily, but he wouldn't. That was the whole point.

"I bloody heard ya!" I snapped back. "And you're a fuckin' eejit!"

"Huh?" He looked confused by the change of topic.

"Ya *obviously* trust me."

"That's a load of—"

"Then why did ya come?" I flapped my arms to encompass the house.

He stared, then looked around like he was confused. How had he come to be in this place? Finally, he looked back at me, blinking and uncertain.

We looked at each other a moment longer, and I swore. I walked into the kitchen and grabbed a sticky note out of the utility drawer, with a pen. Maria usually used these to leave notes when she was going grocery shopping or something, but they came in handy. I scribbled directions on the tiny neon square and returned the supplies to the drawer before returning to the living room.

"I'll be here." I handed the note to Gabe. "If ya show up, I'll answer your questions, as promised. If not, then don't come around askin' for any more help or any of my clues. We're done."

"Why not talk now? I'm right here." Gabe took the note from my hand and reviewed the information.

"Yeah, and ya just pissed off my best friend." I hooked a thumb towards the closing door of Alex and Darren's room. "You've lost your right to pick the location."

And I really didn't feel like talking about any of this here. I headed upstairs to change out of my pajamas. Maybe the detective would follow me, maybe he wouldn't.

He either trusted me or he didn't.

But either way, I could use the motorcycle ride to calm down.

CHAPTER 25

GABE

*F**ucking rapist.*

The words hung in my head like a talk bubble in a comic. What had Alex meant by that? What the hell was the truth?

I stared at the sticky note, angling it in the cab light. She'd be there, I knew she would be. But would she answer me? Would she give me a real reason to trust what she said?

Isaac.

The name had nagged at me since she screamed it this morning. She said would answer anything I asked.

And she was right.

I'd come to her home. I hadn't brought Harper or anyone else. I'd instinctively known I would be safe, even though I was confronting her. Even now, I'd just pissed off her little vampire friend, and I was debating my next move in her *driveway.*

"Gah!" I crumpled the note and jammed my fingers through my hair. The paper scraped my scalp before falling into the passenger seat.

Even when Alex had gotten in my face. Somehow, I still hadn't been alarmed. Just really annoyed. What the hell was happening to me?

I looked back at the bright green sticky, as though it would answer my unspoken question.

It didn't, but it could tell me where to find those answers

I could go home, wash my hands of this mess and all her help. I'd be able to help Harper more and get off the captain's radar. Life would become simpler. Or...

"Door number two," I sighed, retrieving the crumpled directions, and sticking them to the dashboard before pulling out of her driveway.

I parked next to the blue Harley, killing the engine, and slamming the door to my car when I got out. I grabbed the fob to lock it but decided against it. The plastic covering the back window of the driver's side fluttered in the breeze. I was still debating if it was worth an insurance claim for this clunker. I could put in a claim through the department, but our resources were already pretty thin and the window wouldn't be that much. I put the keys back in my pocket and took the sticky note out. Crickets chirped in the dusk air, and I heard something skittering through the bushes to my side. I looked up, absorbing the autumn leaves of the mountainside I stood on before looking back down at the directions.

A crudely drawn map took up the bottom half of the note, indicating I should walk about fifty feet north from the dirt trail I was parked on. I pocketed the note and began walking into the thick of trees and brush. The animal noises grew louder and the sky darker, but I could still see the yellow and orange leaves surrounding me.

The smell of dirt and pine-filled my nose, and I sallied forth until I found the destination she'd drawn so poorly. Most people think of mountains in the United States, and they think of Colorado. It'd been a while since I'd come up one of the

Oregon trails, but just the sight made me think the Rockies could never compare.

Lily sat on the edge of a large stone cliff overlooking the hills I'd just driven through. The only green in sight were the pines, unaffected by fall as always. The rest of the hills rose and fell with waves of yellow, golden brown, and red, the individual leaves shifting in the wind and making the whole sight come alive. Had the colors just changed, or had I'd just missed the whole transition? Had I really been so lost in this case?

Lily let me absorb the complete change in my surroundings before she spoke. "I come here when I'm homesick."

I nodded wordlessly, as though I knew what she meant, and headed over to the cliff. I sat about two feet from her, dangling my feet over the ledge. Lily sat with her legs crossed, her eyes fixed ahead.

"So, ya came."

"What happened with Anna?" I asked without preamble, scared if I waited that I might change my mind.

"She was using her gaze to make one of the donors have sex with her." Lily looked like she'd swallowed a roach. "Rape would normally be a death sentence from the Court. Anna should count her lucky stars she's still upright."

"Why didn't they kill her?" I certainly could understand the harsh reaction. Anna's self-centered words rang in my mind. No one got hurt, my foot.

"I asked them to spare her. I had a lot of credit built with the Court, and they owed me for forcing me to do somethin' I didn't want to. I cashed in."

"Why?!" Part of me wanted to ask what the something was, but I was flabbergasted that she would have used the favor on that.

"She was a friend." Lily looked down at the ground and flicked rocks away. "I hoped she would learn."

"People who pull that kind of crap don't change." As old as she was, she couldn't be that naive to think otherwise.

"I told ya—" she smiled into the distance, "I'd like to think people can still surprise me."

So, she wasn't naive. She was willfully ignorant to what her friend might be capable of.

"Anna felt like I should have worked harder and kept her from being banished. Ever since, the Court's hires me to make sure she's following vampire law and see if I think she qualifies for a donor every year since."

"Can't you turn them down?" The term *hires* implied she might.

"Who exactly do ya think provides me with my papers and background?" She shook her head. "It's Ritti's way of gettin' me back for calling in the favor. She's not a big fan of people pressin' any advantage with her."

"Like working with me." Now I understood Alex's earlier anger. Ritti probably toyed with Lily any chance she could, just to make it clear who was the boss. And I'd given her any easy in.

Now for the million-dollar question. "Who's Isaac?"

She snapped her head up, her eyes wide. "Who the *hell* told ya about that?"

For a second, I debated taking the question back, but it would just nag at me.

"You were screaming that name when you woke up this morning. You said it about five times before you finally opened your eyes. Who is he?"

Lily looked away again, grinding her teeth. "Why do ya want to know?"

"When someone screams a name over and over in their sleep, call me intrigued."

She snorted and looked at the sky, "He was my husband."

"Was?"

"Yeah." She lowered her voice and looked down the side of the cliff. "Ya ever heard of the Great Famine?"

I shook my head. It sounded familiar, but I couldn't quite place it.

"I was born in Ireland. The year was 1823. Ya can do the math." Her look dared me to comment. Her eyes were so sad. Even my curiosity broke at that look.

"You don't look a day over fifty." I smiled sarcastically and her eyes narrowed.

"A lesser woman would smack ya for that, but I don't want to break ya." Her tone was teasing but dark moisture rimmed that blue gaze. "Some just called it the Famine. Essentially, our crops failed due to a nasty fungus and the English crown rulin' us at the time raised the cost of other supplies so high that we starved."

Okay, that rang a bell. "Oh, yeah, didn't one of you write a letter to the Pope suggesting cannibalism as a solution?"

I remembered my father going over it for history class while my mother explained the subtle differences between satire and sarcasm. Still, the name of the writer escaped me.

"*A Modest Proposal.*" Her lilt colored the sad chuckle as it escaped her lips. "Yeah, but that was several years before my time. Anyway, my family was hit pretty bad by the on-again, off-again nature of the famine. We weren't doing great even before the fungus started hittin' the crops and ya can imagine how bad it was after."

She gulped. "Suffice to say I had a lot of siblings and my parents didn't have a lot of food. When I turned sixteen, my family was more than desperate. I'd started getting noticed by the men of our town. One man, in particular. Lord Isaac Edwards. He was an English baron and doing a hell of lot better than my family. Still, he was having trouble securin' a wife. Not surprisin', since most people blamed the English rule for our problems. So, he struck a deal with my father, and I was married in exchange for a decent bride price."

I stared in mild shock, and she gave me a sardonic smile. "Eighteen-hundreds, remember? Anyway, Isaac turned out to be a perfect gentleman. Sure, I thought he was odd. He never pressed for me to produce an heir, which was a big surprise. I just figured he didn't want to have kids during the famine. By the time I was twenty, I'd gotten used to Isaac and his odd habits. I'd grown to really enjoy his company. Besides, our marriage had probably given my family their best chance at livin'. But then..."

Her voice caught, and she stared down the side of the mountain. She opened her mouth, then closed it several times.

"What happened?" I prodded, not really sure what else to do.

She swallowed and tried again. "The famine got worse and there was a fever killing most of our town. It was only then that my husband showed me the truth. He begged me to let him bring me over. By then we'd grown on each other and we'd fallen into a form of love. He didn't want to lose me.

"I asked him to change over the rest of my family, but he refused, sayin' it was too much to handle at one time. I didn't understand what it was like to contain a new vampire then, not until I turned Alex years later. Now I see his rationale, but then I figured I could change them myself when it was done." A dark tear streaked down her face and her voice quivered.

"He changed me and locked me up to keep me from killin' anyone. I was left in solitude for two straight weeks. When I finally emerged, I ran straight to my family. They were all so ill. I made them the same offer that Isaac had given me. They turned me down, callin' me a demon and a hellspawn. I was so angry. How could they just choose to die? It didn't even occur to me how they'd react when I left.

"When I went home, Isaac asked where I had been. I said I'd been visitin' my family. I left out what I'd told them. If only I'd fuckin' listened, or even just told him the truth..." She took a deep breath and talked faster, like if she stopped to think she wouldn't be able to say anymore. "Days later, my sister Neasa wrote me. She wanted to take me up on my offer. She apologized for her reaction and said that she loved me no matter what. I went to her, so glad I could rescue at least one." She paused and looked up at me. Streaks shimmered on her cheeks in the orange light of dusk. "It was a trap. My family had turned the whole town against Isaac. The minute I entered the house, they swarmed me. I'm not sure how long I was out, but I was awakened by this sudden surge in my chest.

"It's called a tether. A link between the sire and sired, informin' the younger vampire of any pain and suffering for the older one." She clutched her chest, the same spot I'd seen Alex reach for just that morning. "I woke up, just *knowin'* Isaac needed my help. They'd tied me up, which was useless. I think they might have thought killin' Isaac would change me back or somethin'.

"Either way, I was out of my restraints and runnin' to our home before the people watchin' me could even yell. Not that it did much good. It was under siege. Our house was burnin' to the ground, and I could smell it miles away. Even taste it. The only thing missin' from the whole mess was their pitchforks. I'm not sure how they took Isaac out, only that they did."

"How?" I leaned in curious, fascinated, and swallowing so many emotions.

She swallowed. "The pull in my chest suddenly went ice cold; right when I heard a victorious cry from one of the villagers inside our home."

"Your family got the entire town behind them?" I couldn't help sounding surprised.

"It didn't take a lot to turn a group of starved Irishmen against one English noble. My family didn't have to work hard at convincin' them to kill the beast." She let out a shaky breath.

"What'd you do to the villagers? To your family?" I wasn't sure I wanted to know the answer, but I had to.

"What do ya mean? I left. I ran away like the coward I am. I trekked almost two hundred miles and black-eyed my way onto the first passenger ship to America."

"You didn't, I don't know, retaliate?" Surprise laced each word. I couldn't help it.

"Why would I? It was my fault!" Her voice had risen slightly, and the last word echoed back to us a few times before silencing.

I stared at her. My blood seemed to slow as a familiar ache burned in my own chest. One I could never seem to forget for more than a few minutes.

"So, what's my prize?" She looked at me, deep sorrow swallowing her gaunt features. "Do ya trust me now?"

I looked at her for a moment, unable to really answer. I finally understood what I had seen reflected in the shopping center window.

Just as before, I didn't see a vampire, even with the twin streams of red flowing down her cheeks. I didn't even see the snarky PI. I saw another reflection. But this time, it was one of myself, staring back at me through those sky-blue depths.

CHAPTER 26

LILY

The sky was starting to sparkle like someone was poking holes in a cobalt sheet overhead. Crickets chirped behind us. I rubbed my arms with my palms, grateful Alex's spare jacket fit over me at all even if it was a bit snug. I really should have fattened the guy up before turning him.

Gabe's eyes moved back and forth, like he was reading something printed on my skin. Or maybe he was just staring at the bloody tears. They had to be freaking him out.

I swiped at them with my sleeve. Probably just smearing the damn things everywhere. We sat in silence a moment longer. I wondered if he would even be able to see clearly. He'd had my blood, but that was days ago. He gulped and opened his mouth, the motion somehow timid. He tried again, finally getting the words out.

"I think I finally understand."

Before I could question his sanity, Gabe stood, dusting the dirt from his jeans blindly. He missed more than half of it. Nope. Couldn't see, not well anyway. He held out a hand to me. I held back a snort. It was a nice gesture, even if it was pointless.

He reached just past my hand, wrapping his thick fingers around my wrist to better support me. His pulse was strong, beating through his skin into mine. Thump, thump. Thump, thump. For a moment, it felt like having a pulse of my own. The rhythm of his heart beat into my fingers and his skin warmed mine as he gently heaved me from the ground. And then, he let go of me. The illusion vanished under the cold air on my skin.

"Read to go?" I shook my head, trying to clear my thoughts as I brushed the dirt from my ass and legs.

"Yeah." He nodded. "I still have questions, but it's getting chilly."

We walked in companionable silence, the various bugs and random rustling of critters louder than the crunch of our footsteps. I walked ahead, my vision making better use of the tiny rays of moonlight between various leaves. Gabe followed closely, slipping once. I turned and grabbed his elbow, steadying him. His eyes widened, and I smiled before I realized he wouldn't really see it.

"Good?" I let go of his arm, keeping my hand at the ready, just in case.

He looked down at his arm in awe. "The morning after you fed me your blood, I could see Harper in the dark. Every detail, just not the colors. Is that what it's like for you?"

"Pretty much." I shrugged, still not really used to being around people who couldn't.

"Huh." His brows drew together, and he walked again, his steps more cautious this time. "What else?"

"Let's see. I'm loads stronger and faster. All the obvious stuff you've seen. And..." I drew the word out. Alex was right. Our little adventure last night had proved that. "I'm a lot harder to kill than you."

"I kind of noticed."

"No, I mean if someone jams a stake in my heart, I'll not only live. I'll either yank it out and stick up their ass—"

"Nice image," he interrupted.

"*Or* I'll play possum. If I'm in a good mood."

Gabe seemed to be chewing on a thought, the silence stretching a few steps.

"I thought that Joey just hadn't done enough damage. That there was some kind of threshold." His voice trailed off, and he walked in silence another moment. He turned his gaze back to me, his brows knitted together. "So, why does every movie in my car say something about the heart?"

I tried to think of a good way to explain it. It took me a moment. He didn't push me to respond quickly, not like he had in the car last night. Finally, a comparison came to mind.

"If everyone knew ya had a superpower but they weren't certain what it was, how would ya conceal it?" I tilted my head.

His eyes darted back and forth again. His words came slow, like he was working it out as he spoke.

"I'd let them think it was something else. Something that would make their reactions predictable."

"Exactly!" I nodded once. "We realized we couldn't keep our existence a true secret for very long. Instead, we planted a bunch of red herrings in literature."

"Giving us a bunch of bogus ways to kill you." He looked up at the inky sky in wonder. "Like the sun?"

"That one's *kind of* true." I couldn't help my giggle at his look of shock.

"But yesterday—" He squinted at me, like he was trying to find something, "you didn't seem to have any trouble."

"Does my skin *look* like it holds pigment?" I snorted. "We might not burst into flames, but we get a nasty sunburn. It uses a lot of energy continuously healing the damage."

"Huh." He brought his eyes back to the hillside. "Is that why all the massacres happened after sundown?"

"I'm guessin' they wanted all their strength in case the Court caught up."

"And the seizure last night?" He flicked his eyes to me for just a moment.

"Allergic reaction." He gave me a surprised look, and I almost laughed again. "It won't kill me, but silver is a natural allergen."

"But Ivan said I probably saved your life?" His tone was confused.

"Ya did, but not like you're thinking. Silver will drive a vampire mad if it's not removed quickly. Our circulation is a bit odd. When I take in something besides blood, my body begins breaking it down to expel it. Except with silver, for some reason. If it's loose, it runs straight for our brain cells."

"Silver bullets." He shook his head. "That would cost the department a fortune."

"It's not even common for vampires to carry it. Joey came to that campus expectin' a fight. I'm still not sure how he knew."

"That's a good question. We'll have to work on that." Gabe gave me a hesitant look before he spoke. "So, how do I..."

"Headshot." I pointed between my eyes. "Think of us like zombies in a video game. Aim for anythin' but the brain, we keep comin'."

"Noted." He nodded, looking mildly entertained and sickened.

We finally reached the parking area. A third vehicle sat next to Gabe's. The two people inside caused the large truck to rock. The smell of sweat and loud moans were redundant, but I hardly noticed the ruckus. The flapping plastic of Gabe's back window had halted my steps.

"Gabe..." I tried to keep my tone level. "What happened to Kimberly?"

"Yeah..." He put a hand on the back of his neck, rubbing it as he explained what his captain, and Harper had told him this morning. I groaned.

"Sounds like Joey had a partner." I looked up at the sky in annoyance. Really universe? Really? "Not like this case wasn't already convoluted as it was."

"Well, we still have the 911 calls to listen to and St. Claire's contraband." Gabe gave me a hopeful smile and headed towards the trunk of his car. He pulled his key out and clicked the button to pop the trunk. He pulled out the laptop bag I'd seen earlier and motioned with a hand for me to get in the passenger side.

"Maybe we should discuss this elsewhere." I bobbed my head towards the rocking truck next to him. He turned his attention to the couple and their romantic interlude. His face twisted in annoyance.

"Fine, I know a place about ten minutes into town. It's nothing fancy, but it's private." He tossed the laptop case into the passenger seat and pointed to the road. "We'll go left to get out of here. Think you can follow me?"

"You're not seriously askin' me if my baby can keep up with your clunker." I crossed my arms and gave the flapping plastic a meaningful glance.

I'd have to ask Ivan about the expense. I might not get my coat, but Gabe definitely deserved to get his window fixed.

"Shut up and follow!" He climbed into the car. The cabin light shined on his amusement before he shut the door and it extinguished.

He turned the engine over and pulled out, waiting patiently. I mounted the bike and pulled my helmet from one of the saddlebags. I revved the engine, harder than I needed to. The loud rumble caused the girl in the truck to shriek in fear. I laughed and followed the detective into the city.

CHAPTER 27

GABE

We pulled up the quiet street. I watched the single head-light of her bike die in the rearview mirror before climbing out with the laptop case. A couple teenagers goofed off in the garage light of their driveway to my left and a few men talked in low tones on a porch several houses to my right, their cigarettes glowing like red cherries in the late hour. The kids waved at me enthusiastically, and I gave a polite little wave back.

"This your home?" Lily came to stand next to me, her accent laced with curiosity.

"Yes and no. My folks left it to me, but I don't live in it."

"Why not?" She stared at the house in awe. I didn't answer her.

The tiny rambler loomed in the darkness, gray paint and natural stone hiding their warm hues in the deep night. The French windows and doors were dark, except for the light I had left on in one bedroom. It wasn't a high-tech security system, but I figured it might discourage the occasional break-in. I walked forward and thumbed through my keys.

I'd thought about taking Lily to my apartment for our little chat. It was closer, but the place was so small, and the insulation was awful. Plus, I wasn't really sure I wanted her to know where I lived. We could have gone back to her place, but I was fairly certain I would get the stink-eye from at least two people if we did. We had too much to go over and had lost enough time. I didn't need any more distractions. Of course, the memories here might provide a new set of them anyway.

I found the right key and opened the door. It squeaked a little, and I reminded myself to pick up some WD-40 for the hinges. I flipped the lights of the entryway and kicked my shoes onto the entrance rug. My feet turned to ice as my socks met the ceramic tile.

"Um, bathroom." She pointed at her face, and I grimaced.

The lines of red clung to her chin, eyelashes, and even dripped off her nose. Thick smears covered her cheeks from when she'd tried to wipe them off. She looked like she killed someone.

Great mental image.

"On the left." I pointed down the carpeted hall.

"Thanks." She disappeared and the water rushed through the pipes for just a few minutes before she returned rubbing her arms and shivering as she kicked her boots off. "Okay, I'm surprised ya keep the place at all if this is as warm as it gets."

I walked in a few extra steps and tapped the screen of the thermostat. It lit up, a faint blue screen telling me the internal temperature.

"It's fifty-four degrees." I turned the temperature to seventy as I spoke, "Considering your core temperature, it can't be that bad."

"That is such a male response." She gave me an annoyed look and walked around. Her footfalls turned nearly silently as her feet exchanged tile for carpet again. She walked past the dual couches, her hand running across the worn leather. She lifted her hand away and rubbed her fingers together before giving me an odd look. "Do ya hire a maid service?"

I shook my head, and she nodded in thought before continuing her surveillance of the room. She looked at the large oak shelves, one lined with several books and the other holding a few films before more books. A big screen sat between the two shelves. She walked over and stood in front of the first shelf, her eyes scanning the spines for a moment.

Lily raised a hand like she was going to touch a novel, but drew it back immediately. I looked past her, not even needing to read the title to know which one she'd been considering. My mother's copy of *The Adventures of Sherlock Holmes* was so worn, I could barely make out an *S* on the spine. Lily tossed me an apologetic look before turning her attention to the second shelf. Her brows rose slightly as her eyes scanned the titles.

"Was your mum into nonfiction as well?"

"No, those are my dad's. He loved history. He picked those up after Mom passed. Said it just didn't feel right not seeing new books in the house." I walked over and scanned the titles of several heavy textbooks. Lily's eyes drilled a hole into my head, and I saw her worrying her lower lip with her flat teeth. I smile sadly. "Just ask."

"Ya don't want me to." She shook her head a little.

"You didn't want to tell me about Isaac." I shrugged and kept my eyes ahead. "Fair is fair."

"How?" She left the question at the single word.

"Brain tumor took my mom." I turned my eyes to the first bookshelf, the one littered with fantasy, mystery, and romances alike. "About five years ago. She saw me graduate from the academy right before she was diagnosed. We had to read to her at the end. Us and the nurses."

"Oh." Lily made a surprised little gasp. I turned my attention to her, my brows meeting in the middle. She swallowed a few times before speaking. "I'm so self-centered. I just assumed ya joined the police force because of us."

"You're not far off. I joined the VPB because of him." I bobbed my head to the bookcase in front of me. "We were at the outlet mall during the massacre."

"Oh, God." Lily placed a hand in front of her mouth, like she tried to hold in her horror.

"Yep." I nodded. "I didn't even have enough of him to bury."

"No wonder ya hate us." She stared at her feet.

I debated telling her that I was having trouble mustering up any hate. Especially after tonight. I didn't know what the deal was, but hate wasn't what I distinctly felt. God knew I'd been trying.

"We have work to do." I held up the case, grateful for the easy change of subject. "Let's load this up."

I turned and walked around the sofa, stepping back onto the tile and walking into the kitchen. I used my free hand to switch the light on and laid the case on the table. Then I started digging out the power cord and wireless mouse.

Lily surveyed the oak table and matching chairs before walking around the room and eyeing the marble counters and stainless-steel appliances. She approached the task with the same intense stare as the living room. I wasn't sure why. I kept the place spotless.

She finally took a seat next to where I was setting up, tossing her leather coat over the curved back of one chair. I placed the pile of DVDs and a thumb drive to the side while the device powered up, the soft fan the only sound aside from the quiet thumps as I laid the evidence out.

"Tech put the calls on the USB." I motioned to the thumb drive. She reached over and picked it up, twisting it in her hand.

"God, technology is incredible." There was more than a note of awe in her statement. I paused in my setup.

"It's a memory stick, not a lost artifact."

"Please remember I'm almost two hundred years old." She put the thumb drive back down and looked at me. "I didn't even see a car until after I immigrated and it wasn't immediate. Ya can't understand the difference if ya haven't lived it. This thumb drive, it's one more symbol of how far we've come. How far we're goin'."

She looked in wonder at the tiny piece of plastic, seeing something I just wasn't. I let out a soft chuckle at the childlike delight in her eyes.

"Are all vampires so fascinated with technology?"

"Nope." She snapped out of her reverence and smiled up at me. "A lot of the older ones don't do well with it, especially if they don't keep up with the constant changes. The Court had to start offerin' computer classes."

"Wait, you're telling me the mighty creatures of the night are like my grandmother with a cell phone?" I finally sat down.

"Essentially, yes. Except, your granny probably doesn't have hundreds of years of experience doin' math in her head instead of using a calculator. Or a whole eternity ahead of her to keep up with the latest and greatest. Some of us just don't feel like dealin' with it."

"Not you, though?"

"Ya kiddin' me?" She snorted. "I haven't had to accept a check in over ten years. That helmet ya keep sneerin' at, it has Bluetooth so my passenger and I can talk when we're on the bike together. It's wonderful."

"I guess it kind of is." I snickered and picked the thumb drive up, popping it into the side of the computer. "Let's use the modern wonders to figure this out, shall we?"

"Yes, let's. Ya got some gloves?" She nodded towards the stack of DVDs. "I don't want my fingerprints on those. Not after how your captain was acting."

"What do you mean?"

Captain Murphy was usually very good with interviews. I couldn't imagine what he could have done to make Lily's tone drop like it was.

"I went through a lot of effort to make my hands look badly injured. Wrapped them up and applied fake blood." She wiggled her fingers. The only thing on them now was the remnants of something in blue ink. "Your captain tried to shake my hand then almost made me open the door to the interview room for myself."

"He suspected something." Shit, that wasn't good. That man didn't give up on any hunch he had. "It can't be about your species, though. The compulsion took care of that."

"It seemed to, but there are workarounds. Take ya, for example. Impervious to compulsion naturally. Though that's exceedingly rare."

"How rare?"

"I know of one more person like you." She shrugged. "Then, of course, there are the Renfields and donors."

"What about them?"

"Well, once ya give a human vampire blood, they can't be mesmerized for weeks. Sometimes months. Only the compulsions they were already given beforehand would stick. Anything new would slide right off."

"I kind of doubt Captain Murphy has a tap of vampire blood at his disposal," I mused.

"Agreed, but he does suspect something about me. Watch it be my luck that he's like you." Lily gave a sardonic smile. "So, gloves?"

I reached into my pocket and drew out a set. She gave me a quizzical look as she took them.

"What?"

"Just an odd place to keep them."

"I need them a lot for work. This way I never have to run out to the car for them. Where do you keep them?"

"I keep a box in my saddlebags, just in case."

"Fat lot of good that's doing you now."

"Fair enough." She pulled on the gloves, but instead of reaching for the stack of movies, she reached into her pocket and pulled out a gallon-sized Ziploc bag. Kimberly Ashland's burner phones thumped on the table as she set them down.

"Took me forever to find a charger that would work for these things."

"I don't doubt it." I eyed the ancient flip phones. "Anything useful?"

"I haven't looked yet." Lily shrugged as I gave her scrutinizing look. "Between yer captain callin' me in and findin' the charger, I hardly had time. Then you came over in a huff, and I got a bit distracted."

She gave me a pointed look. I shook my head and reached across the table for the phones.

"You take the laptop. I've got the calls pulled up, but I've listened to them already. Should be some headphones in the case."

She reached over and fished through the pockets of the case before producing the plastic headset. She inspected the buds, probably checking for old earwax. Satisfied, she popped the tiny buds in and listened.

Meanwhile, I went through the phones. The first of four had one text, someone looking for a hookup and wondering what was up with the evacuation. I took down the number and moved on to the next phone. The second and third had nothing on them, not even a contact. She probably hadn't switched to them yet.

Lily started clicking with the mouse rapidly, and I noticed she was replaying a section of the last call. It was the shortest one, she'd be done soon. I opened the fourth phone, finding a new voicemail from yesterday and several texts. I had just finished reading the texts and was debating what to do about the voicemail password when Lily hissed. She tore the headset away from her head.

"That little shit!"

"What?" I'd listened to those calls several times. There was nothing special about them. Lily practically shoved the earbuds towards me.

"Listen to the voice."

"911, what's your emergency?" The operator toned.

"I live in Rockwood." The woman's voice was soft and familiar. Of course, it was familiar. I'd listened to these calls a few times, trying to pick up anything odd. I'd even had tech enhance the backgrounds. All they found were traffic noises and the faint chime of a store door opening. Considering each call traced back to a payphone at various Rockwood gas stations, none of those noises were exactly helpful.

I gave Lily a puzzled look, and she held up a single finger, telling me to wait.

"Yes, ma'am, and what's happening in Rockwood?"

"I think we have vampires. People are talking and someone was plucked right off the streets."

"Who was taken, ma'am?"

"You should really send someone." God, that voice was familiar. Lily was looking at me expectantly, and I listened closer. Where had I heard it?

"Who was taken, ma'am?" The operator's voice was less patient.

"They can take any of us. Children for example."

My blood froze. I remembered the short Hispanic vampire in teal scrubs. She'd told me how the Court had wronged her. Lily nodded once.

"Anna."

CHAPTER 28

LILY

"**F**uck!" Gabe tossed the headphones away from him, glaring at the monitor. "She was right there, and I didn't even notice. I've listened to this call how many times, and I didn't even notice!"

"You?" I snorted. "I've known that woman longer than you've been alive!"

"So, what do we do? Report her to your superiors? Have them take her in for questioning? Or do we have the VPB take her in?"

"I think we should report her to the Court, but I don't think we should bring her in." I looked at the monitor, worrying my bottom lip as I thought. "Not yet anyway."

"Why not?" Gabe looked surprised.

"That woman falsified records for us this mornin' and gave me one of my earlier leads in this case. If she's workin' for the bad guys, she's bein' awfully helpful."

Gabe leaned back in his chair, his eyes moving back and forth like he was reading the air again. "You think she's playing both sides."

I nodded. "Anna has never let an opportunity pass her by, but she doesn't like big risks."

"What about the donor she forced to have sex with her?"

"She was younger and probably saw that as low risk. " I snorted. "She'd implanted a command before we'd given the donor blood. Donors are kept clean of vampire blood for at least the first two years, in case they decide they want to return to their old lives."

"That's messed up." Gabe's face wrinkled in disgust. "Leaves people open to being used."

"True, and obviously it does happen. But the punishments are incredibly severe, and we can usually erase the memory. That's not to say everythin's all better, but it happens so rarely." I spun one of the DVDs, giving my hands something to do. "It was a twisted form of luck that Anna hadn't told the man to forget what was happenin'. She only instructed him not to tell anyone and to do what she said. His friends noticed some odd behavior, like taking long showers or throwin' up after every time he fed Anna. We pieced it together while I was checkin' to see if she qualified for a personal donor."

Gabe looked at the laptop, his face turning shades of green and red interchangeably, like his body couldn't choose between revulsion or rage. I waited.

"What did you do with the man?"

"He and his friends were weaned off the blood, their memories of the events were erased, and we assigned them to a new house. It was what they requested."

"Why even feed them blood in the first place?" Gabe's eyes grew dark and curious.

"Because of the added years. It's easier to keep one donor alive for centuries than it is to find new ones every lifetime. Not all of donors take the blood, but most do. Between that and their entire life being paid for, it's usually a win-win situation."

"Okay. So, Anna took the risk because she didn't expect to be caught. Kind of like now. She's working with the bad guys, who are apparently tangled up with that Elias prick you mentioned. At least according to Kimberly." I nodded, and he pressed on. "So, what if she thought she was caught by Elias's people. Playing for both teams I mean?"

"I like the way you think." I gave the detective a wicked grin. "We can work on the details of that after we go through the rest of this rubbish. Anything interestin' on the burner phones?"

"Not really. I mean there were some texts talking about Joey picking up money or dropping off product on this one." He held up the phone he'd been fiddling with when I'd interrupted him. "Includin' one from yesterday morning. Maybe that's why he was there."

"Doubt it. Like I said, it's not common to carry a gun with silver bullets. It's not exactly cheap ammo. Plus, if he was there for a pickup, why'd he have backup? Someone broke Kimberly out of your car after ya left, and we know it wasn't him."

"True," he acknowledged, staring back at the tiny pink phone. "I'm not sure what to do about the passcode on this thing. It's an old voicemail system, the kind with a four-digit pin."

"Not surprisin', considering the phone." I shrugged. "Could yer tech team sort it out?"

"You want me to hand this over as evidence?" Gabe's eyebrows both raised a fraction.

"Why not? Kimberly is already written on record as yer suspect. May as well use the resources available. One of my roommates could toy with it, but ya could use the lead at work more."

"Okay then." He stilled sounded a little surprised, but he put the phone back in the Ziploc bag and turned his attention to the next task, handing me one of the DVD cases. I flipped the case over in my hand, reading the back of *The Lost Boys*.

"What is with all the old technology? First, with the flip phones. Now we have a pile of DVDs, not one Blu-ray to be found among them."

"Yeah I was starting to wonder about that too, but something you just said kind of made sense of this." Gabe held up the case for *Blade*. "What if the vampire running the show is one of the ones you mentioned, the ones who don't keep up with times very well? I mean, to me this is practically prehistoric. You can't even buy these new anymore. But to some of you, these are still a fairly new invention."

I worried my lip. Possible, but it still left one question. "Ya got these from the kid, though, right? These were Adrian's. He wasn't even twenty. He had to have grown up with the newer stuff. Why would he bother with these?"

"His mom said he was growing enamored with vampires. Probably wanted to be one. This stuff—" Gabe gave the DVD a little shake for emphasis, "isn't even being manufactured anymore. Sure there are some older Blu-rays of these before you guys came out, but the police confiscated every copy in stores and on shelves once they were banned. I bet our vampire offered Adrian these as a form of payment."

"But then, that still leaves two more questions." I looked at the stack of movies sadly.

"What got Adrian killed and why did the vampires draw us out to him?" Gabe nodded.

"Okay, three then." I blew out a breath. "What got Adrian killed, why was he left out, *and* how does this tie into Elias?"

We sorted through the stack of DVDs, even popping a few into the laptop. Luckily, they all played, but they were exactly as they appeared. No hidden messages or secret files in plain sight, just a stack of movies ranging from decent to downright awful. I'd really wanted to keep the copy of *Buffy the Vampire Slayer*. My copy was scratched beyond watching, and I didn't want to ask Darren to download it.

"It's just not the same!" I pleaded.

Gabe snorted.

"Tell you what, if I come across another copy in the future, I'll try to sneak it over to you *before* it's been logged into evidence. As it stands—" he plucked the 90s cult classic from my hands, "this is already on file."

"You're no fun." I glared before something clicked into place. "Wait, in the future?"

"Yeah." He shrugged and piled everything back into his laptop case. "From the sounds of it, we might be working together quite a bit."

"You're takin' the queen's offer?" I couldn't help the mild shock in my voice.

"Debating it." He crouched to unplug the power to the computer before standing again. "I can't deny your expertise is useful. I've learned more about vampires in the last three days than the department could teach me in the last year."

I nodded. He wasn't saying he trusted me, but he was at least saying he might be willing to try. Granted, I didn't particularly like the idea of getting drawn away from my business any more than I already was. Still, I'd take it. Or maybe that was my tired mind trying to find a silver lining.

"Time for this vampire to catch a serious nap." I got up, grabbed my jacket from the back of my chair, and stretched.

"Can I ask you something else?" His tone stopped me mid-stretch, and I looked over. His dark green eyes were locked on mine. Dark circles underlined each one. Guess the blood was finally wearing off.

"Sure. I thought that's what tonight was for." I slithered my tongue and grinned. "A little quid pro quo?"

He looked at me confused. "What was that supposed to be?"

"Ya know, Hannibal Lecter." At his expression, I sighed and waved a hand. The drug dealer was funnier than me. That was just sad. Or was the movie that old? "Pretty sure that wasn't your original question. Shoot."

"Why'd you save me?" He looked like he was waiting for a snake to bite.

"What do ya mean?" I tilted my head, confused.

Gabe's eyes searched mine for a long moment, and then he shook his head.

"Never mind."

"No, really. What do ya mean?"

"I mean, you've stuck yourself in this awkward position. And from your queen's tone earlier, she's about to stick you in a worse one."

"What exactly was the alternative?" I was more taken aback by his tone than the line of questioning. If he'd had some anger mixed in, then this would have made perfect sense. But he sounded genuinely confused.

"You could have let me die or killed me when you figured out the problem." Gabe gulped.

I blinked, a little rage boiling under an ocean of sorrow. What had this man seen at that shopping mall? He'd been in the heart of the carnage. I'd only seen the aftermath, the pieces of bodies taken away. Had I seen bits of his father? Maybe, given his earlier description.

I swallowed, trying to think of a way I could say this where he might believe me. I wasn't certain anything I could say would make the point clear, but I had to try.

"Ya didn't do anythin' worthy of a death sentence. Ya just happened to be in the wrong place at the wrong time with that damned immunity." I shrugged. "I don't know what else to tell ya."

We stared, unblinking for several seconds.

"Okay." He nodded and looked away. "I'll see you tomorrow."

CHAPTER 29

GABE

"**W**hat do ya mean?"

I stared at the ceiling of my apartment, watching the fan go 'round in the dark. I popped up and punched my pillow before lying back down and blowing out a breath. I turned over. 5:00 AM flashed, blazing through the dark in garish red from the bedside table. I fought the urge to throw the clock at the wall and turned on my other side. Our last conversation just kept replaying in my head.

"What exactly was the alternative?"

Her response to the original question had said it all, the subsequent responses only served as confirmation. Lily had never even considered the idea of letting me die. Sure, once she'd grabbed my jacket collar, to make a point. But that same strength had kept me from sliding off a rocky path tonight. It was weird, instinctively understanding that she would never hurt me. Not unless I posed an actual threat.

"I don't know what else to tell ya."

"Shut up!" I growled the words into the dark and pulled a pillow over my head, trying to silence the relentless lilt that echoed in my skull. Instead, someone pounded on the wall and repeated the directive from the apartment next door.

I sat up and stared at the opposite wall, running a hand through my hair. Jesus, had I been wrong this whole time? I'd just assumed all vampires were predators. That they all thought of us the way she said this Elias did.

Yet there it was. Evidence to the contrary. Evidence piling up with every new vampire I met. I'd only had one of her people do direct damage to me, and that was to get things moving along when Lily needed medical attention. I swung my legs off the bed and stepped across the studio floor.

The light of the fridge swallowed all the shadows of my apartment, and I dug around for a brown bottle towards the back. I found it and unscrewed the lid before leaning against the counter and taking a long swig.

Five grateful swallows later, I let out a long sigh and wiped my mouth. I wouldn't normally indulge in alcohol as a sleep aid. I'd struggled for months after the massacre to stay away from it, so I could stay sharp and deal with the required therapy for work. Then again, I didn't normally debate if vampires deserved more of a chance. But revelations or not, desk duty or not, I had to work in four hours. My brain needed to shut down. I took another swallow.

———————◆◆◆———————

"Sleep much, pal?" Harper's voice was too cheery. I blinked at him, his dark form a little fuzzy in my sleep-deprived eyes. My stupid brain had only negotiated to give me two hours. Harper held out a large paper cup, too big and expensive to have come from our break room. I took it, grateful for the taste of double red-eye.

"Thanks, I might need a couple more to survive the day." I ran a hand over my face and looked back at the computer screen. Harper hadn't been lying. Four hours in and our inbox was still swelling. Too bad none of the information I was combing through was exactly riveting. I'd almost passed out mid-sentence a few times.

"Late night?" Harper sat in his own chair and used his feet to roll it towards me.

"You could say that. But I got a lot of good questions answered." I paused, debating on if I should tell him this next bit. "I showed her my parents' place."

Harper whistled. "You never even took Michelle there."

"Michelle and I didn't date that long," I reminded him. "Besides, it's not like that with her. We needed a quiet place to do our work and the apartment's insulation wouldn't have given us that."

"And her place, in the middle of nowhere didn't work because..." Harper let the words hang in the air.

"I started a fight when I got there." I shrugged. "Her roommates probably would have been glaring at me all night. I didn't need the distraction."

"Yeah, because you've never learned to ignore anything while you were working." Harper gave the rest of the bullpen a pointed look. There were phones continuously ringing and people talking in various pitches. Occasionally we'd even get someone causing some ruckus when they realized they were under arrest. I hardly noticed anymore. Easier to ignore that racket, especially now that the volume was back to normal.

"That's different."

"Yeah, sure, buddy." Harper leaned back in his seat. "I don't know why you're still paying for the mortgage on that place if you're not going to bother living in it. It's nice for poker, don't get me wrong, but you could get decent money from the sale. Maybe even stop living in that storage shed you call an apartment."

"I know." I just couldn't do it. So, I opted to pay the remaining mortgage, utilities, and the homeowner's insurance, leaving just enough money for the studio apartment that Harper and everyone else mocked. I changed topics. "Tech find anything on the phone?"

"Oh, yeah." Harper snapped his big fingers. "That's what I came to tell you. Tony says he should have the passcode before tonight, and he'll put any voicemails on the same thumb drive as the 911 calls."

"There was only one." I took another sip of the liquid heaven.

"Just repeating what he said." Harper shrugged. "Captain didn't seem happy when he heard who turned the phone over to you."

"Yeah, I didn't think he would be. But it wasn't like I could say I was holding onto it and forgot. Still, the texts had some good spots for us to watch later. Maybe we can get some good info from the PI, do some sting operations later."

"Possible." Harper nodded and sipped his coffee. "So, anything else new?"

"Lots, but we can talk about it later."

I didn't want to risk it in the middle of the station. Harper smiled and looked at his watch.

"Nah, I got no one to interrogate for a little bit. Let's get lunch."

He stood and waited. I smiled and grabbed my coat.

"The usual?"

"Of course." Harper downed his coffee with three audible gulps and shook the empty cup in front of me. "Your turn to buy, right?"

I snorted but followed Harper out of the building.

Hammy's Pizza didn't light their sign, but they kept it clean. The big white and red bubble letters were surrounded by cartoon stars in matching colors. The print contrasted sharply with the polished black metal behind them. The exterior of the building was covered by old red brick on the bottom third and an off-white siding the rest of the way up.

Inside, the floor was concrete and covered with a clean rug that hardly ever saw foot traffic. This place focused on delivery, almost exclusively. The floor had been painted red once, a few bits of the old color peeking out around the edge of the rug and order counter.

I could see clear back to the kitchen from our position in front of the register. A woman was cleaning, twirling the mop like a dance partner and humming lightly to herself. I didn't see any headphones and doubted she was wearing a wireless set. We'd seen her little routine before. Harper struggled not to laugh, and I just smiled. An old bell sounded further back, and someone shouted a greeting from the back entrance.

"I'm back!" An old man walked through the kitchen entrance, started to say something, and then smiled at the scene before him. He shook his head in mild bemusement before looking at the girl. "Hannah?"

"Yeah?" The girl continued her humming but looked up at her boss. He chuckled and pointed at the register.

"You have an audience."

The woman stopped mid-twirl, dropping the mop and stiffening. She turned and her face changed shades, matching closely with her hair after a couple of transitions.

"Oh, dear!" She scrambled over to the register, nearly tripping over the mop she'd discarded. "I'm so sorry."

"Don't be." Harper barked out a big belly laugh. "I enjoy getting a show with my lunch."

"What'll it be, Detectives?" Hannah glared at Harper, but her amber eyes sparkled with amusement. We ordered our usual and Hannah tapped it into her touchscreen register before turning it for me to sign. No way the coffee was an even expense. I thought about grumbling but decided to let it be. He had driven us over here and would be driving back. I used the pad of my finger to scrawl something that didn't even remotely resemble my signature.

Hannah shouted the order back to the old man. David already had his apron on and was putting the mop away. Hannah went behind the counter and pulled out two coke bottles from a mini-fridge, her fairy features lighting up as she handed Harper his. "We'll have that right out, guys."

There were no tables inside the establishment. Only a metal picnic table outside and a lot of big carry-out bags behind the counter. Harper and I walked outside, brushing the dead leaves off the metal table and seating ourselves.

Harper let out a satisfied burp and smiled broadly before he put the pop down. "So, what else is going on?"

"I was made a unique business offer," I explained the queen's offer, covering my words as best I could when people strolled by or when Hannah dropped off our food. By the time I finished, my calzone was half-gone, and my stomach edged against my khaki's top button. Harper chewed his barbecue chicken pizza slowly, relishing each bite with a happy sigh. Tiny flakes of crust and drops of sauce were already littering his facial hair.

"Huh, that is a hell of an offer. What are you thinking?"

"That our solve rate for the authentic cases is pathetic. If it weren't for all the fakes and Renfields, our department probably would have been shut down."

"All true." Harper chewed again, slowly like he was using it for time to think. "But you'd probably end up splitting your time more often. You've been pulling double duty ever since the nightclub burned down. No offense, you look like shit."

"I just didn't get great sleep last night."

"And forgot to shave?" Harper gave my chin a pointed look. "Either that or you're trying to copy me because that five o'clock shadow is at least three days old."

I reached up and felt my chin. The rough hairs curled around my fingers, almost encircling them. Yeah, that was a bit longer than I liked. Had I even looked in the mirror this morning?

"I'll trim it when I get home." I waved him off and boxed my leftovers in the Styrofoam container Hannah had provided.

"And *sleep*. At least take a nap before poker night."

"Oh, shit!" That's right. It was Thursday. "God, I completely forgot."

"Why am I not surprised?"

"You mind hosting? I'd hate to cancel on everyone last minute."

"You're not canceling. Tell Lily you need a night off." I opened my mouth to refuse but Harper cut me off. "You look like shit. I'm thrilled you're finally getting over some of your hang-ups, but you need to do something besides play detective with your little sidekick tonight."

"Hang-ups?" I gawked at my partner, tempted to check him for a temperature. "What hang-ups?"

"Them and us." Harper shrugged. "I've watched you hold your little vendetta for over a year. Ever since we became partners."

"So, what? You're completely fine with what happened at the massacre?" I fought to keep my voice low and level. Mostly because it was Harper I was talking to.

"No, and I didn't lose anyone like you did. I can't even begin to imagine." Harper chewed his pizza, and his words, before he spoke again. "I also kind of agree with Lily. I can't see how they only come in one flavor. We don't."

I stared at Harper like I didn't know him for a moment. "So, why even join the VPB?"

"Because too many cops join the team thinking like you do. They're the enemy. All of them. Truth be told, I almost asked for a new partner a few times, but it became pretty clear you were one of the lesser zealots available." Harper gave me an apologetic grin. I continued to stare, not sure what to say.

"Look, pal." Harper wiped barbecue sauce away from his face, missing the tiny drops in his beard. "You can ask for a new partner if you want. But before you do, I want you to go back to the place in your head that led you to take *Lily* to your childhood home. The same place that had you considering working with her not two minutes ago. For now, let's get back to the precinct. I've got an interview coming up."

I nodded, not sure what to say. Did Harper really believe I would discard him so quickly? That was almost more concerning than being lectured for my supposed prejudices.

Harper tossed his crust in the trash and waved goodbye to Hannah before we headed back to the car. He was right about one thing. I did need a night off.

CHAPTER 30

LILY

"**S**orry for the last-minute cancel." Gabe's voice did sound kind of strained.

"No worries." I tried to sound nonchalant. No reason to add unnecessary guilt. "We got a lot done last night. I'll go talk to Ivan about setting a trap for Anna. Enjoy your game."

"Sounds good. See you later." Gabe disconnected the call, and I pocketed my phone.

"Canceled on you?" Maria stood next to Alex at the cooktop.

"Yup, poker night with his friends." I smiled and shrugged. "Probably for the best. He was looking a little beat last night."

"Yeah, probably." Alex poured the box of noodles into the boiling water like the dry pasta would bite him. Knowing his luck, it might.

"Are ya really still trying?"

"Hey, just because I don't eat doesn't mean he doesn't deserve a nice meal." Alex gave me an embarrassed look. "You know, something candlelit."

"Ah, as opposed to being lit by the entire contents of the oven?" I smiled brightly and Alex glowered at me.

"That wasn't my fault." Alex brought a wooden spoon out of the pot and pointed it at me.

"Oh right!" I threw my hands up in mock surrender. "I forgot, the tenderloins burned themselves."

"Children..." Maria drew the word out and snapped her fingers in front of Alex's face. "Hey! Pay attention or you'll boil the noodles to the side of pot again."

Alex narrowed his eyes at me but turned his attention back to the task at hand.

"Alex, if ya want to sweep Darren off his feet, ya know what he wants." I gave my best friend a sympathetic look. "And it's not fancy dinner with some smelly wax."

"Butt out, Lils." Alex kept his back to me and stirred his noodles. "No offense, but you're the last person I am taking relationship advice from."

I stared, my jaw slightly lax. Wow, that stung. Alex turned back to me, an apology written all over his face. He opened his mouth to speak, but I held up a hand to stop him.

"It's alright." He didn't mean Isaac. He'd never bring that up. "You're right, it's been a while since I was on a date."

"A date?" Maria snorted. "Honey, I love you. But you don't date. The last guy you *saw* was Cyrus, and we all know how that's turning out."

"As Alex so eloquently put it, butt out."

I slid off my barstool and headed towards the back of the house. I didn't need reminders of my infamous one-night stand with Cyrus. One stupid slip up fifty years ago and my friends acted as if it was the only evidence of any relationship.

I turned and headed towards the back of the house, stopping to knock on a thick door.

"Enter." Darren's low voice.

I turned the knob and walked into his lair. Several lights and wires greeted me, the guts of a seriously advanced computer plastered to one wall like some kind of technological mosaic. Two cords led away from the device, one to the power outlet and the other to the four monitors that lit the room brilliantly.

Three average ones sat on the corner of Darren's desk and a large TV hung overheard.

The TV was playing one of the Lethal Weapons movies, maybe the third one. Mel Gibson wasn't sporting a mullet. I could hear the audio blasting through Darren's fancy headset. No wonder he kept the device on his shoulders instead of over his actual ears.

Darren sat at his glass desk, tapping away at his keyboard like a mad pianist. He held up one big finger, his chair not even twirling as he did so.

"Hang on Lils. I'm almost done."

"No worries." I closed the door behind me and walked over to examine the computer on the wall. It looked different from yesterday. I surveyed it in silence until I heard the rapid clicking behind me stop.

"'Sup?"

"Did ya upgrade it? There are more shiny squares and a lot more blue wires."

"Seriously? You're the brilliant woman who caught me hacking the Courts, but you still can't remember those are *memory*." Darren took a long swig from a *Mountain Dew* can and shook his head. I shrugged.

"I followed your paper trail and bank accounts. Not my fault ya didn't think to change them after ya bought the gear." I gave him a smug smile. "Why do ya keep this on the wall anyway? I know it's not meant to be art."

"In case I need to purge it. Computer cases can get in the way when you're trying to beat the clock." Darren smiled. "I thought I was going to uncover a government conspiracy. Instead, I get you and uncover that vampires exist."

"Hey, ya got it pretty comfy." I smiled over my shoulder. "Besides, how else would ya have met Alex?"

"True." Darren raised the can in cheers and drank again. "By the way, did I hear correctly? The cop's immune, too."

"Yup."

"Wow." Darren stared at the wall in wonder, not even seeing his computer parts. "Wonder what causes the immunity. Maybe some hidden vampire genes or something?"

"Who knows." I shrugged. "Hey, did ya finish runnin' that check I asked for?"

"Yeah. You're not gonna like it." Darren turned back to the three monitors and began typing again. Mel Gibson's face disappeared from the overhead screen and a giant list came up, instantly scrolling. It was far too long.

"I only asked for the ones from Portland."

"This is it." I stared at Darren in shock, and he winced. "Told ya you wouldn't like it."

"*All* of these people?" I kept staring but waved a hand at the overhead monitor. "All of them meet the criteria?'

"Yeah." Darren nodded. "Each one of these names was admitted to a hospital in the last couple weeks and either had notes about vampire blood explicitly in their chart or their charts show medication you would give someone who was coming down from a blood high."

"Shit." I looked back up at the list with a fascinated sort of horror. There were at least a hundred names on it. "Have ya sent this to Ivan?"

"Not yet, I only got it back a few minutes ago. I hadn't double-checked it yet."

"Send it to him. Now."

"Sorry it wasn't better news."

"Not your fault. Thanks for finding it for me." I squeezed his big shoulder and left the room, closing the door softly behind me. Shit, shit, shit.

"Hey, Lils..." Alex caught me as I was pulling the phone from my pocket and dialing Ivan.

"Not now." I held up a hand to silence him.

"What happened?" Alex's face contorted from apology to worry in a flash. I waved him off.

"Kid?" Ivan's thick accent filled my ears.

"Boss." I fled up the stairs, taking them two at a time. "Check your email. We've got a serious problem."

I heard a little tapping, nowhere near the speed of Darren's keystrokes. Granny with a cell phone was right. Ivan must have finally found the document. His next words were practically a growl.

"Tell me this is not what I think it is."

"Can't do that." I reached my bedroom and used my free hand to dig through my shoe pile, searching for my boots. "At least a couple hundred people have been treated in local hospitals in the last month. All of them have the same fluids that Anna gave Adrian and the others after they showed up. This shit is out of control."

We'd thought we caught this case in the beginning stages. Catching the problem early and nipping it in the bud. We were way off.

"How quick can you get over here?"

"Faster if ya let me hang up now."

The line disconnected with a sudden click. An answer as much as I needed. I placed the phone on the floor next to me and stuck my whole body into the closest, continuing the dig for my boots. I needed to buy a damn shoe rack.

Abba's "Dancing Queen" played from the tiny speaker of my phone, and I froze with one boot in hand.

The chorus played as I pulled my head out of the closet and stared at my phone for a moment before snatching it up. Sure enough, *Dance Partner* lit my caller ID. I pressed my thumb to the screen and swiped left to answer.

"Hello?" I donned the bad sorority voice, just in case.

"You can stop that, dearie." Just as cheery as the voicemail had been. "No need to play games now."

"Fine." I let my tone turn deadpan. "What do ya want?"

"Oh, it's not what I want." The voice let out a chuckle that was part purr and part cackle. My skin tried to crawl away from the sound. I heard the phone shift around a bit, like it was being handed to someone new.

"Goth girl?" The new voice was hoarse, like the owner hadn't seen water in days. My stomach sank. I knew that voice. Last time I'd heard it, he'd been calling me baby and making stupid little promises.

"Dean?" I dropped the boot and held the hand up to my lips, the tips shivering. "Is that you?"

"Please." Dean stopped to cough, a pathetic little noise. "Just give them what they want."

The phone shifted again before I could respond, the throaty chuckle returning.

"So, Miss Edwards, do I need to gather your little investigator friend, too?" A loud slap echoed in the background followed by Dean's muffled groan of pain. "Or will this hostage do?"

"The one is fine." I swallowed, picturing Peter Andrews. He was probably on the job right now, making lewd comments about a cheating spouse or their technique. Now I understood why they'd relayed the message through him. "What do ya want?"

Dean was in this mess because of me. I didn't know how they'd found him, but I had to get him out of this.

CHAPTER 31

GABE

A stack of money took up the middle of my dining room table, several bottles covering the oak. Tony tapped the edge of his two cards against the surface. He strummed his fingers on the stack of bills next to him while he reviewed the three lying face up. I rolled my eyes.

"Would you just check already?"

"Fine." Tony gave me an annoyed look, his sand-colored brows bending as he placed his cards on the table and slip them towards the middle. "I fold."

Harper barked out a single laugh. He shook his head and took a long swallow of his beer while he looked at his own hand. He considered it briefly and placed the set face down and tapped the table twice.

"Check."

"Oh, come now, Harper." Sean Murphy leaned forward, his jeans and T-shirt making him appear like a rogue when compared with his expensive suits at work.

"Now, now." I grinned. "No need to pressure him, Captain."

"I'll stop pressuring him when you stop calling me that during poker night." The captain smiled at me, displaying every perfect tooth in his mouth. I gave his confident posture an assessing glance and looked back at my hand. I nodded once and put the two cards on the table, picking up my own stack of ones to count.

"I raise." I tossed the bills into the middle. "Five."

Sean Murphy looked at me and my cards interchangeably for a moment, laying his cards down to count out his own stack.

"Call."

"Hey, Gabe." Tony got up, grabbing something from the fridge.

"Hmm." The captain was dealing the turn, and I was debating my chances as Tony spoke.

"Harper tell you about the CDs?" Tony was short, maybe a little five feet tall, and pretty skinny. The little tech guy plunked back down, looking like a mouse among men. He was a nice guy and easy to win a few bucks off. Good poker company.

"Raise." I added a dollar to the middle "What CDs?"

"Now, now." Captain Murphy placed the fifth card down. "No talking shop at the table."

"It is one of the rules." Harper raised his beer. "Also, I fold."

"Still, the CDs were really interesting!" Tony's soft voice raised an octave with excitement.

"What could be so interesting about some CDs?" Damn, I'd been hoping for another six on the river. Oh well, I could still make this work. I tossed in another bill. "I raise again."

"I see your one and raise you three." Captain Murphy tossed four dollars into the middle of the table.

"It's not the CDs, it's what's on them! They weren't music. We found them in your suspect's home, the college girl."

"Huh?" I stopped considering the cards and looked at Tony. "What about Kimberly?"

"Hey, shop talk." Harper grabbed a potato chip from his bag and tossed it at my head. It bounced off me harmlessly, and I ignored it.

"What about her?"

"The CDs were filled with files. First one had a bunch of articles from cases around the country." Tony sounded excited now. "I mean there's some in there about the recent scare on the drugs. She'd even highlighted spots about public reactions."

"That's it?" Didn't sound like anything to get excited about. The girl had been obsessed with vampires. Or at least idolizing them. Her reactions had given that away. Of course, Tony hadn't been there.

"No, they were also missing-persons cases and maps. Someone had circled a few cities on the maps with a paint application, using a variety of colors. And the missing person's fliers are old."

"How old?"

"Before the massacre." Tony looked triumphant and sad. "Some were over ten years old but everyone I found on that list was either found dead well before the massacre or is still missing."

I drew my eyebrows together. Okay, that was noteworthy.

"Anything else?"

"Yeah, the girl had a third set of files, these were new missing person cases after the massacre, but none of those people have turned up."

"Hey, Collins!" Captain Murphy gave me a light punch to one shoulder. "You gonna call or what?"

"Oh, yeah. Sorry, Captain." I tossed in five bills and placed my hand face up. "Two pair, you?"

"Ha! Full house!" Captain Murphy placed his hand out like a fancy fan. He reached over and pulled the money towards him. "Tony keep me up to date on those files. But now gentlemen, I say we call it a night."

"Of course, you do." Harper back the large stack of ones in front of the captain a sad look. "You're ahead by forty."

"Don't worry, Harper. Barbara will make sure it goes to good use." Captain Murphy elbowed me. "In other words, I'll never see a dime after I bring it home."

I smiled but my mind was still on what Tony had said. Using the CDs for storage made sense, giving the other weird tech Lily and I had noted last night. But the files. That puzzle piece just seemed out of place with everything else. I couldn't see how or where it fit. I got up and cleared my side of the table of a few beer bottles and grease-soaked paper plates. The left-over calzone had been great, even microwaved.

"Well, thanks for coming guys. Captain, always nice to be robbed by my boss."

"Always a pleasure to rob you." Sean Murphy smiled, his bronze skin spreading for those perfect teeth. The captain stood and stretched. Tony and Harper followed suit before clearing their own trash. The table was cleaned and my guests started shuffling out, the captain was the first to go as always.

"Oh, yeah." Tony stopped and dug into the pocket of his baggy jeans before handing me a thumb drive. "I got the voicemails added for you."

"Wait, there was more than one? When was the second one left?"

"No, there were three. The last two were left early this morning, like around six. I haven't listened to them yet, but I know how you like to look into things ASAP. I'll start tearing apart the background in the morning."

With that Tony left, and I stared at Harper.

"Yeah, yeah. I'll load the computer," he groaned. "You really need to develop an off switch, buddy."

"I know." I headed back into the kitchen and pulled two more bottles from the fridge. "Tell you what, if it's not mind-altering, I'll let it be and deal with it tomorrow."

"Define mind-altering." Harper curved his lips in a knowing smile and raised one brow.

"I think I'll wait until I hear the voicemails." I smirked. "We are who we are."

"Yes, we are." Harper raised his bottle and reached in his motorcycle bag. The backpack was black and armored with thick Denier pads, making it harder for any contents to be damaged in an accident. The material matched his gray jacket. He pulled out his tablet, flipped a black keyboard cover open, and powered the device on.

He propped the device on the table and snapped his large fingers. I handed over the USB, and he plugged it into the side of the tablet. He used the mouse pad of the keyboard, his broad hand making the tiny buttons seem even smaller. He opened a *Start* menu and accessed the files.

Two folders were on the USB. One labeled *911* and one *Voicemails and CDs*. Harper double-tapped the mouse while highlighting the ladder and several files appeared on the screen. The first three files were labeled with a date and time, Tony's way of indicating when the voicemail was time-stamped. The rest were names of people or places. There were at least fifty names of people on the screen, and Harper could scroll down a lot farther. I hunched down to look at the screen.

"What the hell is this?"

"No idea, pal." Harper shrugged. "Let's listen to these messages."

He double-clicked the first voice mail. The software opened and the message played.

"Kimba!" a male voice filled my parent's kitchen. He sounded reassured and casual with the simple nickname. Probably Joey, but I couldn't be sure. I'd only heard the guy once, and there had been a fire alarm covering most of what he said. *"Someone's onto us. Don't worry, I'll take care of it. The idiots left a human around to ask questions. Poor asshole's stuck on a loop."*

The recording ended and Harper's broad face scrunched in confusion.

"A loop?"

"Not a clue." I shrugged in return. "I'll ask Lily later. Next."

Harper went back to the folder and double-clicked on the next file. The second recording started.

"Goth girl." The voice was dry and young. Poor kid didn't sound like he was old enough to drink. *"Please, help me. They said to tell you..."*

A loud thump sounded in the background and the dry voice yelped. Harper and I both jumped at the new sound, my hands were balled into fists, the knuckles were turning white.

"Please, I'm doing it." The boy whimpered, his voice a little further away, like he'd pulled the phone away from his mouth to say it. *"They said to tell you if you don't come to them, you're going to need a new dance partner. Please..."*

The voice broke into sobs and the voicemail stopped halfway through the cry. I already had my phone in my hands, dialing her. It rang. And rang. And rang. God, was she in the shower? She never took this long to answer. Three more rings and a beep.

"You've reached Lily Edwards with Strictly Confidential Investigations." Lily's voice was calm and slow, lacking the usual energy. Like she was tired when she'd made the recording. *"I am currently out of the office for the foreseeable future. If ya need help, call Peter Andrews. He can be reached at..."*

She rattled off the number twice, and I waited for the beep to sound.

"Lily, we got the voicemails from that burner phone. You need to hear this. Call me back." I hit the end icon and looked at the tablet with new horror. "Play the third one."

Harper went back to the folder and double-clicked the third file

"To the assholes holding my phone." It was a woman's voice this time, her voice shaking like a leaf despite the word choice.

I could hear her crying. Kimberly. *"They want me to tell you, this is what happens when you get into their business."*

I heard a soft *thud*, like the phone was being put down. A few soft steps walked away. The new voice, further away this time.

"I'm sorry, child. But I need the boy to lure her in." The new voice was more reassured than Kimberly and older. Much older. But it didn't shake. I looked up at Harper, our faces mirroring one another. Our eyes were wide as realization struck. *"You're dying for the cause, my dear. Your pain will prevent the suffering of others going forward."*

"I understand." Kimberly didn't sound like she understood anything. Her voice stopped shaking as she spoke, sounded robotic and canned.

A loud smack sounded, and Kimberly's screams were anything but canned. A sharp cry of pain filled the room, followed by another, and another. They came like an awful tidal wave, with no end in sight. Ugly rending sounds filled the few gaps between screams. My stomach curled in on itself.

I stood and grabbed my phone to dial again. No shower was more important than this. Her phone rang to voicemail again, and I swore. Where was she? I dialed again. It rang again and again but only that business tone of hers ever responded. I tried again, and someone picked up on the third ring.

"Hello?" The voice was unfamiliar. I pulled the phone away from my ear, Lily's contact info blinked back at me with the ongoing call.

"This is Detective Collins of the Portland VPB. To whom am I speaking?"

"Whoa, whoa, man." The voice sounded rattled. "I didn't steal this phone or nothing. I just found it."

I stopped pacing and stared at Harper. "Where did you find this phone?"

CHAPTER 32

LILY

The night was dark and my ride felt like it took years. Rain pattered against my helmet and visor, trying to obscure my vision and hearing. The cold of the evening sank right through my hoodie and into my bones. Maybe I should have borrowed Alex's jacket. It wasn't like he would need it.

I turned my motorcycle down Washington Street and parked it several houses away from my destination. I got off the bike and ran a hand over my Harley. I really hoped no one screwed with her. I didn't want to bring her into this side of town, but the guys would need the car and it would have been suspicious if I'd taken an Uber. I was supposed to be going to Court, after all.

I left my helmet on as I walked down the streets. It was a bit conspicuous and it wasn't bulletproof, but it was better than nothing. The concrete was cracked everywhere, my boots touching the splits in several places as I went. Would the maintenance of this area to become a priority or would it always be a ghetto? I might never know. I passed several decrepit ramblers before a voice halted my steps.

"Stop there." The voice sounded ancient but didn't shake like the typical elderly would. I held my hands up and looked in the direction of the voice. I almost snorted, my vampire vision making quick work of the night around me.

"So, tell me, do ya use the old tech to keep up with appearances or is your brain just stuck in the nineties?" I was worried my snark would be muffled by the helmet and drizzle of rain. That was until a loud crack broke through the patter of droplets against my helmet. I cried out as sharp, hot pain sliced through my knee. I collapsed to the sidewalk.

"Any more smart comments?" The cheery old bat walked towards me, a .38 pointed at Dean's skull as she dragged him along. The boy didn't struggle. He barely moved his limbs. His jaw was slack from the lack of thought.

"Can you stand?" She used the gun to indicate my leg. I tried and fell to the ground instantly. I reached to cradle my wounded leg until she spoke again. "Ah, ah you little hussy. You think I don't know what you keep in those shoes. Anna told me all about your little weapon stash."

"Hussy?" I smiled despite the pain. "There's one I haven't heard in a while."

"Remove the helmet." She used one thumb to cock back the hammer, the tiny click blending in with the sound of rain surrounding us. I nodded once and reach up and pulled my kitty helmet off, slowly trying to think of any way out of this.

I placed it on the ground before me and held my hands up. Rain slicked my scalp, plastering my hair to my face and neck. Little droplets clung to my eyelashes and I fought the urge to blink them away.

"Remove the boots." The old woman's deep brown eyes were filled with menace as she stared at my still bleeding knee. "Quickly now. Someone will have heard that shot."

"This is Rockwood." I leaned on my uninjured knee and removed my motorcycle boot, laying it next to my helmet. I winced as I leaned on the bleeding knee, the rain on the concrete clouding with red while I removed the other. "We both know no one's coming to my aide."

"Smart girl." She gave me a smile that made me think of a deranged Betty Crocker. "Of course, if you were really smart you wouldn't have come. But you Court types are awfully sentimental about the livestock. It's like you're trying to go vegan or something."

"If ya had a heart, you'd get it. Since ya obviously ripped that out long ago, I won't bother explaining it to ya, you ancient old biddy."

Okay, not my best insult, but it wiped that stupid smile off her face.

"Enough chatter. Drop your phone in the boots."

I did so.

"Good, the rain should kill it." She smiled triumphantly. "Get in the house, quickly."

"If ya wanted it quick you shouldn't have shot me with silver." I pointed at the gaping hole where my knee should be. It looked like raw hamburger wrapped in jeans, bits of bone splintering from where my kneecap used to be.

"If you want this boy to live, you'll move it!" She indicated the screen door behind me. I stood, gasping at the new pain. I limped up the walkway, favoring my right leg. My socks slapped against the ground, unable to absorb any more moisture. I walked past the old lady, and she shoved the .38 into the small of my back. "Faster."

I yelped as I tried to move faster on the mangled leg. It would heal once I got the bullet out. That would be difficult if she stuck a bullet in my spine and screwed up the nerves that told my brain how to move my arms. I really needed the universe to throw me a bone.

I reached out and pulled the screen door open with one hand. The floral decor was almost enough to make me dry heave. The couch, recliner, doilies, and even the teacups were all covered in one form of flower pattern or another.

It was a shock the coffee table was merely ornate, except for what was on it. Those restraints weren't a mere conversation piece. My wet socks sank into the thick shag of the rug, making little squishy sounds.

"Sit." The old lady stuck the gun in my back again, and I move forward, towards the sofa. "No, the chair."

"Bitch." I shuffled the extra steps, wincing at the extra two feet she just insisted on. I turned and sat, almost letting out a grateful sigh as pressure eased off my leg. I kept my hands raised.

"Put the manacles on."

I gave the heavy links a dubious glare. These weren't like Gabe's cuffs. They wouldn't snap under tiny little tug. These were heavy-duty steel, the insides lined with bright silver barbs that would dig into my flesh and make it almost impossible for me to pull free. They were designed to bleed me and sap my strength simultaneously. I'd seen Cyrus put my dance-club captives in a set just like them for transport. Their skin had bubbled at the instant contact and they'd screamed so loud we had to gag them both. They wouldn't poison my brain terribly fast but every second would be hell. I gulped.

"Now!" Betty Crocker yelled, and I jumped. I locked my eyes on Dean and reminded myself why I was here.

He looked so gaunt, covered in fang marks up and down each limb. His skin was filthy, in several shades of brown and grey and his clothes were torn. I'd seen him less than a week ago. She'd done all this that fast.

I reached out towards the table, each second passing like a long minute.

The metal was gold and I was a little grateful the outside was pure steel. I wouldn't feel the bite of the rash until those barbs dug into each wrist. Not that it was going to tickle. The thick cuffs scraped the lacquer on the table as I slid them towards me. "How'd ya even find that poor kid?"

"You forgot to set a timer." Betty Crocker smiled and I gave her a confused look. She pointed at the cuffs with the barrel of her gun. "Keep going."

I looked at the cuffs and gulped again. No more stalling. I slapped one metal loop closed, the manacle snapping shut. My scream was instant; I couldn't stop it. Tears welled in my eyes and overflowed onto my cheeks. It was like someone had sliced me open and poured lava in the wounds.

"The other one. Now!"

"What did ya mean, timer?" My lip quivered as I grabbed the other open manacle. My hands shook and the chain rattled. I worked the cuff slowly trying to think of anything that might help this situation.

"Stop stalling and put the cuffs on!" She poked Dean's head with the gun.

I slapped it over my other wrist. White-hot pain sliced into me again, the barbs pulling my tendons part and trails of red pooling on both wrists and beginning to trail down each arm. The right was worse than the left, but not by much. I stared at the little rivers in horror. One thing the lore almost always got right; blood was our strength and mine was staining her hideous furniture.

"There, was that so hard?"

I glared at her, shivering in anger, pain, and actual chill brought on by my soaked clothes.

"As for your question, you apparently asked this kid to help you interrogate my son."

I looked at Betty Crocker more carefully, blinking away some of the pain to take in the details. The only vampire I'd involved Dean with was Joey. Joey had been white as bone. This woman's skin was the color of year-old chocolate. Not an actual family relation then; must have been Joey's sire.

She shook Dean, his jaw remained slack. The front of his pants soaked and the air mixed with the smell of fresh urine with the metallic scent of blood.

Jesus.

She must have instructed him to be compliant, but she hadn't bothered to tell him not to be scared. Poor kid. He was seeing everything going on in front of him but couldn't react. He had to be silently screaming behind that vacant stare.

"He showed up at a party asking Joey to give him a hook up so he could help the lady in the back relax. Then, the kid got all confused because there was no lady in the back." Betty Crocker snickered. The blood drained from my face and it had nothing to do with the cuffs. "Didn't take long for my kid to figure out what was going on. A vampire had given him a direction but hadn't given him a time limit. Probably the same vampire who'd handed my other two kids over to the Court."

"Oh, God." I stared at Dean, my face pleading. "I'm so sorry. I didn't think. The cops showed up and I completely forgot about ya."

Vampire directives were ongoing unless the human died or the vampire in charge put a time limit on it. Otherwise, our directives to forget what people saw would be lost and we'd have been exposed a long time ago.

A single tear flowed down his cheek.

A second vampire could remove the glamour. These assholes hadn't gone that route. Now Dean was being tormented. All because of my stupidity. I let the tears flow freely. She didn't deserve them, but Dean did.

"I'm sorry." The words were hollow, but they were all I could offer him. I'd done this to him.

"No, you're not." Betty Crocker pointed the gun into Dean's temple, the hammer still pulled back. "But you will be."

I tried to lunge but my injured leg went limp and I fell to the ground. A loud blast filled the room. Tiny bits of skull and brain pelted me right as Dean's limp body sank to the ground. I screamed, half-anguish and half-rage.

"Ya already have me." I rested my head on the carpet and growled, "Ya could have let him go! Ya didn't have to kill him!"

"You didn't have to kill my son." Betty Crocker grabbed my ponytail, using it to pull my entire weight off the ground. I groaned as several roots pulled away from my scalp. Her eyes were lifeless and wide, a look of purpose filling each one. "Now, you're going to tell me where to find the rest of my family."

Great, I was going to die for nothing.

CHAPTER 33

GABE

I stepped out of the passenger seat, slamming the car door and running up the driveway. I didn't even need to ring the doorbell. A kid, maybe thirteen years old, opened the door as my feet hit the patio step.

"I swear I was going to turn it into the police." His voice shook and his face was so pale the few pimples on his chin stuck out like beacons. His mother stood behind him, her arms crossed and her face pinched.

"Don't care." I pulled my badge from my pocket and flashed it. "Detective Collins, Portland VPB. Do I have permission to enter?"

The mother leaned past her son and pushed the screen door open. Heavy steps sounded behind me, and I looked over my shoulder, motioning for Harper to follow. We walked into the house, the state of badly used furniture and dirty carpets unsurprising. This kid was probably planning to hawk the cell phone and anything else he found the moment he saw it. Standard practice on this side of town. I didn't care. Right now, he was my only witness.

"Show me the gear you found with the phone."

"Boy." The woman backhanded her son across the back of his head. The slap was light, just enough to gather the kid's attention. He flinched as she spoke, "What did I tell you about taking things that don't belong to you?"

"It actually might be lucky that he did, ma'am." Harper scraped his shoes and stepped forward in a rush. He stuck out one large hand. "Detective Harper. We believe your son might know where an informant of ours is being held. He might be able to help us save her."

"See mom!" The kid whined, throwing both hands over his scalp protectively. "I might have saved a life."

"You better hope they're right. If they're not, you're grounded 'till you die!" The mother placed both fists on her hips and shook her head. "Well, get what you need from Tommy. If he did steal anything, you feel free to stick his butt in jail for the night."

Tommy's face lost even more color.

"Tommy," I interjected. "What did you find? You said you found a whole bunch of stuff."

"Yeah." Tommy nodded and walked behind the worn couch. "This is all of it."

He came back, holding a set of leather boots and a motorcycle helmet. My heart sank into my stomach at the sight of those fiberglass-kitty-ears. I'd known that he had her stuff. Seeing it was something else entirely.

"Hand me the boots." Harper put out one hand, waggling his fingers in a gimme motion. Tommy handed the boots over, almost dropping the helmet. I held my hands out, and he handed over the helmet. Harper rummaged in the boots, roughly checking the liner. I positioned the helmet under one elbow and held out one hand, palm up.

"Phone."

Tommy jumped like a scared rabbit and dug in his pockets. He pulled out the device and handed it over, screen side up. The phone was sopping wet, even after being in his jeans. Thank God she loved the updated technology. My high school phone would have been fried if it had been half as wet.

The little zombie bear smiled at me, a digital dial pad overlaying his features. She'd taken my advice and put a password on it. I turned to Tommy.

"How'd you unlock this?"

"I didn't, it just let me answer the phone when you called!"

Shit, that's right. I'd called her. I glowered at the phone before pocketing it. I couldn't reach her friends or the court. *Me and my big mouth!*

I turned to Harper. He held one of the boots open for my viewing. A leather stripe lined the inside of the boot, sewn into the inside to hold several throwing knives in place. We'd seen the same setup the first time we'd questioned her. All the loops were empty.

"Did you take those knives?" I barked the question at Tommy and pointed at the boot. His mom yelled at him, and he defended himself, practically crying. I held up my hand, signaling for silence as best I could. "Ma'am, let him answer. It's important. Tommy, did you take those knives?"

"I'm sorry, they looked like they were worth a lot." The kid's eyes were wide with fear.

Probably because of the look his mother was shooting him. The woman was a volcano ready to blow. He walked back to his place behind the couch and held up two stacks of throwing knives. The mother glared at her son. I nodded at Harper.

"Okay, Tommy." Harper smiled, looking merry as ever while he took the knives. "Now where did you find all this stuff?"

"In front of the old woman's place!" Tommy pointed up the street. "It was just piled outside. I swear."

"And how long ago was that?"

"It couldn't have been more than five minutes before you called. I swear."

"Thank you." I bobbed my head and filed out of the house. I pulled out my key fob and popped the trunk of my Toyota. I tossed the helmet and boots in and slammed the cover shut. Harper came out, his heavy steps splashing in the fresh puddles behind me.

"Do we call it in?"

"No. They'll take her down too." After all, that's what I would have done. "It's just us"

"What about their gaze." Harper swallowed. "You're immune, buddy. I'm not."

I gave him a sympathetic look. "I'm not asking you to do this."

Harper nodded and reached into his jacket, taking his gun from the shoulder holster. "Fourteen rounds, one in the chamber."

"Fifteen." I took mine off the gun belt. "No siren."

He nodded, and we both popped magazines out, checked them, and popped them back in.

I walked around him and opened that passenger door before climbing in. Harper took the drivers side. I was more wound up than he was. Harper turned over the engine and pulled a narrow U-turn back up Lincoln. A few houses away, he slowed our pace to that of a crawl and killed the headlights. He parked two houses away. I climbed out and started up the sidewalk.

We got to the lawn. The driveway was barren of any vehicle. Even a motorcycle. The curtains were drawn, two figures making blurring shadows that stretched unnaturally against the folds of fabric. One was kneeling before the other, a long line stretching between the two. The standing party shook what I thought might be someone's hair. Someone cried in anguish. It was her.

Harper and I stopped. I made hand gestures, silently urging Harper to take the back. He was right. I was immune. It would be best if the vampire was focused on me. Harper nodded and moved like a cat despite his broad size.

I watched my partner go for a second before looking back to the building. The screen door was shut, as was the interior.

Shit. It would have been easier if I didn't have to deal with the front door.

I stepped forward, forcing myself to go slow and quiet as Lily screamed obscenities and insults at her attacker. I opened the screen door. It squealed, a low pierce in the silent night. I lifted my gun and aimed towards the standing shadow. The attacker didn't even halt, bringing something down on the kneeling form before them.

I opened the screen door a little further and propped it open with the doorjamb on the bottom. Lily screamed again, and I tried to ignore it as I assessed the door, sizing up the right place to kick. I needed to get this right the first time.

I lifted a leg and shot my foot out. My heel landed next to the doorknob and the wood crunched. The door slammed open with a heavy *thud*, the metal plate flying away. I aimed my gun towards the attacker.

"Police, drop the gun!"

Miss Stafford looked surprised, but only for a moment.

"I told you not to bring him!" She shook Lily by her ponytail. Red was already soaking into her roots. Lily's face was covered in fresh bruises and lacerations. Her hands were low to the ground, large metal restraints covering each blood-soaked wrist. The carpet and chair closest to her were covered in a red pattern, ranging from drops to full splatters. A body lay on the ground, a quarter of the skull missing.

"She didn't bring me. I got your voicemail." I kept the gun level with the old woman's head. "Seems like you don't take it well when your staff messes up."

"I really liked Kimberly." Miss Stafford smiled sadly. "She was going to be my next child."

"Child?" I didn't bother hiding the confusion in my voice.

If I could keep her talking, I might be able to get a shot off before she moved. Lily had dodged my bullet's intended path in the club. I'd barely hit Joey's shoulder the other day, and he hadn't been trying to dodge. Miss Stafford probably had the same abilities. I needed her distracted.

"She considers the ones she sires her children." Lily spat blood, foamy red drops blending with the ruined carpet. "Took it a bit personal when I killed Joey."

"It is personal, you cumbersome girl!" Miss Stafford shook Lily's hair again.

Lily groaned in pain. A single drop of blood ran down her forehead and over the tip of her nose. Miss Stafford smiled, looking like she was baking cookies. She looked at me and aimed the gun at Lily's head.

"I said drop it!" I split my legs into a shooter's stance.

"You drop it or I'll kill her."

"No." I shook my head. "You won't. She's your bargaining chip."

Something clicked behind me and the cold barrel of a gun pressed to the back of my neck.

"Put the gun down, Collins." Rocks fell in my gut. "Now."

I bent at the knees and put the gun on the ground of the living room.

"Kick it away."

I did.

"Let's go inside and talk about this." The authority in that voice sent a shiver through me as I stepped forward. I went forward until he told me to stop. I turned around. He was still in the jeans and T-shirt he'd worn to my house.

"You've got to be fucking kidding me!" Lily hissed. "You?"

"Me." Sean Murphy shrugged his massive shoulders, his gun pointed at my heart.

CHAPTER 34

LILY

"**W**hy'd you give him the phone?" Miss Stafford glared at Captain Murphy, her gun still drilled into the side of my head. "He said he heard my voicemail. I left that to make the Court back off."

"I wanted to see what he'd do with it." Captain Murphy gave Gabe a sad look. "You were my best cop, Collins. How could you work with *that*?"

He sneered at me. I tried to glare back, but the silver was now burning in every cell. I didn't have long.

"You're one to talk." Gabe gave Miss Stafford a meaningful glance.

"That's different." Sean Murphy smiled at Miss Stafford, a flash of teeth. "I need her."

"What are you talking about? You're the captain of the VPB. She's a vampire who's killed at least twice, probably three times. What could you possibly get from her?" Gabe looked like someone had just told him there wasn't a Santa Claus.

"I can save Barbara." The captain's face seemed to droop, his laugh lines turning into harsh wrinkles in a flash. "My wife's been diagnosed with MS. It's a progressive disease. She's slowly losing herself. You know what it's like to watch your family die."

Gabe swallowed the lump in his throat.

"Imagine watching it in slow motion. Angela here offered me a way out. All I had to do was assign my best cop to one case. A cop that wouldn't ever think of vampires as anything but scum. Of course, I picked you." Captain Murphy gave that sad smile again. "I had my doubts about Harper, but I was certain you would stay the course.

"Then you went missing after the dance club. Sure, this one and her merry little friends gave everyone a new memory, but you were different after that night. All you gave me all week was tiny little clues. You were out of the office every night. You were going to scenes without calling it in first. It wasn't like you."

He jerked his head towards me again.

"Then Kimberly said that Lily here gave you blood. Must have been at the club, right?"

Gabe nodded once. I gulped. Shit, shit, shit.

"I figured that, because of that, she couldn't fix your brain. But that didn't explain why you would work with her. When you showed up with Kimberly's cell phone, I asked Angela to leave a little message, just to see how you'd respond. And here you are."

"Here I am," Gabe acknowledged. His voice was cold and angry.

"Can we kill him?" Miss Stafford sounded gleeful at the prospect.

"No." Sean Murphy nodded. "You sure Anna's cocktail worked?"

"Works every time. Gets the blood out in no time." Miss Stafford gave Gabe an assessing look. "He should be clean."

"Good. Clean his mind and we'll get the bitch down below. You can send your threats to the Court later."

"They have my family!" Miss Stafford's eyes widened.

"Yes, I know." Sean Murphy smiled indulgently. "I'm sure they'll still be there in the morning. But I need him back to work. He's the best pawn to stir up the herd. Make them easy picking, right?"

"*That's* what all this was about?" I choked out the words. "Scaring the humans."

"More like priming them for panic." Miss Stafford grinned proudly. "Much easier to overthrow a panicked population."

"So, why do you need me?" Gabe stared at his captain, his face turning various shades of red.

"Because." Captain Murphy smiled with satisfaction. "You're likable. The rest of my men are more enthusiastic, but they don't look as good in front of a TV screen. And you really hate vampires. At least you will again."

Captain Murphy stepped away from Gabe and nodded at Miss Stafford. "Do it."

Miss Stafford stepped forward, finally letting go of my hair. I collapsed to the ground, my body landing over my arms, putting all my weight on the cuffs and digging those awful barbs further in. I needed to get them out before the reaction set in. Miss Stafford stood before Gabe; her dark eyes barely seemed to change as power filled them.

"So, ya told us how Gabe knew to come here!" I tried to think of anything. Anything that might save our asses. I just needed a little time. "Ya didn't tell us how ya knew to come here."

"I tailed him and Harper."

"I didn't see you behind us." Gabe's face drained of color.

"Of course, you didn't, you were too busy bustling about to come get your little friend." Captain Murphy snorted. "Speaking of which, I can hear your breathing Harper. Get out here or I'll plug a hole in your partner's heart."

Harper came out of the kitchen, his hands up and his expression dark. I strained, trying to keep my body still as I pushed the cuff down my right wrist. The weight of my own body made the cuff feel like it was a hundred pounds heavier.

What I wouldn't have given for a bobby pin. My skin boiled and bubbled as the barbs dug new paths up my hand.

I could feel the blisters pop as I kept pushing the cuff up, my hands trembling. I kept my eyes on the two detectives ahead of me and reminded myself not to scream. The silver had been in me too long. I would start seizing soon, becoming about as useful as a sitting duck. But I might be able to give them an opportunity before that happened.

"Drop it!" Sean Murphy eyed the gun in Harper's dark hands.

Harper dropped his gun to the ground. It landed with a soft *thud* on the carpet and he kicked it away. It skidded and stopped at the captain's feet. Miss Stafford looked at him like a steak in a meat case.

"So, I guess I know why the memory change didn't take." The puddle of my blood grew beneath me, moist and chilly against my belly. "No way you heard that naturally. She's been feeding ya."

"Of course." Miss Stafford smiled that friendly-old-lady-grin again, her eyes still trained on the dark detective. "You said Detective Collins was driven by the loss of his family?"

Captain Murphy nodded. "Why?"

"Do you think it would help his motivation if he also lost his partner?" Miss Stafford's smile widened. Her canines extended a centimeter at a time.

"Huh, I hadn't thought of that." The captain gave Harper a quick glance. "Could be an option."

"You bastard!" Gabe spat the words.

Sean Murphy waved Gabe's comment away with his free hand. "It's not like you'll remember this later."

"So, I can eat him?" Miss Stafford made a show of licking her lips. Harper gulped, loudly.

"Not yet, for now, just put him under. We can do the deed somewhere we'd like to have evidence."

Miss Stafford pouted, a weird expression on her aged face. Still, she complied and turned her black eyes on Harper. He snapped his eyes shut. She snorted rudely.

"Open your eyes or I'll do it for you."

Harper popped each eyelid open slowly and swallowed again. He was shivering.

"Stay here, stand still, and be quiet." Miss Stafford nodded sharply, apparently satisfied with her work. She turned her attention back to Gabe.

"Two more questions, before ya fuck with my friend's memories!" I snapped out the request.

"What now?" Sean Murphy sighed, exasperation written on his features.

Well, I'd been expecting him to tell me to fuck off. Beggars couldn't be choosy.

"Why kill Adrian?" I aimed my gaze at the aged vampire in front of me. "He was one of yours. Did he step out of line or something?"

"Oh no." Miss Stafford shook her head fervently, a small grin tugging at one corner of her lips. She looked like she was sharing a secret with an old friend. "I'd intended to kill him since day one. That boy always thought he was so important. I suppose he was in the end, but it was still a blast tearing the grin off his face."

"Your second question?" The captain's tone was deadpan.

"Why haven't ya killed me yet?" One of the barbs caught on a knucklebone and I swallowed a gasp. "I'm not good for anythin'. Not unless you're looking for a prisoner exchange. And let me tell ya, the Court and I aren't on the best of terms."

Miss Stafford finally looked at me, a little shock in her wrinkled features. "You truly don't know, do you?"

"Know what?" I didn't really care. The lady didn't seem all there. I just wanted them distracted while I scraped that bloody barb through the bone. It was almost...there...

"Don't tell her." Captain Murphy gave me a smile meant for awards ceremonies. "I think she might enjoy the surprise."

"That's me. I love surprises." The barbs snapped over my knuckles, and I slid the cuff down my fingers. Blood trickled down my hand as the tip of each barb etched a new little trail across my skin. I let the cuff fall to the carpet and reached into the left sleeve of my hoodie, grasping the hidden knife with shaky fingertips. I grinned, hope bubbling in my chest. "I'm just full of them."

CHAPTER 35

GABE

Lily's eyes flashed black and she flipped onto her side. A silver glimmer sliced through the air before a knife jutted from Captain Murphy's shoulder. He howled in surprise. I lunged forward, tackling the old woman to the ground. She clawed at my throat, her dark hands raking my skin and carving painful grooves through my skin.

"Harper, do what you fuckin' want!" Lily's lilt was even more garbled.

Captain Murphy swore and a loud blast filled the room. Lily howled in pain. I couldn't look up, not with a vampire snapping and clawing from under me. Miss Stafford reached for my neck again, and I pulled my arm back, ready to punch her in the face. She pushed me upwards like I was a rag doll. I toppled next to her on the floor, my lungs losing all their air on impact. My spine cracked over a hard, irregular lump.

Miss Stafford climbed on top of me, grabbing my throat. It was like yanking free from a steel trap. I pushed to get up; she smacked my head against the ground. Pain rocketed through every nerve. She lowered her face, her nose almost touching mine as I struggled. The irregular lump dug further into my back and I realized what it was.

"Stay still! I won't heal your boo-boos like that floozy." She smiled, her fangs still extended, gleaming against her bottom lip. Her breath was rotten like she'd been chewing on old meat.

"Make me!" I growled and punched her in the stomach. She didn't even move. Just grinned.

"I think I will." Her eyes turned back into those pools of ink. Her tone became that of a hypnotist. "Stay still."

A feeling of violation overcame me and my mind tried to cloud. I stopped punching, letting my hands fall straight to the ground. I relaxed under her; letting her round form rest all her weight on my hips.

"You're gonna watch me kill your partner." She sat up, an eerie smile of satisfaction filling her features. "You may not remember it later but it'll be fun while it lasts."

Oh hell no.

I bucked my hips up with all their strength. She toppled forward, instinctively bracing herself against the ground, those ink-black eyes wide in shock. I reached under my raised hips and nabbed the gun. I pulled the hammer back with my thumb, barely pointing the muzzle into her skull right as her hands left the ground.

"That's not possible!" Shock shifted to anger, contorting those wrinkles into savage lines across her face.

"Next time, try poking me in the eye." I started to squeeze the trigger.

"Stop Collins." Sean Murphy's voice was filled with dark promise. I paused, my finger still poised.

"Why should I?" I kept my eyes trained on the vampire astride me.

The hammer of the gun clicked. My guts went cold.

"Stay still," I mocked Miss Stafford's earlier tone and looked out of the corner of my eye. Lily was kneeling on the ground, Captain Murphy's big hand the only thing holding her upright. A large chain on one of her wrists jingled maniacally as her body shuddered. Streams of foam dripped from her mouth, mingling with the fresh blood all over her face.

"Let's talk about this." Captain Murphy nuzzled her temple with the barrel of his pistol.

"Nothing to talk about. You want a pawn. I think I just proved I don't have the necessary qualifications for that position."

Maybe we wouldn't make it out of here. Maybe only a couple of us. But I would go down fighting dammit.

"Doesn't mean you can't learn on the job." Captain Murphy's voice was silk. "Think about it, Collins. You saw what they can do firsthand."

"Your point?"

"We're in war humanity can't win." Captain Murphy chuckled, the low amusement mixing with the rattling chain in a disjointed melody. "Get on the right side of history before it's published."

I couldn't help the snort that escaped me. "Here I thought this was about saving Barbara."

"That was the start of it, sure. But you've seen what they can do. The power they hold over us."

I swallowed the retort that came to mind, darting my eyes away from Miss Stafford for just a second. A second was more than enough. Lily was still shaking, the blood and foam bubbling down her sweatshirt and pants while she looked right at me.

I looked back at Miss Stafford. "We're going to get up now, nice and slow."

"No, Gabe!" Lily's shout was muffled; I barely understood the words. A loud smack sounded in the room and she let out a garbled cry.

"Shut up!"

Miss Stafford smiled and nodded, slowly removing her palms from the ground. She sat up and stood, stepping to the side of me. I kept my gun trained on her skull the whole time.

I sat up, using my free hand to push myself up before leaving the ground.

"You say we're on the losing side, Captain? You certain about that?"

"Have I ever led you astray?"

I didn't answer right away, just let my arm go limp with the gun hanging by my side. I could die or I could go back to the way things were, more or less. "If I agree to help, would you let Harper live?"

"Possible. Especially since he can be conditioned to act how we need."

Conditioned, like he was a piece of software that needed reprogramming. But still, he'd be alive. Harper scowled at me but kept his mouth shut. That just left Lily.

She nodded once, a single red tear trickling down her cheek. "I understand."

I didn't see the vampire, even with her shivering and bleeding on the carpet before me.

In my mind, there was a disheveled blonde girl in tattered clothes trying to urge me to drink from a water bottle. Or her enthusiastically clapping as she successfully picked locks in the seat next to me, that single dimple I don't think she even knew about. The sorrow in her eyes while looking at a watch display, such a familiar feeling to my own. All of these were in the woman before me, shaking, battered, and cake with blood.

"I don't know what else to tell ya."

She could have let me rot beneath that lighting fixture, but it hadn't even occurred to her as an option. Now, she was ready to die. Just so Harper and I could walk out of here. I turned my attention back to Miss Stafford.

"Thanks for standing."

I raised the gun and pulled the trigger, a single fluid motion. She tried to dodge; it wasn't quick enough. The back of her skull exploded. She flopped to the ground, her brown skin starting to gray and shrink.

The gunfire echoed.

Hot pain pierced my chest.

"No!" Lily's shriek tore the air into tiny pieces.

"Collins!" Harper's voice was a loud wail I'd never heard from him before.

"Don't move Harper!" Sean Murphy's voice was a bark of pure authority.

I looked down. A pool of red was quickly swallowing my tie and shirt. I dropped the gun and fell to my knees.

I turned my gaze, landing on my captain. He shook his chiseled head sadly.

"I really wanted you with us, boy."

My heart beat; each pulse slowing with an ever-growing ache. Tears streamed down Lily's face, mixing with the red foam. Her lip quivered and I didn't think it was the seizure. Too bad. She really did have a nice smile.

I didn't have a chance to turn to Harper.

CHAPTER 36

LILY

Gabe collapsed. Harper let out a gasp of sharp pain. I screamed, the dread tearing through the foam and blood in my throat.

"You killed him!" Harper shouted, his dark face turning red. "You fucking killed him!"

"He didn't give me any choice." Sean Murphy looked between us. I shuddered more and more furiously. He snorted. "I guess I'll take care of you first. She seems to be having troubles. Besides, my boss still wants her alive."

"Your boss fits into a dustpan!" Harper screamed, anguish filling his voice.

"Nah. She was just my supervisor. I'll get another one soon." Sean Murphy let go of my shoulder and I collapsed to the ground, my head slowly lulling to each side with the convulsions. "Maybe I'll even get one with all their screws in the right places."

His ankles came into view.

I struck, my fangs sinking through denim and socks, into the tender flesh of his Achilles tendon.

"Fuck!" The captain sank on the injured leg and I bit harder, shredding the tendon while fresh blood filled my mouth. It tasted foul, mixed with the dirt and sweat of his clothes. The silver still shook me, almost ripping my teeth through his flesh. I locked my mouth in place, biting in as deep as I could.

"Let go, you bitch!" He aimed his gun at my head.

I swung my arm. The limb still quivered but the heavy manacle slammed into his face. He howled in pain. I yanked my head back, my jaw still clenched. My teeth ached as jean, sock, and muscle tore beneath my bite.

A loud *boom* sounded and the captain stilled. I looked over, hope surging.

Gabe!

But no, he was still prone. Harper knelt by his side, one knee on the floor and the gun in both hands.

I hefted out a pitiful little sigh. Gabe's voice was raspy as he let out several pained gasps on the floor. It was little more than a wheeze.

My limbs jerked as I tried to crawl; the manacle thumped against the rug twice before Harper rushed over. He hoisted me to my feet and I screamed as all my weight landed on my ruined knee, but he didn't stop.

"You can fix him?" He tossed one of my arms over his big shoulders.

I nodded slowly. "Just get me over there."

Harper deposited me next to Gabe in a hapless heap. His eyes were already clouded, even if they were fixed on me. I bit down on my wrist, pulling the flesh open in a jagged hole as I continued to seize. Gabe reached up and placed a hand over mine.

It was so cold.

I pushed the gaping wound towards his mouth. He just smiled sadly.

"We can fight about this later! " I shouted at him, pushing my wrist past his grip. "Fuckin' drink!"

A few drops hit his lips but none went in.

He coughed, his own blood littering his lips with mine. "I wish you'd smile more."

His head lolled and his eyes rolled back.

"No, no, no!" Harper knelt next to me, lifting Gabe's head. "Come on, buddy."

I reached past Harper and placed two fingers against Gabe's throat. His carotid pulse was silent. I sat back, my blood running cold and my body shivering for a whole new reason.

"Fix him!" Harper screamed.

I shook my head once. "His heart stopped."

"No!" Harper sobbed, his body overshadowing his partner's. His laugh lines grew deformed with grief. "No, he's whole! Last time, he was a puddle and you fixed him!"

"He still had a pulse." Could I risk it? Would Gabe forgive me? Could I forgive myself? "Vampire blood reacts to the life in the cells and amplifies it. That's why it moves through the body so fast. The minute that life is gone..."

I let the sentence hang.

"Then we try CPR!" Tears rolled down his eyes and snot littered his burly beard. "Get the heart going again and then give him the blood."

"CPR might jostle the bullet in his heart, cause even more damage." And I needed that heart for what I was thinking. I pushed the other cuff down my hand. Pain sliced through me and not just from the barbs this time. I gasped a little as I shoved it down. I didn't have time to take this slow.

"So, what then?" Harper's voice was a loud demand. "There's got to be something!"

"Ya have a choice to make." The cuff thumped next to me.

"What choice? Anything, if it will save him!"

I threw the offending cuff to the side before starting to dig into the raw flesh of my leg, groaning between each word. "Would Gabe want to live if he weren't human?"

The pain was becoming a welcome distraction to what I was plotting.

Confusion slashed through Harper's anguished wrinkles, but only for a moment. Understanding stretched them back out.

"Oh, shit..."

"If I will the blood into him with the intent to change him, it changes the design. I don't know why." The tips of my fingers shook as I prodded the bullet. It was like pouring liquid fire into my veins but I forced myself to keep going. It wasn't fair to ask Harper, but I couldn't make this decision alone.

"Normally, it would start to instruct his organs to close shop instead of doing the repairs. His organs have already shut down. It's just a matter of willin' undead life into the ones he still needs."

And hoping that fucked-up heart would do the trick for us.

My fingertips sizzled at the contact as I pushed the bullet to the surface. The bullet was probably about half the size it had been going in. My body must have broken it down already.

Shit, I couldn't do this under silver poisoning. The blood would only transfer it.

I looked at Gabe's rapidly paling face.

Shit. Shit. Shit.

There wasn't another option.

"I don't know him well enough, but ya need to choose now. His brain has already been deprived of oxygen for too long. If we don't move fast, he could wake up chewin' tablecloths."

He might still, between the time elapsed and the silver in my body. There was just no way to be certain. I didn't know which outcome would be worse. A Gabe that couldn't control his drool or a dead one. I gulped and gave Harper a hard look.

"Do it." He nodded sharply. "If he hates it, he can stake himself in the morning."

"I need blood." I nodded and indicated the corpse behind me. "Bring me yer captain and his gun."

Harper got up and obediently dragged the body to me, positioning it in a sitting position before me. He went back for the gun as I sank my fangs into the crook of Captain Murphy's neck. I drank in long, heavy gulps. Harper paled and his lips thinned but he said nothing.

The blood was disgusting. Whatever Captain Murphy liked to eat, I would be too happy if I never tasted it again. Or maybe that was just my imagination, knowing the source of this blood.

Finally, I dropped the body to the floor with a heavy *thud* and turned my attention to the gun in Harper's grasp. Standard Glock but not police issue. Probably the gun the captain used whenever he was doing something he didn't want linked back to him or the department. I wouldn't be surprised if the serial number was missing.

I took it and ejected the magazine and looked at the rounds. *Fuck.*

"Rip his shirt open."

Harper did so, his dark features a bit green. I dug into the hole in Gabe's chest, fishing with my fingertips for the bullet. Harper gasped in horror and I held my free hand to silence him.

"The bullet's silver. If I turn him and that's still lodged in there, it could cause more damage to his brain. He probably wouldn't be himself." The trace amounts in me were bad enough. If this even worked.

I pulled the bullet to the surface and flicked it away. It clunked against something. Blood trickled from the wound, and I plugged the hole with my free thumb as I scored my wrist with my fangs, the wound from earlier already gone.

I held the trickle of blood over the gaping hole of Gabe's chest, giving the blood its quickest path to victory. Digesting it wouldn't be enough. Too slow and his body wasn't set to distribute that way anymore. I needed the blood directly in Gabe's circulatory system.

"You said ya know CPR?"

Harper nodded once, his face still gaunt. "Standard part of police training."

"You gotta do chest compressions while I add blood directly to the heart." I lifted Gabe's legs and held them at a slope, hoping to drive the blood towards his heart. "It's going to be messy as hell, but we need to get the blood to circulate fast."

Theoretically, it could work.

"Ready?"

"And you have no clue what surprise they were referring to?" Queen Ritti tilted her head, scrutinizing me like a new game piece of some kind.

"None. They acted like I ought to." I shrugged. "I assume it had something to do with exchangin' me for Thomas and Ami, but they didn't exactly clarify. Plus, the old lady was bat-shit crazy."

"What were you thinking?" Ivan stared down his nose at me, his arms crossed as he stood behind the queen's chair.

I kept my eyes trained on my boots. Harper had been nice enough to give them back to me. Along with my helmet and copies of all the files that he and Gabe had compiled. Even after everything.

"I was thinking I had gotten the poor kid into the mess. I needed to get him out." My tone was hollow. "I think ya can skip the lecture, considering how that turned out."

"Jesus, kid!" Ivan drew his hands down his dark face and paced. "And then, you try to turn a human. No Court authorization or even a request from the human. After the human was dead!"

"Again." I finally looked up, my eyes brimming with tears. "I think ya can skip the lecture, all things considered."

"That—" The queen's tone was imperious. Ivan stopped pacing behind her chair, "depends on what happens when Detective Collins wakes."

CHAPTER 37

GABE

I woke to a barren concrete ceiling instead of my ceiling fan. It took a minute for me to realize where I was.

It was all a dream.

Lily had never gone missing. Captain Murphy hadn't betrayed us. It had all been my brain sorting through this last week in a fucked-up dream.

Then thousands of tiny paper cuts formed inside my guts.

I doubled over onto my side, but I rolled too far and fell to the concrete floor. I gasped, a loud sound of agony as the pain intensified. I looked around but everything moved in blurry waves, like I'd had a thousand too many. This was far worse than the blood hangover. The visual cloud made me nauseous, increasing the pain and bringing it to unfathomable heights.

I had died.

I had died and this was hell.

Through the agony, I felt someone's hand behind my shoulders. I tried to resist the motion but that sizzling pain made it too hard to pull away. Something was being pressed against my lips, something soft and cold.

"Bite down," a raspy voice urged me. "The pain will go away."

Relief rushed through me. All I had to do was bite something; I would have done anything to make that pain stop. It was like biting into a water balloon, with a sudden gush of ambrosia bursting in my mouth. The pain lessened, though the feeling of being drunk did not. I sucked until the heavenly nectar was gone. A hand tapped my cheek lightly. "Okay, give it here."

I assumed *it* referred to the remaining plastic in my mouth. Glad to simply recognize the material, I opened my mouth to let it fall. The now recognizable male voice chuckled. "Feel better?"

"What are you doing here?" I groaned as I saw the round ears through the blurry haze. "Where's...Lily? Why's she give...me blood again?"

"She's having some trouble at work." Alex's ears seemed to droop. "As to that last part, I think it had to do with wanting you to live."

"Huh?" I sat up and placed a hand over my chest.

Great, I've ruined another shirt and tie.

Blood stained what was left of my shirt in various hues, thick red blotches in my eyes. Some of it was still wet. My hand came away soaked.

So, it hadn't been a dream. "He...shot...me."

"'Fraid so." Alex sat on the floor with me.

"This hangover... is a *LOT* worse than last time. Everything's all furry."

"I think you mean fuzzy." Though the blur, I swore I saw Alex smiling. I just couldn't be certain. I couldn't even be certain what color the bedspread was. "It's not a hangover."

"What do you mean?" I slurred. "Because I'm not...puking yet."

"Vampires don't puke." Alex's tone was dreary. "Not unless you count that foam we spew with silver poison."

We sat in silence, my eyes failing to focus on his.

"Waiting for...the pun..." I burped, the taste noxious. My stomach tried to convulse around the flavor.

"You're not the first one to ask for a punchline. I'm sure you won't be the last, but I can't offer one." Alex leaned back on his arms.

I stared at him another moment then dropped my head to review the red smeared across my palm. So fresh crimson. And it smelled...

"Arghh." An animal sound escaped my throat as I slurped and licked my hand with the fervor of a dog after peanut butter. I didn't even realize what was I doing until the blood was gone, shiny pink-tinted saliva coating my palm. My whole body turned to ice. I finally gulped and looked back to Alex, my eyes wide as dinner plates. He gave me a sympathetic look and nodded once.

"Welcome to vampire rehab."

CAN'T WAIT FOR MORE?

TRY BLOOD RENEGADE

How does one deal with life after death when death doesn't seem any different than life... except the need for blood? As Gabe struggles with his new role, Lily avoids all her responsibilities to him. But soon, their newest investigation makes confrontation inevitable, as they are forced to run from human authorities and the vampire Court, all to protect a new comrade. Can the two resolve their differences and come together for the common good?

Turn the page to find out...

CHAPTER 1

LILY

When that silly book came out with the sparkly vampires, a lot of my kind were pissed. Not me. After all, inaccuracies just like it had saved my ass more than once. Then there was the whole insta-romance. It was written for teenagers, what did people expect? I mean the stalky bits were creepy, but that was about the worst I could say about that.

No, I wasn't upset about any of the cliches or disco-skin. I just wondered, why Washington? Why not Oregon?

Oregon was just as overcast and our landscapes were just as beautiful. Maybe better. The November rain was chilly, yet the clouds still weren't thick enough to block all of the sun. I might need to reapply my sunscreen if this kept up.

Most of the leaves were green and lush, excess moisture making their fallen brethren stick to my boots everywhere I went. While the rest of the country changed colors or forfeit their foliage, Oregon took on a healthy sheen as the heavy rains nurtured them, giving the hills a wild look. The few trees that did submit to Fall broke the vast expanse of green with deep bursts of scarlet and honey tones. It was breathtaking.

Even from a mall parking lot.

I flicked my eyes back to the building ahead, snapping photos repeatedly from my motorcycle. I usually brought the car to stakeouts, but Maria had needed to do some shopping. She couldn't exactly balance the grocery bags on my handlebars. Not that I would have trusted her to take my Harley. Ever.

So I snapped pictures with my cell phone, trying my best to look like I was trying to figure out my GPS. How exactly does one look when they're lost? That was one look I hadn't practiced before. My phone made a little bird noise and a text appeared on the screen. Alex.

He's out of the basement today.

Another chirp issued from the phone's speaker. Maria this time.

He's still asking for you. Just saying.

Gabe. I swallowed and flicked both texts off my screen. I still couldn't handle that face-to-face. Not yet. So I continued to watch the mall entrance across the asphalt. It was probably another dead end, but at least it was something to do. Correction, something *else* to do.

The large entrance swooshed open and the double-glass doors slid away from each other. A short woman with a large handbag walked out. A fuchsia scarf peeked out through the thick mass of hair that shrouded her face. I sat up straighter, trying to see her features. I couldn't, that damn hair blocked my line of sight.

The woman had the stance of someone who was insecure, trying to turn herself into a tiny ball while still walking. She hunched her shoulders, staring at the ground and shoving her hands deep into her pockets. She could just be hiding her face because she was used to doing it. I hardly wanted to go after a woman with self-confidence issues. But that scarf... It was a bit irregular for someone with low self-esteem to wear something like that. The bright color drew just about every eye right to her. Then again, would a vampire on the lam wear it?

The light wind rustled the woman's hair and she lifted a hand to smooth those dark strands. The skin of her hand was the right shade of olive. She started to push the loose hair behind an ear before finger combing it back over her lovely face. Too late. I snapped three photos in quick succession. Click. Click. Click. I pinched my fingers to zoom in on the image, just to be certain.

"Gotcha."

I grinned and dismounted my bike. I could chase her on it, but she might run somewhere the bike would become a handicap. Better to leave it here. I double-checked my saddlebags to ensure they were zipped up and pulled on the hood of my sweatshirt one more time, making certain my hair was hidden. Finally, I shoved my too-huge sunglasses up on my nose, obscuring my features as much as possible.

I kept my distance, wanting to see where she was going. The background checks I'd been running had given me some surprising results. The twit had stayed in Portland, though I had no clue why. The whole Court wanted her ass on a silver pike. Still, she hadn't used any of her credit cards to rent a room. So where had she been hiding out?

My target strolled down through the parking lot, that large bag smacking against her waist as she moved quickly. She turned a corner, exiting the large parking lot. Past the large gate of the hospital and their large lawn of thick fall grass, she walked past several houses. I reminded myself to give her plenty of space, even more than I would if I was following a human. I didn't skulk or crouch behind cars. That shit always made me laugh when I watched a movie.

No, I walked casually, looking at the overcast sky like I was considering the various hues of gray instead of the woman ahead of me. I nodded politely to the people who greeted me, not wanting to actually speak. I could hide my hair. I couldn't really hide my lilt, and my query knew me pretty well.

A group of children ran past me, maybe playing tag before they shot past me and my target. They stuck their tongues out at her and called her some silly playground title that made me smirk. She looked down at them for a moment before looking away.

My query turned a corner. I sped up, just a little. I turned the corner and scanned the few people walking on the sidewalk. No fuchsia scarf. No short Latina woman.

Shit.

I ran, throwing caution to the wind. I didn't know if she'd just turned another corner or actually realized she was being followed. It didn't matter. I needed to find her. Aside from her, all I had on this case was a bunch of files that made no sense.

I bumped a man on the sidewalk.

"Watch it, lady."

I held up a hand in silent apology and surged forward, still not wanting to risk speaking. My gaze darted down each alley and street corner I passed.

Nothing. Nothing. Nothing.

Dammit. Dammit. Dammit.

A flash of black hair caught my eye and I turned a corner, then another.

Smack!

Her fist shot into my face, shattering my sunglasses and crunching my nose. Several tiny shards scored my skin, barely missing my eyes.

"Heya Lily." She punched again.

My cheekbone cracked and I staggered backward. Anna sprang forward, trying to land another blow. I shot my foot out. It landed squarely in her gut and she flew backward, into a fancy brick fence.

"Heya, Anna." I smiled, a shark showing its teeth. "How's tricks?"

She hit with a heavy thump and let out a gasp as the impact forced the air from her lungs.

I ran forward, trying to slam her against the wall. She raked her nails across my face, catching me off guard and embedding some of the shattered glass in my eye. I yowled. I don't care who you are, glass in your eye fucking hurts.

I reeled backward shaking my face wildly to free it of the busted shades and howling as my eye worked to repair itself and push the glass out. My cheek and nose started to snap back in place, audible little clicks as the bone mended itself, and I growled at the added pain. My eye welled with tears.

"I'm not going back!" Anna came forward, a blurry shadow in my good eye right before her knee slammed into me, shooting my stomach through my spine. I coughed blood, scrounging to grab her leg before she could go again.

"Yes, you bloody are!" I barely grabbed her ankle in my half-blind attempt.

She must not have been ready for that, because she fell to the ground, her body slamming into the walkway. I snatched her throat and pushed all my weight into her windpipe before she could scream. She flailed and kicked against the ground. I looked both ways down the walkway, my eye finally shoving out the last sliver of glass.

No audience. Not yet.

She continued to kick wildly, gasping out little words without any air to carry them. I kept my grip firm. We were about the same in strength, but only one of us had bothered learning how to use that strength. She clawed at my hands, tiny trails of my flesh ripping under her well-manicured nails.

When that didn't work, she pounded her fist on my side, like a feverish toddler in the midst of a tantrum. She kept mouthing something with every blow, but I didn't let up to find out what, just let the wordless squeaks as I tightened my grip. I swallowed the lump in my throat. How had I ever called this woman a friend?

I leaned towards her, just enough to whisper. "We need to talk."

I shook her once snapping her head into the walkway. Her body went limp in my grasp and she glared at me. Pure hate-filled those copper eyes as her head lolled and a little spot of blood stained the ground in a deep splatter.

I sat back and looked her over. Her right hand looked like she'd broken her thumb, the bones slowly coming back in place with tiny snaps. Her clothes were washed and her skin was clean. Even her make-up was perfect.

"Well, you haven't been living on the streets." I continued my examination, trying to ignore the itch on healing claw marks on my hands. They'd be gone soon enough. "So where the hell have you been all this time?"

I looked up and down the alley again, deciding it would be best to continue this later. I patted her down, not finding anything but a single card. Seriously what fugitive doesn't carry a weapon or even a burner phone?

Finally, I swung off Anna and lifted her, one arm supporting her knees and the other under her shoulders. Her head remained loose in my grip.

She could be faking it, but I wasn't worried about that. As long as she didn't turn into a pile of ash. I had some questions first. Or at least, the Court did. The back of her head would heal, but if I was lucky, she wouldn't wake right away. I cursed my lack of a car. Next time, Maria could take the damn bus.

I looked around trying to find a place to hide my old friend, my eyes landing on a set of rubbish bins. They were tall with big company logos on the side. There was enough space between them to shove Anna's limp body out of immediate sight. I looked up and down the alley once again.

The neighborhood was clean and well kept. If someone saw me sitting here with an unconscious woman between the bins, they wouldn't just ignore us and keep walking. They'd stop, probably call 9-1-1.

"Shit."

It was kind of annoying that I had to worry about people being decent to each other. I gave the rubbish bins another look. But if Anna was inside the bin...

I kicked a few before the sound echoed back to me. I plopped her on the ground and kept a wary eye for any movement, lifting the lid. Empty or not, the receptacle stank. Good. It was no less than she deserved. I checked my surroundings again and hauled Anna up, letting her fall none too soft on her head. She slid in with a heavy thump, her body contorting into an unnatural shape to fit the container.

I closed the lid and hoisted myself on top of the bin, seating myself over my captive. She would move the bin if she woke, giving me time to react while I waited.

I pulled out my phone and hunted through my contacts, stopping at the Cs. I hit the little green phone icon and pressed the phone to my ear.

"Hello." The male voice was like melted butter. It also echoed, bouncing off whatever surrounding he was standing in.

"Cy! How's it goin'?"

"Lily." The smooth tone dropped and Cyrus' natural speech took over, rough with his Norse accent. "That is not the way to greet someone you're about to ask for a favor."

"Who says I'm askin' for a favor?"

"Drop the act. We both know you need something."

"Yeah but it's not a favor. I need a pickup." I used my phone's GPS to relay my location to him. "I found her."

"That only took you two weeks," Cyrus grunted and I heard someone howl in pain in the background.

"I've had a lot of balls in the air, asshole." I winced at another howl. "Are ya seriously torturin' someone while we're talkin'?"

"It's called multitasking," he grunted and another wail issued from his captive. I held the phone away from my ear as someone pleaded for mercy. The cry finally stopped and I tentatively brought the phone back to my face.

"Knock that shit off. I don't want to hear it. And send someone for Anna." I barely heard him say it would be twenty minutes as I hung up. The screen filled with the normal background and I saw the time.

"Fuck." Now, on top of everything else, I was going to be late for my meeting with the new Captain of the VPB. I gave the overcast sky an annoyed look. "Okay, I get it. Thanks."

I hunted through my contacts again, stopping at the Hs this time.

ABOUT E.H. DRAKE

Visit our publishing website at http://www.ehdrake.com/

You can join our mailing list (no I won't spam you or sell your information) and learn about E.H. Drake's next fantastic book.

If you love the cover, please check out our artist's website https://nicoleyork.com/, check out her amazing photography and art work.

Thank you again!

Acknowledgments...

are a pain. Seriously, who do you thank for helping you through such a process as writing a book?

Who made this possible?

Should it be my mom, who introduced me to vampires and nurtured my inner nerd and love of literature?

Or maybe my husband, who has listened to me rant about my imaginary friends on and on for years and still signed on for more?

Should I dedicate this to my critique partners, Aisling Wilder, Nicole McKeon, and Lauren Sevier? Maybe the countless Beta Readers who helped me deconstruct this story sentence by sentence and rebuild it too many times to count?

Or, perhaps, I'll cheat and go with option "D", all of the above.

This is for every one of you. Anyone will tell you, a book takes a freaking village.